CONTENTS

MURDER AT THE MANOR HOUSE

CHAPTER ONE – CHRISTMAS EVE MORNING 1930 – THE MORNING ROOM

The room at the Manor House that had been designated as the morning room, had purportedly been done so as, logically, it was the room that received the most sun between the hours of eight a.m. and twelve noon. On the morning of Christmas Eve 1930 however, the sky was decidedly grey and threatening.

Lord David Mountjoy was sitting contentedly in his favourite armchair, smoking a pipe and reading a newspaper. The door from the hall opened to reveal Alice, one of the Manor's two kitchen maids, carrying a large tray containing all the requirements for The Mountjoy's morning coffee ritual. He was pleased to see that it was Alice who had brought in the tray and not the younger kitchen maid, Jane, who had a tendency towards clumsiness. However, his heart sank a little as he realised that his precious peace and quiet would soon be disturbed by the arrival of his wife, Lady Serena Mountjoy, their two children and his cantankerous mother-in-law.

Sure enough, Lady Serena flounced into the room announcing, 'You may pour coffee for myself and Lord David, Alice and a slice of walnut cake,' before taking a seat on the sofa opposite her husband. Meanwhile, Lord David continued to read his newspaper, holding it up so high that it completely covered his face, hoping for a few more moments of peace before his wife started up. Alice placed their cups of coffee and plates of walnut cake on the coffee table between Lord and Lady Mountjoy which neither of them acknowledged, both of them having far more important things on their minds.

Just then, the door to the morning room opened and the Mountjoy's widowed daughter, Amelia Jayne Cavendish appeared. She walked into the room supporting Lady Selena's cantankerous old mother, Sonia Ferguson, whose face was currently wearing an expression that could have soured milk.

'Mummy, Amelia,' announced Lady Selena. 'Come and have coffee and a slice of cook's delicious walnut cake. David do put that newspaper down and try and be sociable for once. Amelia, have you seen your brother?' She had barely completed this mini diatribe when Stephen Mountjoy burst into the room.

'I'm here, Mummy,' he announced. His presence brought a renewed energy into the room.

'Some coffee and cake please, Alice, then you may return to the kitchen. Amelia will see to any refills.'

Alice nodded with a half-smile and an awkward curtsey to acknowledge the request and turned to busy herself with pouring and slicing. Amelia, Sonia and Stephen had taken their seats on either side of Lord and Lady Mountjoy. The latter, waiting for Alice to depart before speaking.

'Right! Here we are then. It's Christmas Eve and in an hour, or so, our guests will be arriving. Such wonderful people, so we will be guaranteed a marvellous time. Now, I would just like to go over the itinerary whilst you are enjoying your coffee and walnut cake.' So enthusiastic was she that she failed to notice how utterly bored her mother and children looked at this precise moment.

'Serena dear,' her husband interjected. 'Could you please just remind us all of who we are expecting this year?'

'Certainly, David,' came the rather curt reply. 'Even though I have already mentioned it countless times, I will tell you once again.'

'Thank you, dear,' Lord David replied, somewhat woefully. Realising that once again he was in his wife's bad books.

'Well, firstly we have the bank manager, George Rochester. You really will find him quite charming.'

'THAT remains to be seen,' whispered Sonia Ferguson loudly enough to be heard by all.

Lady Serena chose to ignore her mother and continued. 'Then we have Doctor John Hollis.'

'Oh good,' Sonia interrupted once again. 'He is a tremendous fellow and probably the only one I shall wish to speak to.'

'Really, Mummy,' Lady Serena retorted. 'You must make an effort with all our lovely guests.' Sonia failed to comment but raised her eyebrows to the ceiling. Serena once again ignored her mother and carried on. 'Of course, Reverend Joseph Smith will be coming as usual.'

Upon hearing that, Stephen burst out laughing. 'Honestly, Mummy, you invited him ten years ago when he first arrived in the village, out of pure courtesy and now he expects an invite every year. Now he really is an old bore. You should just tell him.'

'That really is quite enough of that kind of talk,' Lady Serena admonished him. 'For your information, I don't invite him, he just informs me that he is coming. However, we all attend his church service every Sunday and therefore it is the very least that we can do. Especially as Lord and Lady of The Manor.'

Stephen Mountjoy remained silent but raised one eyebrow, a characteristic he had inherited from the paternal side of the family.

'Is Uncle James coming down, Mummy?' Amelia asked her.

'Yes, of course,' Lady Serena replied, blushing ever so slightly.

Lord David's younger brother, Colonel James Mountjoy, was an absolute charmer and both Lady Serena and her daughter enjoyed his company enormously.

'Any females coming to join our seasonal festivities?' Stephen asked whilst helping himself to another rather large slice of walnut cake.

'Of course, there is, Stephen,' Lady Serena snapped. 'You know how I must have a balanced dining table on all social occasions, especially at Christmas.' She drew a deep breath before she spoke again. 'My oldest and dearest school friend, Clarissa Llewellyn-Jones, is finally able to join us for the Christmas period. She has just been so busy touring all over the world that it must be years since we have seen her.'

'Oh, how simply marvellous!' Amelia exclaimed. 'A world-famous opera singer gracing our humble table. I wonder if we'll be able to persuade her to sing for us.'

'She is here for a good rest darling, so we must not bother her by suggesting such a thing.'

Lord David gave what could only be described as a guffaw. 'Get a few sherries inside her and I bet she'll be more than happy to sing for her supper.'

Lady Serena tutted. 'Lady Eliza Ross and daughter Susan are our final two guests.'

Stephen's eyes immediately lit up. Eliza Ross was the widow of Lord David's deceased best friend, Lord Duncan Ross. Their daughter and only child, the beautiful and headstrong Susan Ross, abhorred the country and therefore spent all her time in London, only returning to her mother's home when absolutely necessary. Lady Eliza insisted that Christmas up at the Manor House was indeed absolutely necessary. Stephen was completely besotted with Susan, who didn't know he was alive. He suddenly became aware that his mother was speaking again.

'So, I suggest that once you have finished your coffee, you all go and get changed, ready for lunch. We will all wait in the drawing room for our guests so that when they arrive, they can see the beautiful Christmas tree. When they are all here, we shall have lunch in the dining room. After lunch, the gentlemen shall enjoy an afternoon of shooting and the ladies shall enjoy a stroll in the gardens before taking tea. Now, best behaviour at all times everyone. Have you got that Mummy?'

Sonia Ferguson gave a wry smile and a slight nod that Lady Serena acknowledged as agreement.

CHAPTER TWO

Alice had returned to the morning room to collect the morning coffee remains and then taken them back below stairs. The Manor House kitchen was probably the cosiest room in the whole place.

Alexander Jameson, the Mountjoy's family butler, was seated in a comfortable old rocking chair by the hearth, polishing his already spotless shoes. His good lady wife and Manor House cook, Agnes Trelawney, was busy rolling out pastry for the plethora of mince pies she was making.

Jane, the Manor's other kitchen maid and younger sister of Alice, was stirring a heavy pot of soup on the stove.

A clatter of footsteps could be heard on the stairs leading down into the kitchen, along with the sound of giggling as housemaids Betty, Mary and Rose appeared.

'Now, now simmer down there,' Agnes gently reprimanded. 'You've taken your time. Is everything spick and span above stairs now?'

'Yes, Mrs Trelawney,' the three of them replied in unison.

'Sit yourselves down at the table then and have your morning tea. Jane, you too. Just leave that soup simmering awhile.' She turned to the sink where Alice was just finishing washing up the coffee things. 'You too, Alice. Have your tea and then you can help Mr Jameson polish the silver.'

All the girls took a seat at the table. Agnes picked up the big teapot that she had placed on the table a little earlier, giving it the time to brew nice and strong, just as they all liked it. Not strictly her place to be pouring the tea, but she didn't trust a single one of those girls to do it without making a complete mess.

'Alice, pass the milk and sugar around now. Jane, there's a plate of shortbread in the pantry. As it's Christmas Eve and we are going to be extremely busy for the next few days, you may all have a slice,' Agnes told them.

Once they were all settled with cups of tea and slices of shortbread Betty asked, 'So who is coming for Christmas this year Mrs Trelawney?'

'Well, let's see now. Some that we see most years with a few new faces thrown in,' she teased.

'Is the vicar coming then?' Rose asked.

'Yes, the Reverend Smith will here once again. Must be nigh on ten years he's been coming up to the Manor for Christmas now.'

'That's good,' Rose continued. 'I know some people think that he is boring and beneath them but he's a very kind man and always really nice to us maids.'

'Yes, well he is a simple God-fearing man.' Agnes confirmed.

'So why would he choose to come here then?' Betty cheekily asked.

'Don't you be asking such questions young Betty,' Agnes scolded her. 'Know your place.' Betty reddened and looked down at her empty plate.

The butler, Alexander Jameson had finished polishing his shoes and placed them back on his feet whilst the female chatter had been carrying on. Now, he stood and addressed them all. 'Now then. I am going to speak a few wise words that will assist you as you go about your business for the next few days. As you have already observed Rose, the Reverend Joseph Smith is a very nice, kind man who will be most grateful for all the service you provide for him whilst he is here.

'The new doctor in the village, Doctor Hollis will be here for the first time this year. Some of you may already know of him if you've had cause to pay him a visit. Now you will find him much like the vicar, a quiet and kind man. You might think he is a little forlorn. He doesn't appear to have any family to speak of which might account for his sadness. I believe he moved down here from Harley Street to try and find some peace. So please do not mistake his sullenness for rudeness.

'The bank manager, Mr Rochester is also coming here for Christmas for the first time. I understand that the people he would normally spend the Yuletide with are away in Yorkshire this year. I do not know the gentleman but have no reason to believe that he would be anything other than a nice kind man.

'Lady Eliza Ross and her daughter Susan will not be staying over at the Manor House, as I am told that they will return to the Gate House every evening. Lord Mountjoy or his brother, the Colonel will most probably accompany them.

'Now, the final house guest is Lady Mountjoy's oldest and dearest friend that she has known since her very early days at school and who just happens to be the world-famous opera singer, Clarissa Llewellyn-Jones.'

All the maids' eyes lit up with excitement, although Agnes appeared completely uninterested. Alice was the first one to recover and exclaim, 'Oh my! Jane and I have seen a picture of her in a magazine. She is so beautiful and so famous.'

'Now don't you be getting ideas above your station, young Alice,' Agnes told her. 'She's a reputation of being a complete diva. The likes of her don't notice the likes of us I can assure you.'

Without giving anyone the chance to reply, Agnes rose to her feet and continued. 'Right girls, finish up your tea and let's get on. Goodness me, all these guests will be arriving before we know it and expecting a proper good luncheon, I dare say. Chop, chop now.'

Everyone stood up and went about their duties. Jane checked the soup, from which some lovely aromas were beginning to emerge, before preparing vegetables. Alice went to join Mr Jameson for some silver polishing and the housemaids went above stairs to prepare the dining room.

CHAPTER THREE

Lady Serena Mountjoy stood staring out of her bedroom window at the front of the house. It gave her a view of the sweeping drive, down which the guests would soon be arriving. She would not have proclaimed that she particularly enjoyed these seasonal gatherings and, in actual fact, found the majority of the guests quite tiresome. But, as her self-appointed role of 'The Lady Bountiful', felt somewhat obliged. This year however, she was delighted that her oldest and dearest friend, Clarissa Llewellyn-Jones would be joining them all.

Lady Serena felt blessed and was content with her life. A happy enough marriage to Lord David and two children she adored. However, she would have much preferred a life of travel and adventure, like her dear friend. But unlike Clarissa, she had no particular talent or skill. So, as a young girl, her father point blank refused to support what he considered to be a decadent and worthless lifestyle. Nothing more than mere folly.

Turning from the window with an audible sigh, Lady Serena turned her attention to the matter of dressing in something suitable for greeting their guests.

Her husband, Lord David, was currently happily walking his Golden Retriever, Chester, around the grounds. Glancing up, he was pleased to observe that the sky had not become any darker. Whilst he was sentimental enough to wish for a white Christmas, he would like the snow to abate until after their traditional Christmas Eve shoot this afternoon, which he so enjoyed. He started whistling a jolly Christmas Carol as he continued his walk around his estate, seemingly without a care in the world.

Mr George Rochester was currently sitting at the large desk, in his office, at the bank where he was the branch manager. As he planned to leave the premises before the bank officially closed that day, he was briefing his assistant manager on the actions that needed to be completed in his absence which his assistant was enthusiastically recording on a notepad. List complete he left the room, leaving Mr George Rochester to quietly pack away that morning's customer files that he had been working on, before he left to attend the festivities at the Manor House.

At only thirty-two years of age, he was considered quite young to have been made a branch manager. He was, however, smart, diligent and a hard-working individual who had been promoted to an assistant manager on his own merit, shortly before the war. He was drafted about halfway through the conflict and returned from the trenches a decorated hero. Although exactly why he never talked about.

He was deeply saddened on his return to discover that his branch manager unfortunately did not return from the front, having perished in the Battle of the Somme. So, once back to work, he found himself promoted to the bank manager role.

Now, as he placed the last file into his desk drawer and locked it, he glanced up at the clock on the wall and thought about the lovely young lady that he had recently become engaged to. Sophie Westchester was his childhood sweetheart who, at this moment, was on a train to Yorkshire with her parents. They would be spending the Christmas period with Sophie's grandparents who resided there. He would have loved to have joined them but as they would be staying in Yorkshire for a couple of weeks, it was simply not possible for him to have taken the time away from the bank to be able to join them. He did feel a little regret about that as he did so enjoy the long walks the whole family took in the beautiful Yorkshire Dales. Never mind. It couldn't be helped and instead he would spend an interesting few days with Lord and Lady Mountjoy and their fascinating array of guests, up at the Manor House.

Back to the present, he realised that he must get a move on as he needed to call at his house before going on to the Manor and it simply would not do to be late. Rising from his desk, he paused just long enough to bow before the portrait of King George V that adorned the wall of his office. Passing quickly through the branch he wished staff and customers 'Seasons Greetings' before hurrying out of the door and up the High Street to his residence.

Doctor John Hollis had just treated his last patient and so the waiting room at the surgery was finally silent from the seasonal coughs and sniffles he had been treating all morning. Typically, it was Mrs McAllister who was his last patient. The hypochondriac of the village who, although in her sixtieth year and actually in perfect health, tended to call on the doctor at least once a week with some supposed ailment or other. Ostensibly though, her main purpose appeared to be to deliver a home-baked Victoria sponge cake or a plate of fruit scones.

As Doctor Hollis was thought to be a bachelor and living alone in the premises behind the surgery, Mrs McAllister was desperately trying to glean as much information about him as she possibly could. He, however, was simply not at all forthcoming about his life outside of being the village doctor. She had even tried to pump his receptionist, Darlene for information. But Darlene could not tell her anything because she quite simply did not know. All anyone really knew was that Doctor John Hollis had arrived in this sleepy village from a practice in Harley Street. Of course, he had been asked by practically the whole village why he would have made such a move. Every time he was asked the question, he responded with alacrity just how much he loved the countryside and was ready for a change from the hustle and bustle of life in the city. Other than that, nothing was known about his private life and that suited him just fine.

The truth of the matter was, that even though he was only forty-two years of age, he was very much enjoying the peace and solitude that the country afforded him and the uncomplicated village folk that he treated in his practice. He shuddered when he recalled some of the Lords, Ladies and other assorted dignitaries that he had had the misfortune to treat in the Harley Street practice. Doctor Hollis looked up as he heard a knock on the door. His receptionist Darlene entered the room.

'Is there anything else you need, Dr Hollis?' She asked him.

'No thank you, Darlene. You go and enjoy the Christmas break with your family.'

'Thank you, Doctor Hollis and I hope you have a really nice time up at the Manor.'

'Thank you, Darlene. I'm sure it will be most interesting. I will tell you all about the festivities on my return.'

'I'll look forward to hearing all about it, Doctor Hollis. Happy Christmas to you.'

'And a very Happy Christmas to you, Darlene,' he responded as she left the room.

'Right then,' he said out loud even though he was all alone. 'Time to go indulge myself with the posh people.' He gave a light laugh and left the room.

The Reverend Joseph Smith was sitting in his favourite armchair in the parlour at the vicarage where he resided, having been the parish vicar for over ten years now. As it was Christmas Eve, the evensong service would be conducted by the curate. However, the Reverend was busy adding the finishing touches to the short sermon he would deliver at that evening's midnight service.

The vicarage was attached to a beautiful, old sixteenth century church, which in turn was only a short walk from the Manor House, home of Lord and Lady Mountjoy. He smiled inwardly, recalling previous Christmas Eves when he had walked with the Mountjoy family and their guests across the Manor estate and into the little church for the midnight service. Hopefully, the dark threatening skies would not empty their contents down on the village and the service would take place as planned.

Extracting his pocket watch from the small pocket in his vest, he gave a satisfied nod, delighted that he had perfected the sermon at exactly the right time to now be making his way up to the Manor House. Although perhaps he should leave his sermon with his curate, Thomas Mason, just in case?

Clarissa Llewellyn-Jones stared vacantly out of the carriage window of the train that was transporting her towards her very oldest friend for the festive period. Clarissa adored her friend Serena but could not abide the rest of her family and the last time she had joined them all for Christmas, had found all the invited guests to be the most intolerable bores. She had vowed never to return and indeed had spent the intervening Yuletides partying with the rich and famous, on the arm of a young beau.

However, not one single invitation had come forth this year. Added to which, there was currently no young beau dancing attendance on her. Plus, her singing engagements for the following year were not nearly as many as in previous years. Worried that her star might be fading along with her looks, she simply could not face this time of year on her own. For these reasons she finally accepted her dear friend's annual invitation.

She really was quite looking forward to seeing old Serena again and, if her memory served her well, Lord David did keep an excellent wine cellar. Plus, if they had retained their old cook, the food would be jolly decent as well.

All alone in her first-class carriage, Clarissa felt cheered enough to practise a little aria and look forward to a nice break in the countryside.

Lady Eliza Ross was waiting patiently in her sitting room at the Gate House for her daughter Susan to descend from her bedroom above, so that they could walk across to the Manor House together for Christmas Eve lunch.

Lady Eliza enjoyed Christmas up at the Manor House enormously. She knew that Lord David admired her and was always most attentive. This gave an added bonus of annoying

Lady Serena, which was evident to Eliza by the fixed smile she kept on her face whenever she came across the two of them talking and laughing together.

Then, of course, there was David's younger brother, Colonel James Mountjoy. The Colonel always flirted outrageously with her, and she could not help but be flattered by the attentions of such a handsome, charming and distinguished younger man. Of course, she realised that he was hoping to woo her and then somehow extract funds from her. She had heard rumours that this was his modus operandi. Affairs with wealthy married women who, once the affair had petered out, would pay him to buy his discretion. Lady Eliza would enjoy the flirting for as long as it lasted, but not one penny would he be able to extract from her.

Looking up she saw that her daughter had finally entered the room. 'Goodness what took you so long?' Lady Eliza asked her.

'Calm down, Mummy, we've got ages yet. Anyway, I've just been arranging for some overnight things to be added to the evening clothes that the servants are taking up to the
Manor House. If you ask me, we are in for one heck of a snowstorm and may well need to spend the night there.'

Lady Eliza sighed. Her thirty-year old, headstrong daughter would do as she saw fit. It would not have even occurred to her that there might not be any room for them to sleep up at the
Manor House, or how it might inconvenience their hosts.

Sometimes she wondered about the wisdom of the terms of her daughter's trust fund that her late husband, Lord Duncan Ross had arranged. If Susan had married before reaching the age of twenty-one, she could not access the funds until her thirty fifth birthday. Presumably, to ensure the devotion of her chosen husband. However, if she remained a spinster of the parish until she was twenty-one, the trust fund was all hers to do with as she pleased.

Whether Lord Duncan assumed that once someone turned twenty-one, they automatically acquired some common sense, she did not know. But she was pretty sure that, like herself, he would not have approved of their daughter's chosen lifestyle. Her musings were interrupted by her daughter's shrill tone.

'Come on then, Mummy, if you are in such a hurry. Let's get up there before it starts snowing.'

Lady Eliza rose from her chair and followed her daughter out of the room.

Colonel James Mountjoy was currently driving, way too fast it must be pointed out, in his bright red sports car along the country lanes that would take him to his brother, Lord David's residence. Very glad to be escaping for a while from his bachelor lifestyle, which sometimes rendered him in a spot of bother. For example, his latest liaison had ended with a gun being pointed at his head and, although he was sure that the fuss would all die down soon, felt that it might be wise to lie low for a while.

On second thoughts, maybe it would be wise to find himself a rich wife and take a break from all his philandering. The Lady Eliza Ross was a fine woman that he had always enjoyed flirting with, even though she had always rebuked his advances up until now. Perhaps this time he could use the more subtle approach of undying devotion. His new wife would surely be quite contented at the Gate House whilst he was away on business in the city. The odd discreet liaison needn't bother her, especially if she didn't find out. James started whistling a merry tune and tapping his fingers on the steering wheel as he started to plan exactly how to woo the lovely, unknowing, Lady Eliza.

Sonia Ferguson declined to dress for lunch having decided that she was adequately dressed already. Instead, she was seated at the top of the great stairs, in an alcove with a large window that overlooked the sweeping driveway. She quite often sat in this position and watched all the comings and goings in and out of the Manor House below her. Now she was watching, eagerly waiting for all the guests to arrive.

It wasn't long before she spotted Lady Eliza Ross and her daughter Susan walking arm in arm up the driveway. Sonia

Ferguson tutted. With all the money Lord Duncan left her, you would have thought that she would have left the Manor's Gate House and moved somewhere far more suitable by now.

Sonia was of the opinion, that Lord David liked having her around a little too much. Quite understandable as he had married a shrew. Serena might be her own flesh and blood, but she recognised a shrew when she saw one!

The daughter Susan was dressed up to the nines, she noted, in a very smart fur coat and matching hat. The very latest London fashion no doubt.

Like clockwork, as they were nearing the porchway, both Lord David and Stephen Mountjoy appeared to dance attendance on the first of their guests to arrive. Lord David took Lady Eliza's arm and escorted her through the front door of the Manor House and straight into the drawing room where they would probably both be soused on the dry sherry by lunchtime.

Stephen Mountjoy leant in and kissed Susan on the cheek before taking the vanity case, that had obviously not been trusted with the servants, from her. Her grandson really was like a little devoted puppy dog around that girl. So eager to please and grateful for any morsel thrown back at him. He was just as stupid as his father. Her son-in-law had made a right pig's ear of running the Manor estate and Stephen appeared to be following in his footsteps. They disappeared into the house as well, but Sonia carried on watching.

She did not have to wait too long before Lord David's Rolls Royce appeared in the driveway. Now this should be interesting! Their chauffeur, Robert Milroy, had driven to the local station to pick up the diva, Clarissa Llewellyn-Jones. World famous opera singer apparently, although Sonia personally felt that she sounded more like a strangled cat. What a size she was as well, Sonia noticed as she struggled out of the rear of the Rolls.

Serena immediately appeared from the house and ran towards her oldest friend, no decorum at all, arms outstretched as she enveloped Clarissa in a huge bear hug. Two old lushes reunited, Sonia thought to herself as her daughter and friend disappeared into the house.

Meanwhile, the chauffeur had unloaded Clarissa's numerous suitcases from the boot of the Rolls ready for the servants to carry into the house. He was about to get back into the driver's seat, presumably to park in the garages by the stables, when Sonia's granddaughter, Amelia came around the corner of the house and approached him. The pair huddled together and appeared to be whispering in earnest about something. Amelia climbed into the passenger seat of the Rolls and Robert drove them around to the left of the house where the garages were situated and, also where the chauffeur had a small living space above. Sonia thought that most odd and wondered what on earth her granddaughter could be doing with the chauffeur? Nothing good that was for sure.

Poor Amelia's husband was declared MIA at the end of the Great War. As far as the rest of the family were concerned, Amelia was a widow. But she would simply not accept the fact, and move forward with her life. The girl did little more than mope around the Manor House all day when she should have found herself another rich husband by now and delivered an heir and a spare. You simply had to get on with things in her opinion.

Sonia's attention was drawn back to the drive as a fast moving, cloud of dust came towards the Manor House and drew to a sudden halt. Oh joy. Lord David's younger brother, Colonel James, driving a totally inappropriate sports car. No doubt purchased to woo the ladies. One of these days he really was going to get what was coming to him from some cuckolded husband. Nobody appeared at the front door to greet him or admire his beastly machine. So, he took off again in another cloud of dust towards the Manor's garages. He would then probably enter the house via the kitchen to make himself popular with the servants who appeared to adore his fake charm. For some strange reason it was possibly only apparent to those below stairs.

Talking of below stairs, here was the Reverend Smith fairly

trotting up the drive as fast as his legs would carry him. Heaven forbid that he missed a single moment of the festivities. As dull as ditch water, Sonia would be surprised if she spoke more than two words to him the whole time he was here. Nobody ran out to greet him either. But she shortly heard the ring of a bell and what sounded like one of the servant's footsteps, scurrying towards the door.

The only good thing she had to say about the presence of Reverend Smith every Christmas, was that at least he remained sober, pious and devout throughout. Although, he had arrived in time for a small sherry in the drawing room before lunch. She would bet a guinea that he was indeed imbibing. She found herself quite hoping that he was, as it might make him slightly less boring.

Sonia Ferguson attended church regularly and was a God-fearing woman. But she did not suffer fools gladly and, for reasons she kept entirely to herself, she completely believed that the vicar was a fool and a hypocrite.

Sonia was so lost in thought that she almost missed the arrival of Mr George William Rochester, the bank manager. She did not agree with her daughter that he was a dull little man, for that is what Serena really thought despite what she had said earlier. From the social functions where they had both attended, Sonia had noted a man who quietly observed his fellow human beings and appeared to be more interested in listening than talking himself. Perhaps it was the quietness that made some people assume he was just a dullard. However, when he had something to say, he was extremely articulate and spoke with intelligence. She wondered how much he would contribute to the next couple of days. Let's face it, he would have a whale of a time observing this group of people. The privileged class enjoying its privileges. Sonia stifled a giggle at that thought as GW Rochester entered the Manor House.

Finally, the one person she was looking forward to spending time with, Doctor John Hollis. You didn't get to be her age without needing a little medical intervention every once in a while. Having practiced in Harley Street, she found Doctor Hollis extremely forward thinking in his ideas of how to treat her ailments and she felt better than she had in years. He had taken time with her and appeared genuinely interested.

Sonia was hoping that in this relaxed social setting, she might get to know him a little better. She knew absolutely nothing about his private life and, apparently, his dopey receptionist Darlene knew nothing about him either. She noticed that he was not carrying a medical bag, which some doctors carried with them everywhere. So, he really had declared himself off duty for the next couple of days. Let the real John Hollis reveal himself then.

Rising slowly from the chair, Sonia decided now was the time to make her grand entrance into the drawing room.

CHAPTER FOUR

Whatever the conversation had been ceased the moment Sonia Ferguson entered the drawing room.

'Ah, Mummy, here you are at last,' Serena declared as she handed her a glass of sherry. 'Everyone is here.'

'So, I see,' Sonia replied and turning towards her granddaughter continued, 'Amelia, so glad that you made it in time. I did wonder when I saw you with the chauffeur in the Rolls heading towards the garages.'

Amelia blushed a deep crimson. 'Oh, Robert just gave me a quick lift around to the stables. I just wanted to check on the horses before lunch.'

The awkward silence that followed was thankfully broken by the sounding of the gong, signalling that lunch was now served.

'Spiffing,' declared Colonel James. 'I am simply famished.'

'Right. Come along everyone and drink up your sherry. Lord David and I will lead you into the dining room,' Lady Serena announced.

Sonia Ferguson approached Doctor Hollis and offered her arm, indicating that she expected him to lead her into the dining room. He gave a slight nod and proceeded to do so. Colonel James made a beeline for Lady Eliza, starting as he meant to go on. Stephen Mountjoy and Susan Ross had been standing next to each other, so he was delighted to quickly be able to offer her his arm. Clarissa was determined not to be led in by a vicar, who was heading her way. She managed a quick sidestep and offered her arm to Mr Rochester. That left a slightly shell-shocked looking Amelia standing alone. The Reverend Smith decided that here was a poor soul in need of his attention, as he took her by the elbow and walked her into the dining room.

Lady Serena had considered her table plan most carefully and strategically. As the hostess, she felt it was her due to be immediately surrounded by who she considered to be her most charming guests. Obviously, she and Lord David would be seated at opposite ends of the long dining room table. To her left she had placed her dear friend Clarissa, with Colonel James next to her as she thought that Clarissa might find his boyish charm endearing. Next to the Colonel was Susan Ross, who could handle herself and the Colonel, should he attempt to flirt with her. The Reverend Smith was on Susan's left, which saw him seated between mother and daughter, as Lady Eliza had been placed immediately to the right of Lord David. She did not care for all the attention her husband paid to Lady Eliza but knew that he would sulk if he did not get his wish to be seated next to her.

On Lord David's left, and also at his request, was George Rochester. This suited Serena admirably, to be as far away from this boring little man as possible. She had placed Amelia next to the bank manager and then her son Stephen. This meant that her daughter was diagonal to her father, Lady Eliza and Susan, opposite Reverend Smith and next to her brother. Amelia was often quite awkward in large social gatherings, so at least she should feel quite comfortable at mealtimes. Sonia, she had placed between Stephen and Doctor Hollis, who was on Serena's immediate right This would delight her mother, who Serena had also placed near to herself to keep her in check. Sonia really did say exactly what she thought, at all times, with no filter whatsoever. Nine times out of ten it was completely inappropriate. So, hopefully her fascination with the doctor would keep her out of trouble for the next few days at least.

Looking around the table now that everyone was seated, Serena gave a self-satisfied smile. Her husband was the first to speak as the soup was being served from a large tureen on the sideboard, the wine glasses having already been filled. She noted how Reverend Smith had not declined the wine, having probably got a taste for it after his large dry sherry.

'Welcome one and all,' Lord David announced. 'Here we are, Christmas 1930 and what a year it's been. But now it is time for celebration. So, I will ask you all to partake and enjoy some of the delicious food cook has prepared and some of the finest wines from my own cellar.'

'Yes, thank you, dear,' Lady Serena retorted. 'Now, as everyone has their soup, may I ask you to say 'Grace' please, Reverend?'

'Certainly, certainly,' he replied with a slight slur.

'Good heavens above,' thought Sonia. *'The man is already half cut!'*

The Reverend stumbled his way through a very short Grace, at the end of which Sonia produced an audible snort, loud enough to be heard by the entire table. Serena cast a look in her mother's direction that spoke volumes. Luckily, Doctor Hollis chose to address the awkward silence by commenting on how wonderfully cared for he thought the grounds were looking and had they had any success with vegetables this year?

Lady Serena smiled and puffed her chest out proudly. 'Why yes, Doctor Hollis. We will be enjoying all home-grown vegetables tomorrow with our Christmas luncheon. Of course, it is extremely difficult now with only one groundsman.'

'Ah yes, Nathan Parkes,' Reverend Smith interrupted.

'His name is Nathaniel Parker,' Lady Serena replied haughtily. So furious was she that she had been interrupted, that she failed to notice that George Rochester had raised his eyebrows in surprise and continued before any further interruptions could take place.

'He potters around happily six days a week and does have a quite wonderful way with flowers. Quite frankly, I have never seen roses anything like the ones Parker is able to produce.'

At this point, Clarissa looked around the table with wine glass in hand and boasted loudly.

'Personally, I've never had to grow flowers. I am just on the receiving end of hundreds of bouquets.'

Everyone at the table gave a polite little laugh, albeit mostly false, which brought to an end the conversation concerning the grounds. Clarissa sat back in her chair, annoyed that no one appeared to be fully appreciating her and her fame. Not to mention her very divine presence at this sad old Manor House.

George Rochester, a keen observer of people, noticed that another awkward silence had descended and so turned to Lord David. 'How is your new venture into the antiques business going, Sir?'

Relieved that the silence had been broken, Lord David positively gushed. 'Well, so far, I think. But it is very early days.'

'Oh yes,' Reverend Smith piped up once again. 'I think I saw one of them in the village. Some kind of statue. Very good. You would almost think it was the real thing.'

Cutlery hovered midway between plates and mouths, as everyone's attention turned towards Lord David and the Reverend. Lord David was quick to reply.

'I do not deal in statues or supply to the antique shop in the village.'

'Oh, but I thought....,' the Reverend started.

'Never mind,' Lord David said brightly. 'Let me tell what I have planned for you gentlemen this afternoon.'

The ladies took this time to focus on eating and drinking, whilst the men turned their attention to Lord David as he began to speak.

'Of course, some of you will already be aware. But, for those of you who aren't, Christmas Eve afternoon has, traditionally, always been spent by the gentlemen on a shoot. For generations now as it happens. It all started one lean year when if nothing had been shot and killed on Christmas Eve, there would have been no roast bird on the table at all. In fact, there have been a few years where that has been the case. We are indeed fortunate that this year there is a sumptuous bird just waiting for cook to give it a good stuffing and roast to perfection. However, today's spoils shall be enjoyed by us all, through to the New Year with a bit of luck. So, gentlemen I suggest we leave the ladies now and take our coffee, and brandy with us while the weather holds.

Jameson, flasks of coffee and brandy if you will and we will meet in fifteen minutes in the great hall. Ladies, if you will excuse us, the gentlemen and I will take our leave.'

With that, Lord David rose, gave a nod to the ladies and left the dining room followed by the other gentlemen.

'Right then,' declared Lady Serena. 'If we are all finished, coffee will be served in the drawing room.'

Clarissa had been secretly hoping for some more dessert, but rose and followed the others, leaving just the servants to clear up and ponder on the various snippets of conversation they had just witnessed.

CHAPTER FIVE

The ladies gathered in the drawing room as Alice served coffee.

'Some brandies as well please, Alice?' Lady Serena requested. Turning to the assembled ladies she announced, 'We must not forsake our stroll around the gardens that is taken every year after Christmas Eve lunch. But with the threat of snow in the air it must be quite chilly outside. So, let's have some brandy now to keep us nice and warm inside.'

Everyone was so used to the traditions that were part of 'Christmas at The Manor House', that nobody objected. Apart from Clarissa who would much rather have taken a post lunch snooze! However, the brandy, or even brandies, would go down very well and she might even get more of a chance to talk about herself and become the centre of attention that she always craved.

Susan Ross picked up the newspaper that had been left on the sofa next to her and started reading the front page. 'Goodness me!' she exclaimed. 'Nothing but bad news is there? Worldwide recession: outcomes of the cuts to benefits.'

'Well, what do you expect?' Sonia huffed. 'With a first Labour Party Prime Minister. And as if that wasn't bad enough, Scottish, illegitimate and said some terrible things during The Great War.'

'Well, all that may be true,' Susan retorted. 'But one simply must admire him for appointing the first ever female minister. Very forward thinking. I might just go into politics myself. Put Lord Ross's money to good use.'

'Susan,' Lady Eliza said harshly. 'That is no job for a lady. Your father would not have approved and especially not for this Labour Party.'

Susan shrugged with a half-smile on her face.

'Well, no matter,' said Serena. 'He is our Prime Minister, and we will toast him on Christmas Day, as always. Now no more talk of politics. Goodness me, it is Christmas Eve after all. Everybody out to the great hall. Let's get you all kitted out in warm scarves, gloves and boots and we shall take our walk.' With that, she stood up sharply and strode out of the room, leaving the others to follow in her wake.

Once they were all wrapped up, they left the house via a side door that led directly into the rose garden. Although, of course, there were no roses blooming on this Christmas Eve afternoon. Lady Serena led the way, linking arms with her best friend Clarissa. Lady Eliza followed just behind, arm in arm with her daughter, Susan. Bringing up the rear, Amelia was guiding her grandmother cautiously along the path, out of earshot of the others.

'So, how were the horses, Amelia?' Sonia asked her granddaughter.

'They were fine, thank you, Grandmamma,' came Amelia's weak reply.

'It really is quite inappropriate for you to mix with the servants in that way, Amelia. Even if, as you say, he was simply giving you a lift to the stables, it was certainly not proper to be in the

front passenger seat beside the chauffeur. What if some of our guests had seen you? What would they think? No, that is simply bad form Amelia. You must not do it again.'

'Yes, Grandmamma,' Amelia replied meekly, and they continued walking along in a not so companionable silence.

Lady Eliza and Susan, however, were walking in a comfortable silence as they listened in to the conversation between Lady Serena and Clarissa.

'Oh, it is just so wonderful to have you here with us all this year, darling,' Serena told her friend. 'I just hope you won't find us country village folk too dull.'

Clarissa laughed. 'Who knows that perhaps a little dull is just what I need right now. A little rest and recuperation.'

'Yes of course. Has it all been too tiring this year, darling?' Serena asked her.

'Yes, indeed it has. I am really not sure how much longer I can take playing the role of Cio-Cio Sans mother in Madame Butterfly. Yet the thought of constant travel for live concerts fills me with dread. What is one to do? And to think that I could have opened at The Met in 1907 with Enrico Caruso if I hadn't had my little health problem.'

'Yes, well let's not worry about that now, dear. You can stay here for as long as you want. Things will work themselves out for the best. They always do.' Serena patted Clarissa's hand as they came upon a large patch of overgrown land that was not in keeping with the rest of the grounds.

'Goodness me what has happened here?' Clarissa asked.

'Oh, this patch of land and the fields beyond used to belong to the church. They handed it over to the Manor during the war as we had the WLA, the land girls here, cultivating as much land as possible. It's just too much for Parker to take on as well. In actual fact, I think Stephen is going to sell it all off.'

'Can he do that?' Susan asked. 'Surely the land still belongs to the church and was only lent to the Manor for the war effort.'

'Oh, I'm sure he'll have looked into all that, dear,' Lady Serena dismissed her remark quite haughtily. 'Goodness me. Is that a snowflake just landed on my nose? I do believe it is. We'd best make our way back. Careful now, Mummy, we don't want you slipping.'

Serena and Clarissa led the way as Lady Eliza and Susan followed, Susan with a quizzical expression on her face.

For once, Sonia kept quiet as she and Amelia brought up the rear. Although she could have said an awful lot at that stage.

CHAPTER SIX

Lord David and his brother James were having a whale of a time on the shoot. Fuelled by plenty of brandy, they were missing more birds than they actually shot. Stephen was having the most success as, being the manager of the estate, this was a necessity more than a sport for him and these birds were needed for food.

The Reverend, Doctor Hollis and Mr Rochester had all taken some early shots and were now mostly content to watch Lord David and his brother and try some polite conversation. Reverend Smith turned to Mr Rochester.

'You've had quite some success there, Mr Rochester. Have you done much shooting?'

'A little, Reverend. My fiancée's family have an estate in Yorkshire, and I've shot there from time to time.'

'Ah Yorkshire,' Reverend Smith replied. 'God's county as they say. I spent some time there myself as a younger man. What about you, Doctor Hollis? Have you ever spent any time in Yorkshire?'

'It's not a county I am very familiar with,' the doctor admitted. 'Of course, I was in Harley Street before I decided that a life in the country would be much more appealing.'

'Oh well, that would explain why you haven't managed to shoot as many birds as Mr Rochester here. But I thought I detected a hint of a Yorkshire accent now and again.'

'Unlikely,' Doctor Hollis replied. 'However, I am probably such a poor shot as deep down in my core I believe in preserving life. What about you, Reverend? Does the shoot not contradict your religious beliefs?'

'Oh, I would not kill for sport, Doctor Hollis, indeed. However, this shoot is to provide food and what our Lord tells us in Leviticus chapter eleven, ensures that my conscience remains clear.'

Mr Rochester had spotted the slight needle between these two. Reverend Smith could be a little irritating, he had noticed but the doctor seemed to be particularly irritated by him.

Colonel James gave a whoop of delight after another successful shot, as George Rochester felt the first flakes of snow falling.

'Well done, everyone,' Lord David announced. 'That's a fine haul indeed and just in time. Let's away up to the house and get warm and dry.'

The Gentlemen all made their way hastily back to the Manor House, leaving Alexander Jameson the task of dealing with the rifles and the shot birds.

CHAPTER SEVEN

The ladies had already taken tea and were now resting in their respective rooms when the gentlemen returned. They all decided to give the tea a miss and retire to their rooms before dinner.

Reverend Smith was looking forward to some quality time reading his bible whilst the other gentlemen all intended to take forty winks and sleep off the afternoon's brandies.

Alice collected the remains of the tea things and took them back down below stairs. The kitchen was a hive of activity with preparations for that evening's dinner and tomorrow's Christmas lunch.

'None of the gentlemen took afternoon tea, Mrs Trelawney,' Alice announced as she set down the overladen tray on the kitchen table.

'Well, there's no point letting a perfectly good tea go to waste,' Agnes replied. 'Come on everyone. Sit down at the table and we'll take some tea and vittles.'

Alice, Jane, Betty, Mary and Rose happily ceased what they had been doing and took a seat at the kitchen table. Alexander Jameson had just come in, having dealt with the guns and the birds, and taken a seat in his favourite rocking chair by the hearth. Agnes poured a cup of tea and placed a selection of sandwiches and cake on a plate, which she then took across to her husband.

'There we are, Mr Jameson. Now how did that shoot go this afternoon then?'

'A fine haul, Mrs Trelawney, a fine haul. Mr Stephen was the most successful. I think Colonel James was a little put out by that, him being an army man after all. Reverend Smith managed a couple as usual. But between you and me, the man imbibed a bit with lunch, so I'm rather surprised that he could hit anything at all.'

The girls at the table giggled and Agnes tutted in disapproval.

'Really, Mr Jameson! Gossiping in front of the girls and about a holy man at that.'

'Not gossiping, my dear. Just simply relaying what they could clearly see for themselves.'

'What about Mr Rochester and Doctor Hollis?' Jane asked.

'Yes, they shot a couple of birds each as well. Of course, neither of them has shot at the Manor before. But they didn't look like first time shooters to me.'

'Wasn't the Reverend funny at lunch?' Alice commented. 'He kept getting everything wrong.'

'What do you mean?' Agnes asked her.

'Well, he called gardener Nathan Parkes instead of Nathaniel Parker for starters. Then he told Lord David that he had seen one of his antique statues in the shop in the village. Lord David told him that he didn't sell statues and sold nothing to the local shop.'

Jane and the other maids giggled again whilst Agnes continued to look disapproving.

'That's not all,' added Alexander. 'While they were shooting, he told Doctor Hollis that he thought he spoke with a Yorkshire accent. Everyone knows Doctor Hollis was in Harley Street before he came here. Anyway, he put the man right and told him he had never lived in Yorkshire.'

'Really,' commented Agnes. 'That man really shouldn't have taken a drink at all. He's a service to take later. Now back to work girls. These dinners won't cook themselves, will they?'

The girls rose reluctantly from the kitchen table and set about their chores.

Much as Lady Serena enjoyed playing 'Lady of The Manor' at Christmastime, she always appreciated the moments of solitude she was afforded. A time of reflection and planning. Right now, lying on the chaise longue in her bedroom, she was reflecting on lunch and the afternoon so far.

Generally, she thought she had got her seating plan correct and for the next couple of days the conversation should flow quite nicely. More to the point, her cantankerous old mother had behaved herself. So, placing her next to Doctor Hollis appeared to have worked. It had at least prevented a further interrogation of Amelia.

Really, she did not know what the matter with that girl was. So moody and unpredictable. Her mother was right, hanging around with a chauffeur simply would not do. Perhaps, she ought to have a quiet word with her daughter herself. It was simply too trying. Also, she really must make sure that Reverend Smith didn't drink any more with dinner. He really had embarrassed himself so far and he had a sermon to deliver later. There must be a way to prevent him from coming to the Manor House for Christmas next year.

Thank goodness Clarissa was here this year. She fully intended to have a marvellous time with her friend over the next few days.

Speaking of which, it was high time she started dressing for dinner. She simply could not allow any other lady to outshine her at the dinner table tonight.

Lord David, meanwhile, was indulging in a rather fine cognac and enjoying smoking a large cigar in the privacy of his dressing room. Having foregone tea, he was extremely appreciative of this quiet time before needing to dress for dinner. It wasn't that he disliked these Christmas rituals or his guests, but he was basically a solitary person and needed a respite from time to time.

The shoot had gone well, he thought. His son Stephen always set about it in a very business-like fashion. Personally, he always enjoyed a bit of friendly competition with his brother. Shame about the weather cutting the shoot a little short. Although, he was quite sure that the bank manager, doctor and vicar were more than happy to return to the house. He gave a little chuckle as he pictured them standing outside, freezing half to death.

Glancing out of the window now, he could see that the snow was still coming down thick and fast. Even at this stage, it looked most unlikely that they would all be attending the midnight service at the church tonight. Hopefully, that would not mean that Reverend Smith would drink more wine. He really did become such a buffoon when he imbibed. Lord David really did not need to be watching what that man might be up to when his objective for the next few days was to woo the bank manager and undertake a little harmless flirting with Lady Eliza. Everybody else could just go hang as far as he was concerned. Oh yes, he would be perfectly pleasant to everybody in his 'Lord of The Manor' style. But anytime he could escape on the pretence of taking his beloved dog, Chester, for a walk, he would.

Amelia was pacing up and down in her bedroom, not happy with life at all. It really was too bad of Grandmamma calling her out like that in front of everyone and then going on and on about it on their walk this afternoon.

She'd got it all wrong anyway. Of course, Amelia wasn't fraternising with Robert Milroy, the chauffeur. Her heart still well and truly belonged to her husband, Nigel Cavendish. Even though he had been declared MIA since the end of the Great War, she would not accept that he was dead. She prayed every day that he would return to her, and they could go ahead and live the life they had planned. She fully accepted that he must have been somehow injured during the war and had probably lost his memory. But love could conquer all and so one day his memory would return, and he would come back to her.

Until that happened, she just needed a little help to get her through the day from time to time and that was what Robert was able to help her with. They had both managed to keep it a secret so far and she would never reveal it to anyone.

Although she always managed to put on a brave face,

Amelia had to admit that she found these Christmas gatherings extremely trying. She had absolutely no idea how to converse with Doctor Hollis or Mr Rochester, a bank manager. Susan Ross and Clarissa Llewellyn-Jones completely overwhelmed her. They were just so sophisticated and worldly. Reverend Smith was very nice, she supposed, if a little boring.

Amelia adored her Uncle James, but he would probably be far too busy flirting with one or all of the other ladies to pay much attention to her. Oh well, luckily Robert had been able to fix her up with enough 'tonic' to help her through the next few days. Amelia gave a sigh and started to prepare for dinner.

Her brother Stephen was in his own bedroom watching the snow coming down thick and fast, with no sign of abating and gave a sly smile. As soon as everyone was gathered downstairs, he must impress upon them how attending the midnight service would be impossible for all of them, including Reverend Smith. He could then encourage the man to enjoy a few more glasses of wine.

Stephen required Reverend Smith to be intoxicated in order that he could be easily persuaded to sign the document that Stephen had had the family solicitor prepare. Technically, the land that the parish had given to the Manor estate during the war still belonged to the church. It had been handed over on trust and therefore no paperwork had ever been completed. However, in the twelve years since the Great War had ended, the church had never once asked for the land and honestly, as far as Stephen was concerned, could have no use for it.

He though desperately needed the funds that would come from the sale of that land. He had not made a huge success of running the estate since taking over full time from Lord David and he could not bear to be thought of as a failure by his family. But that was not going to happen. The Reverend Smith would sign his document, and everything would work out just fine. Stephen turned away from the window and walked into his dressing room.

CHAPTER EIGHT

Usually at The Manor House, at least one person would have descended into the drawing room for drinks before Alexander had sounded the first gong of the evening. However, on this occasion it was the sound of the gong that brought everyone from their rooms to start the evening's proceedings.

Perhaps, it was the wine and brandies that had been consumed earlier that made them all require some extra rest in the afternoon. Nevertheless, they all arrived within five minutes of the gong to discover Colonel James, who had obviously been the first to descend, busy mixing up cocktails and pressing them upon everyone.

'Come along, everyone. These are the latest thing in London you know. A Sidecar for the ladies and an Old Fashioned for the gentlemen.'

Sonia took the cocktail that was offered to her and knocked it straight back. 'Delicious, James,' she commented. 'I'll take another one, please?'

Susan looked on in admiration at the old lady. Colonel James had not held back on the liquor as this was one of the strongest cocktails she had ever tasted, and that was really saying something. She looked around her, thinking that now might be the time to start chatting to Stephen and enjoy a little harmless flirtation when she noticed that he had handed Reverend Smith an Old Fashioned and was now leading him to the corner of the room.

'Well now,' she said to herself. 'I wonder what that is all about?' Then, all of a sudden, she remembered about the patch of land that they had come across on their afternoon stroll, that still belonged to the church. 'I'll bet that's what he's doing. Trying to con the vicar out of that land.'

Just then, she was startled by a loud guffaw and turned her attention back to where it had come from. Clarissa had just accepted a cocktail from James and had produced the loud noise as a result of something he had said to her. Susan took a moment to study Clarissa. She was wearing a multi-coloured kaftan that brought to mind Joseph and his coat of many colours. This exotic ensemble was completed with a matching turban that had a peacock feather attached to the front. Her ears, neck, wrists and fingers were adorned in gold jewellery.

'Really, what was she doing here in this country manor dressed like that?' Susan said to herself. James seemed to be quite taken with her though, chatting away as he poured her a second cocktail. Well, it would keep his attention away from her own mother for a while anyway.

Susan was fully aware of his intentions towards Lady Eliza. He had tried to woo Susan first of all after her father, Lord Duncan, had died. But she had very firmly rejected him. Lady Eliza had also resisted his charms thus far, but he might just wear her down eventually when Susan wasn't around to watch out for her mother.

All he wanted was money and wasn't too choosy about where it came from. Perhaps, that explained his behaviour towards Clarissa. He might be trying his luck there.

Susan noticed her mother sitting quietly by the fireplace, dressed demurely in black velvet, with a simple string of pearls her only adornment. She had placed her cocktail on a side table, untouched, as she watched James and Clarissa with what could only be described as a look of disdain on her face.

Spotting that Lady Eliza was alone, Lord David made his way over to the fireplace to talk to her. 'Ah, my mother's other suitor,' Susan chuckled. 'Lady Serena will be pleased.' Her eyes scanned the room looking for Serena and fell once again on Stephen and Reverend Smith.

The Reverend was striding back towards Colonel James with

his now empty glass. Stephen stood staring after him with an expression on his face that could only be described as furious. 'Guess that didn't go well then,' she thought. Probably not a good idea to talk to Stephen now. Turning back towards James, she decided to have another cocktail.

George Rochester stood slightly to one side with his Old Fashioned and did what he liked to do best, observing everyone around him. Although he had only been in the Manor House a few short hours, George felt he had gained some insight into each of the people here for the Christmas festivities.

Take Lady Serena for example. She was doing a grand job playing the charming hostess. But every now and then, her expression would sour when something displeased her. In the short time that they had been in the drawing room for pre-dinner drinks, he had seen her direct that sour look a few times.

Firstly, towards her son Stephen and Reverend Smith when Stephen had handed him a cocktail. Clearly, she preferred the clergyman to be sober, which George imagined the Reverend probably was most of the time as he clearly could not hold his drink, judging by his tipsy comments at lunch and during the afternoon shoot.

She had also looked sour when she noticed that Lord David was over by the fireplace chatting to Lady Eliza, both of whom were smiling and obviously happy to be engaging in conversation with each other. She also looked displeased that Lord David had allowed his dog to sleep on the rug in front of the fire.

Meeting his gaze, her eyes passed over him as she settled her gaze on the group who stood around where her brother-in-law had been making cocktails. All apart from Stephen that was, who stood entirely alone. His face was pale and wearing a look that appeared to indicate anger and utter despair. Of course, George had observed him talking to Reverend Smith just a short while ago.

'Now, I wonder what happened there?' he thought. 'Very curious.' He turned, intending to join the main group just as the dinner gong sounded.

Colonel James's cocktails had clearly done the trick as it was a very jovial group that sat down to dinner. Lady Serena had lost her sour expression and even Stephen had managed a smile. The snow had not abated, and drifts had started to form, some of which were up to five feet already.

'Well,' declared Lord David. 'It very much looks like we could all be stuck here together for the next few days. I can't remember a time when the Mountjoy family and their guests did not attend the midnight service or the service on Christmas morning. I don't think you need to worry about the curate delivering your sermon, Reverend. Highly unlikely anyone in the village will be able to make their way to the church either, including the curate.'

Lord David chuckled before continuing. 'So, let us all eat, drink and be merry. Reverend, would you be so kind as to lead us in thanks please?'

Reverend Smith concentrated hard on saying Grace without slurring. He had previously noted Lady Serena's looks of disapproval and didn't wish to further blot his copybook, so to speak. He so enjoyed his Christmas's at the Manor House and would be devastated if he found that he wasn't to be invited back the following year. He managed to get through it without one single stumble and was therefore delighted to see Lady Serena nodding her approval when he looked across at her.

As they were all being served with delicious food and drink, Colonel James turned towards Reverend Smith. 'I bet you've heard some things in your time at the old confessional, haven't you, Reverend?'

'Ah, well now,' the Reverend began. 'Of course, strictly speaking, confession belongs to the priests of the Roman Catholic faith. However, one is so often seen as a sort of spiritual guide. Many of my parishioners do choose to talk to me and I always encourage them to do so. A problem shared being a problem halved, as they say.'

'Are they hoping you will be able to forgive them their sins?'

Amelia enquired.

'Well, sometimes yes, my dear.' The Reverend continued staring at Amelia. 'But sometimes they are just looking for a little help or advice that will enable them to find solutions to the perceived problems they are facing in their own lives.'

Turning his glance away from Amelia to scan the whole table, he continued. 'But a lot of the time people do so like to inform me about other people's transgressions. Purportedly, under the guise of looking for advice over whether they should take any action themselves. Mostly, I suspect they have just come for a jolly good gossip. It's always been the same in every parish that I have ever worked in.'

'Oh, do tell, Reverend,' Susan encouraged him. 'It doesn't need to be scandal from this village, although that would be rather juicy.'

The Reverend smiled. He was rather enjoying his moment in the spotlight and the drink had certainly loosened his tongue. Just as long as he didn't name names or indeed the parish in which it related to, what harm could it really do?

'Alright,' he nodded around the table. 'I remember being in the church one day, when I heard the sound of high heeled shoes clicking and clacking at great speed down the centre aisle. I went to see who was there and it turned out to be a young girl who was a maid at one of the big houses in the parish. Most disturbed she was. So, I sat her down and asked what was wrong. She told me that she was really worried about two of the senior staff in the house where she worked. They were just married you see, and it was a very respectable house. However, her own mother had just found out that these two couldn't possibly be a married couple as the gentleman in question already had a wife from some years before, but nobody knew where she was.'

The Reverend paused at the sound of something clattering behind him, as a rather red-faced Jameson picked up the knife that had just fallen to the floor.

'What did you advise?' Amelia asked.

'Well, I told her that it was admirable of her to be concerned for their souls, but was she absolutely sure that this wasn't just a bit of gossip started by someone who bore them a grudge? Therefore, she had best do nothing unless she was absolutely sure, as she might just get into trouble herself.'

'That's all very well,' Lady Serena interrupted. 'However, if it was my house, I would have liked to have been informed if there was even a hint of impropriety. I would, of course, investigate and deal with the matter accordingly.'

'Oh, I am sure that kind of thing happens all the time,' commented Susan. 'Living in sin with a curtain ring on the third finger of your left hand. Anyway Reverend, enough with the boring tales from below stairs. Give us something juicy from above stairs.'

Reverend Smith glanced at Susan with a slight twinkle in his eye. 'Well, yes, I suppose I do recall one occasion when I was not required to give any advice or an opinion. The person involved was so totally racked with guilt that they just wanted to speak to someone completely impartial, so to speak. A lady of a rather fine estate had borne her husband the son that he had always wanted, a few years earlier. However, the lady had been somewhat indiscreet, and she had never been sure that the child was actually her husband's. Now that the boy was grown, she was more and more convinced every day that he was not her husband's son and even worse that her husband would realise this himself, or at the very least suspect something.'

'That's more like it,' Susan commented. 'Anyone we know, Reverend?'

'Really, Susan,' snapped Lady Serena. 'That really is quite enough of that kind of talk at the dinner table. Let the Reverend eat his dinner now. Goodness me, he is almost an entire course behind the rest of us. Now then, can anyone remember the last time this much snow fell in such a short space of time?'

The conversation for the remainder of the meal turned to such mundane topics as the weather past and present and how long it might be before the current snow thawed.

As the meal came to a close and the ladies were preparing to leave the gentlemen to their brandy and cigars, Lady Serena rose from her chair and announced, 'As it will be impossible for us to attend the midnight service this evening, I propose that we all gather around the piano later for some carols. Amelia will play. In the meantime, when you are ready to join us gentlemen, I suggest a nice round or two of Bridge in the drawing room. Two tables, I think. Amelia, Stephen, Susan and James, I am sure you would be happier playing that confounded Chinese game you are always talking about.'

'Mah-jong, Mummy,' Stephen told her.

'Oh yes,' James added. 'Much more fun.'

Lady Serena tutted before adding, 'Right ladies, let's excuse ourselves and take coffee in the
drawing room.'

The heavy drapes in the drawing room had been drawn and a fire was blazing in the hearth, the light from the flames reflecting in the glass ornaments hanging from the branches of the Christmas tree. The effect of which made the large room appear rather cosy. The ladies remarked on this as they took their seats to be served coffee and liqueurs.

Lady Serena turned to her mother. 'Mummy, why don't you decide the fours for Bridge with Eliza? Susan, and Amelia, you can set up the tables.' She was hoping to spend a few more precious moments chatting to Clarissa whilst everyone else set about their tasks. Besides which, as much as she hated relinquishing control of any given situation, she fully realised that there would be at least one, if not two people that she would have to be in a four with whose company she could generally do without. Therefore, to her mind, better to let someone else make the decision for her.

Meanwhile, the gentlemen were enjoying their brandy and cigars in the dining room courtesy of Jameson.

'Splendiferous vittles there, David,' James remarked. 'Anyway, now the ladies have left, and it is just us men, why don't you enlighten us, Reverend as to some of your dark tales? No need to be so delicate now, what?'

Further fuelled with fine wine and brandy, Reverend Smith did not need to be asked twice and indeed was very happy to be the centre of attention again as he regaled some more of his secrets.

'Yes, it really is most surprising what people will reveal to you, especially things that perhaps should be reported to the police.'

'What on earth do you mean?' James asked him, rather astonished.

'Well, years ago when I was working in a parish in the North of England, a young lady came to see me and told me that she was terrified that her husband was going to kill her. Now I didn't know her or her husband at all. Apparently, she had travelled some distance to talk to someone who would remain entirely neutral. Of course, I told her that she must report her suspicions to the police, but she replied that she couldn't do that as there was not a single shred of evidence and therefore the police would not believe her.

'Furthermore, her husband was a doctor, extremely popular, well liked, pillar of the community. Also, a member of the golf club and always extremely charming and courteous to everyone he met, including her.

'To all intents and purposes, there was absolutely no reason to believe that he meant her any ill will at all. And yet, she remained convinced that he intended to kill her.'

'So, what did you do?' James asked eagerly.

'All I could do at the time. I prayed with her and advised that she kept on praying for guidance and a solution would surely come to her.

'However, not long after that, I heard that the lady had died of a gastric condition. I felt it was my duty to tell the police what I knew because, if the lady had been correct in her suspicion, perhaps the husband, a doctor after all, had administered some sort of poison that manifested as some kind of gastric complaint.

'The police explained to me that there were no suspicious

circumstances whatsoever as the doctor had been treating his wife for the stomach complaint for some time. It was believed that her ongoing illness had made her a little depressed and therefore prone to all sorts of imaginings.

'The doctor left the area soon afterwards, supposedly for a fresh start. But I am convinced to this day that he somehow murdered his wife and got away with it.'

'Well, that's good to know,' joked James. Turning to Doctor Hollis, he added, 'Remind me to have a chat with you about poisons that manifest as a stomach complaint, Doc. It could come in jolly useful one of these days.'

Doctor Hollis forced a half smile, clearly not amused by James's suggestion.

Lord David was quite obviously not amused either as he jibed, 'Given your philandering, James, you need to make sure that some husband doesn't come after you.'

The Reverend looked somewhat astonished, then added, 'Of course the question of the unfaithful wife isn't always answered by murder now, is it?

'I recall a gentleman, very near to the end of his life, asked me to visit. It turned out that he wanted to confess to me that he had just changed his will so that his wife did not inherit a penny of his estate. Turns out that he had always suspected that his wife had married him for reasons other than love and she was, in fact, in love with his best friend. They had been happy enough, until recent times with the children now grown and fleeing the nest. And now with his own health failing, he strongly suspected that the old romance had been rekindled, even though his best friend was also married. It had angered him so much that he had changed his will as a consequence.'

'What happened to the wife?' James asked.

'Now here is a funny thing,' Reverend Smith replied. 'When the gentleman died shortly afterwards, it appeared he hadn't changed his will at all as the wife inherited everything. Most strange.'

Just then, there was a knock on the dining room door and

Jameson entered.

'Yes, what is it, Jameson?' Lord David asked him.

'Excuse me, my Lord. Gardener is in the kitchen. He was waiting in one of the sheds for the snow to stop and now it is too deep for him to return to his cottage. Would it be alright for him to dine with us below stairs and stay overnight in the servant's quarters Sir? Also, Robert, Mr Milroy has made it to the kitchen for his supper but thinks it would be best if he stayed over as well Sir. He could share a room with Gardener.'

'Why yes of course, Jameson,' Lord David told him. 'It is the season of good will to all men after all. Right, if there is nothing else, we really ought to go and join the ladies. They'll be wondering where on earth we've got to.'

With that, the gentlemen rose and followed Lord David out of the room. Jameson looked around at the vast array of dishes and glasses and with a sigh, left the room and returned below stairs.

Nathaniel Parker and Robert Milroy were sitting on either side of the hearth, desperately trying to get warm, when Jameson returned to the kitchen. Alice and Jane were assisting Agnes with the preparation of the servant's Christmas Eve supper. Betty, Mary and Rose had formed a production line at the kitchen sink of washing, drying and putting away a constant supply of glasses, crockery and cutlery that a Christmas at the Manor House produced.

'Leave that now, girls,' he told them. 'The dining room is ready for clearing, so get that done before we all sit down for our supper.'

'Yes, Mr Jameson,' all three replied before grabbing the big serving trays and hurrying up the stairs to the dining room.

'Gentlemen,' Jameson turned to the hearth. 'Lord David is happy for you to stay at the Manor House tonight. The girls will make up a room for you after supper. Who would have thought the weather would come in like this now?'

'Well, let's look on the bright side,' Agnes chipped in. 'We can all be one big happy family this Christmas Day. Plenty of good food here. And I'm sure Mr Jameson will appreciate a couple of extra pairs of hands tomorrow morning. Hectic is what it is on Christmas Day.'

'Yes, of course,' replied Parker. 'Happy to oblige, I'm sure.'

'Indeed,' agreed Robert Milroy. 'Although, I must make it down to the stables tomorrow and see to the horses. Amelia won't be able to make it down there, I'm sure.'

The family did not employ any stable staff. Mostly, Amelia enjoyed looking after the horses but as Milroy was hardly utilised full time as a chauffeur, it was mainly his responsibility to make sure that they were fed, watered and exercised.

'Aye well, there's snowshoes and skis in one of the cupboards you can use, and we'll give you some sugar lumps to take. Even the horses deserve a bit of a treat on Christmas Day, don't they?' Agnes joked.

Betty, Mary and Rose returned to the kitchen. Trays piled high with dirty crockery.

'Leave all them by the sink and come and set the table,' Agnes told them. 'May as well tackle it all at once after we've had our supper. Mr Parker, Mr Milroy, I hope you are all warmed through now. Come up to the table and get your supper while it's hot.'

Everyone took a seat at the table whilst Agnes, Alice and Jane placed delicious smelling dishes upon it. There was silence as the dishes were passed around and everyone filled their plates.

'Mr Jameson will say Grace,' Agnes advised, and Mr Jameson duly delivered.

'Was the vicar still drinking with dinner?' Alice asked, once they were all heartily tucking into their food.

'Oh yes,' replied Jameson. 'Knowing that he had been relieved of his Christmas duties, he
really had become quite intoxicated. Colonel James was egging him on to reveal some of the secrets people had told him and he came out with all sorts of nonsense about servants and illegitimate children.'

'He was the same at lunchtime, wasn't he?' suggested Jane. 'They was all talking about the garden and what a fine job you do

Mr Parker and vicar called you Nathan Parkes.' Jane laughed and looked at Parker who had raised one eyebrow and had a look of complete surprise on his face.

'Oh, you wasn't the only one,' Jane continued. 'He got it wrong about Lord David and Doctor Hollis too.'

'Now no more about the vicar's foibles, young Jane,' Agnes chided her. 'Let's have a nice catch up with our guests. Tell us about them 'orses now, Mr Milroy. How are they doing?'

Milroy was happy to wax lyrical about the thing he loved, second only to the Rolls Royce he drove for Lord David.

And so, the servants enjoyed their Christmas Eve supper with contented casual conversation.

'Oh, there you are at last,' Lady Serena greeted her husband and the other gentlemen as they entered the drawing room, clearly annoyed to have been kept waiting. 'Mummy and Eliza have sorted out the tables. So, David, if you, Doctor Hollis, Eliza and Mummy take this table here. Mr Rochester, Reverend, Clarissa and I will be next to you here. The young ones can gather around the coffee table for your Jah-pong.'

'It's Mah-jong, Mummy,' Amelia corrected her.

'Sorry for the delay, Serena,' James said with a twinkle in his eye. 'It was just that the Reverend here was telling us a fascinating tale about a doctor's wife in the North of England who thought her husband was going to murder her and then she dies mysteriously, and her husband disappears: And then about a husband who changed his will so that his wife wouldn't inherit a penny, only to find that when he did actually die, his wife somehow got everything.'

'Well, that's quite enough of these ghastly tales now,' Serena admonished. 'Let's enjoy a pleasant Christmas Eve evening with no further talk of such unpleasantness.'

The Reverend, eager to make amends, turned to Clarissa and said, 'My that really is a most
captivating outfit you are wearing. Would you describe it as a kaftan? Perfect for the shape and size of most female opera

singers I would imagine. Is that what makes them such good singers, I wonder?'

'It is not a prerequisite I can assure you,' Clarissa replied haughtily. 'In fact, in my younger days, I was extremely slim.'

'Oh,' Reverend Smith responded. 'But when I saw you. Well, no matter now. It was a long time ago.'

Mr Rochester had been happily observing his fellow housemates all evening. As Reverend Smith had been recanting his tales, some of the guests had looked bored, whilst some had looked mildly surprised. When they had returned to the drawing room and Colonel James had further updated the ladies, George noticed an expression on one face that he couldn't quite identify. Was it fear or anger?

He wasn't the only person who had noticed this. Someone else was staring at that expression with a definite look of puzzlement. George turned away to take his designated place at the card table just as the Reverend was commenting on Clarissa's kaftan and he fought to keep a smile from forming on his face. The Reverend seemed to be getting more and more tactless. He really hoped for everyone's sake that the man didn't take any more drink.

However, as there is very little to do in the country on dark winter nights, all were keen card players and therefore the next couple of hours were passed quite contentedly and mostly in silence, as people focussed on their cards. Just the call of trumps and the east wind rising from the Mah-jong players.

After a couple of hours, Lady Serena called a halt to the proceedings. 'Now then everyone, it's time for carols,' she announced. 'Just move the card tables to the back of the room there and the Jah-pong. Just remember where you are, and we can pick up from where we left-off tomorrow. Now help yourselves to a nice hot cup of mulled wine on the sideboard there. We always take a cup of mulled wine before walking across to the midnight service, so it seems appropriate to have some now. Amelia, is your music ready? Now gather around the piano everyone.'

And so, they all gathered, cups in hand and sang together numerous carols whilst Amelia accompanied them splendidly. There was a pure and simple joy in that good old singsong that brought this odd group of people together and filled their hearts with warmth and optimism.

They had worked their way through Amelia's entire carol songbook before Lady Serena once again called a halt to the proceedings. 'That was glorious,' she commented. 'But it is getting late, and we do need to be nice and fresh for tomorrow.'

'Oh yes,' added Lady Eliza. 'I am definitely ready to say goodnight. Susan, would you accompany me please?'

Colonel James leapt to his feet. 'Allow me, ladies. I will see you both safely to your rooms. Goodnight, all.' With that, James took an arm of both Eliza and Susan and led them from the room.

Sonia turned to the doctor. 'Doctor Hollis, if you would be so kind as to help me up the staircase, I should be most grateful.'

'Certainly, Mrs Ferguson,' and bidding everyone a good night he guided Sonia out of the room.

Lady Serena turned to Clarissa. 'Let me see you up to your room and make sure you have everything you need. David, are you coming?' Turning to the remaining party, she added, 'Don't you stay up too late now. It's a busy day tomorrow.' With that she swept out of the room, Clarissa and David following in her wake.

Remaining in the drawing room were Amelia, Stephen, George Rochester and Reverend Smith. Amelia spoke first. 'Well, I think I'll retire as well now. I'll just pop down to the kitchen first and see if Robert, Mr Milroy is still up. I'd like to make sure that he checked on the horses before he came up to the house.'

'You do make such a fuss about those animals,' Stephen commented. 'I'm sure all the servants will have gone to bed hours ago. Still, it's no skin off my nose if you want to traipse down there.'

'No, it isn't,' Amelia retorted. 'Goodnight, Stephen. Goodnight, Mr Rochester. Goodnight, Reverend Smith.' Amelia flounced out of the room, clearly annoyed by Stephen's comments.

Breaking the somewhat awkward silence that followed Amelia's departure, George Rochester declared, 'I'll just have one more cigarette and finish my mulled wine before I retire as well.'

'Indeed,' commented the Reverend before asking, 'Not with the family this year, Mr Rochester?'

'Sadly not,' George replied. 'My fiancée and my future in-laws have travelled to Yorkshire to be with relatives for the festivities. I myself must return to the bank the day after Boxing Day but consider myself most fortunate to have been invited here to the Manor House.'

'Oh yes,' Reverend Smith enthused. 'Christmas festivities here are really quite splendid.'

'Well, on that note, I will bid you both a goodnight,' concluded Mr Rochester. Upon which he rose and departed the room.

'Yes, well I suppose I should go up as well,' sighed the Reverend, rising unsteadily to his feet.

'Just one moment please, Reverend,' Stephen interjected. 'If I might just have one last word with you.'

Reverend Smith sat down again knowing full well what was coming.

Amelia descended to the kitchen and was pleased to find that it was empty apart from Robert Milroy sitting by the hearth, nursing a glass.

'Ah, Miss Amelia,' he greeted her arrival. 'And what brings you below stairs at this time of night?'

'I just wanted to ask how the horses were before you came up to the house? I'm a little anxious that I can't get down to the stables to see them.'

'Now don't you worry your pretty little head about them,' Milroy replied. 'They were nice and snug in their blankets when I left with plenty of food. Besides, Jameson has offered up a pair of skis and some snowshoes so I shall get down to the stables first thing tomorrow morning to check on them.'

'That's good,' Amelia replied. 'There is just one more thing though.' Amelia bit her bottom lip. 'From the way he stared at me this evening, I think Reverend Smith knows.'

'Knows what?' Milroy questioned her.

'You know what,' Amelia snapped back at him.

'He doesn't know anything. You're imagining it just because he might have looked at you a bit funny. Look, if you're that worried, I'll have a quiet word with him tomorrow. Just explain to him that I get you a tonic for your nerves from a doctor friend of mine to help with the anxiety you've been feeling ever since your husband was declared MIA and the reason you don't get it from Doctor Hollis is to prevent any village gossip.'

'Oh yes that would be a great relief. Thank you. Are you going to stay down here all night?' Amelia asked him.

'Yes, I think so,' Robert told her. 'It's lovely and warm by the hearth here, besides which they put me in a room with Parker. I know for a fact he snores his head off. I've heard him enough times having a crafty kip in one of the sheds.'

Amelia smiled. 'Well, I will say goodnight then, Robert.'

'Goodnight, Miss Amelia,' Milroy replied.

Stephen was just leaving the drawing room as Doctor Hollis descended the stairs from the bedrooms. 'Ah Stephen. Just thought I'd borrow a couple of magazines from the coffee table. Reading helps one to nod off, doesn't it?'

Without waiting for a reply, he walked past Stephen who heard him say, 'Ah Reverend, just come for a couple of magazines. Don't let me disturb you.'

He quickly emerged with the magazines as Stephen was climbing the stairs. 'I wouldn't be surprised if we find him fast asleep in that chair in the morning,' Doctor Hollis commented. 'Looked to me like he had dropped off.'

Stephen snorted, said goodnight and left Doctor Hollis at the top of the stairs.

CHAPTER NINE

The snow had continued to fall whilst everyone slept peacefully and therefore it was a very white world the servants awoke to early on Christmas morning. The dazzling whiteness had made their room so bright that both Jane and Alice thought that they might have overslept as they hurriedly dressed and made their way down the back staircases to the kitchen, which was already a hive of activity.

'Ah, Jane, Alice,' Agnes greeted them. 'Quick now, have some hot tea and a bite of bread before you start. Mary, Betty and Rose have just gone above stairs to do the rooms. All hands on deck here. The gentlemen are trying to clear a path through the snow. Although no one will be going anywhere, you mark my words. Lucky we got them 'ams out of the cold store yesterday morning. Come on now, eat and drink up and start on the crockery and silver. The girls can help me with the breakfasts when they're done.'

Having completed her diatribe, Agnes went to the kitchen door to check on the progress of Messrs Jameson, Milroy and Parker, who were desperately attempting to clear the path of snow with shovels, buckets and wheelbarrows. The problem was that the drifts were very high. So, as soon as they had cleared a little, more snow would fall from the drift above, creating a new mini avalanche affect. Agnes left them to it, closed the door and returned to the warmth of the kitchen.

George Rochester was invariably a light sleeper and he had also woken early, mainly due to the unfamiliarity of the room and the light that the snow had created. He was now gazing at the idyllic scene outside his bedroom window. The undisturbed snow was pristine on the ground and the magnificent evergreen trees now completely white. How majestically they bore their burden and would continue to do so, without any fuss, until the snow had melted away from their branches.

Although it was early on Christmas morning, he already experienced a slight concern about being able to open up the bank for business the day after tomorrow. If he had been in his own little home, he could cheerfully have cleared a path, helped by friends and neighbours no doubt. No, it would simply not do that the bank could not open because he was stuck at the Manor House. With a rueful smile, he set about his ablutions and contemplated what materials might be available about the property for him to build a sled of some description.

Sonia Ferguson was also awake early, although this was normal for her. She too was gazing out of the window at the white world surrounding her and trying to recall if she had ever experienced snow at the Manor House quite like this.

She hadn't minded missing the midnight service last evening. It was becoming too much for her old bones to be out that late at night. However, she would miss attending a service on Christmas morning, even if she did have to listen to that buffoon of a vicar delivering the sermon.

Sonia tutted as she thought about, what she considered to be, the vulgar behaviour Reverend Smith had displayed the previous evening. All those sordid little stories. Sonia did not believe in washing one's dirty linen in public and yet there he was telling tales that had been told to him in confidence. Only he hadn't revealed the secret in his own sordid little past, had he?

He didn't even know that she knew what he had done, that there was a reason why she disliked him so much. Well hopefully, he would be a little the worse for wear after all the liquor he had consumed yesterday and would remain firmly in his place today.

Sonia gave one last look outside and prayed for a rapid thaw.

Little by little, the house came to life and quite a few of the residents and their guests had stirred by the time Jameson had sounded the gong for breakfast, which was to be an informal affair. All the hot dishes had been laid out on the sideboard, from which one helped oneself. Therefore, if you were extremely peckish and wanted to indulge in a full English, you would be ready to descend the stairs by the time the gong had sounded to ensure it was piping hot. If not, then enjoying some additional sleep would not be frowned upon.

George Rochester was a man who delighted in a full English breakfast so, was not surprisingly the first person to arrive in the dining room where Jameson was just placing the last hot dish onto the sideboard.

'Good morning, Jameson and a Merry Christmas to you and yours.'

'Thank you, Sir,' Jameson replied. 'And may I wish the same to you? If you would excuse me Sir, Parker, Milroy and myself are attempting to clear the pathways of snow.'

'Oh yes, don't let me keep you. I can sort myself out here.'

Jameson gave a slight bow and left the room as George started to pile a plate, thinking that he wouldn't mind a couple of hours of shifting snow himself after breakfast. Bit of fresh air and exercise would be just the ticket. He had just started tucking in when the door slowly opened, and Lord David poked his head around it.

'Ah, Mr Rochester. Good morning and a very Happy Christmas to you.' Opening the door wider, he walked in with Chester at his side.

'Just checking Lady Serena wasn't present before I brought old Chester here in. He does so enjoy a sausage and it is Christmas Day after all, even for dogs. It's just that Lady Serena does not approve,' he said with a chuckle. 'So, he might as well enjoy a nice sausage and sleep in front of the hearth as I don't think he'll be going for a nice long walk today.'

'Jameson, Milroy and Parker are attempting to clear a path, but I don't know how successful they'll be,' George advised. 'Thought I might give them a hand after breakfast. I will need an escape route back to the bank after all.' He joked.

'Indeed,' Lord David remarked. 'Perhaps all the chaps should help out with that a little this morning.'

The door to the dining room opened and a very buoyant Clarissa entered. 'Oh, good morning, gentlemen,' she gushed. 'And a Merry Christmas to you both. Isn't it too marvellous? It's like a magical wonderland being all snowed in here together. Lucky you had such a good shoot yesterday, gentlemen. We won't have to think about eating each other.'

Clarissa laughed raucously loudly at her own joke as she piled her plate high with bacon, eggs and Chester's beloved sausages. Taking a seat next to George, she started tucking in.

'Did you sleep well, Miss Llewellyn-Jones?' George politely asked her.

'Oh yes, like the proverbial log, Mr Rochester. And please, Call me Clarissa. Did you sleep well also?'

'Thank you, Clarissa, you must call me George and yes, I did sleep well, although by nature I am a very light sleeper and did wake early. I rather think it was the brightness of the snow penetrating the room despite the heavy drapes at the windows.'

Lord David had been contentedly feeding sausages to Chester whilst this discourse had been taking place and failed to hear the dining room door open once again. This time it was Lady Serena. She held the door open as Sonia walked in on Doctor Hollis's arm. This gave him just enough time to feed Chester the one remaining sausage that was on the plate in front of him and shoo his beloved dog under the table, out of sight, before his wife turned and spoke.

'Clarissa, you are already here, splendid. Merry Christmas to you and to you, Mr Rochester, Lord David and your dog, who I know is hiding under the table.' Lord David looked sheepish but was saved from having to reply as Lady Eliza entered the dining room.

'Merry Christmas, everyone,' she announced only to receive multiple Yuletide Felicitations in return. 'I don't expect Susan will be down to breakfast this morning. With no morning service and what with being completely snowed in. I expect she will sleep until lunchtime.'

'James, Stephen and Amelia will be the same I expect,' Sonia snorted. 'I wouldn't be surprised if the vicar had a bit of a lie in this morning either.'

'Yes. Well, I suppose it's not very often he gets a Christmas off now, is it?' Serena retorted.

'I would not be at all surprised if he was still in the drawing room, fast asleep,' Doctor Hollis commented. 'He was certainly close to dropping off when Stephen and I left him last night.'

'Oh no, that would never do!' Serena exclaimed. 'David, pop through and have a look, would you, dear? And remove that dog while you're at it.'

Lord David called Chester out from under the table and made his way to the drawing room. Upon entering, he was mightily relieved to discover that the room was spick and span with no Reverend Smith in it. There was, however, a glorious blaze in the hearth.

'Come on, Chester, there's a good boy. You have a nice little snooze next to the fire until Lady Serena discovers you.'

Whistling a Christmas carol, Lord David returned to the dining room, now ready for his own breakfast.

'No sign of the vicar, dear,' he announced on his return to the room. 'Even if he did nod off, I expect he woke up at some point during the night and made it up to bed.'

'Yes, I expect you're right,' commented Doctor Hollis rather dolefully causing George to look at him, slightly puzzled by his tone.

'Well, let's just let sleeping dogs lie, shall we?' suggested Serena. 'Now then, as we cannot attend the Christmas Day service this morning and we are confined to the Manor House, I suggest we spend this morning at leisure. Ladies it will be lovely in the drawing room with the Christmas tree and the warm fire. We can have a few hours at needlepoint, knitting, or read a little and of course enjoy some most pleasant conversation. There are some new records for the gramophone as well.

'David, dear. What do you propose for the gentlemen?' Serena asked, clearly indicating that they would not be welcome in the drawing room.

'Well, before you came in, dear, Mr Rochester and I were discussing joining Jameson, Milroy and Parker in shifting a bit of snow. As Mr Rochester correctly pointed out, he will need to return to the bank the day after tomorrow and I dare say Doctor Hollis and Reverend Smith will have essential duties to return to also. Besides which, it might be rather jolly fun.'

Doctor Hollis nodded his agreement.

'Right then, that's settled,' Serena stated. 'Make sure you wrap up warmly. Best take a little flask of something with you to keep out the cold and best have a good breakfast now to keep your strength up. You really could use Stephen and James's help. Never mind, when they come down, I will send them your way.'

'Thank you, dear,' Lord David replied, whilst tucking into his own sausages.

Jameson, Milroy and Parker meanwhile had worked hard at digging out a narrow pathway from the kitchen towards the front of the house. Some snow had been piled and compacted either side of the cleared area, creating a tunnel like effect. The rest had been loaded into buckets and wheelbarrows and carried to one side where a huge pyramid like structure of snow had been created. Into this scene wandered Lord David, Doctor Hollis and Mr Rochester, after having breakfasted and given Agnes and the maids the fright of their lives as they emerged in the kitchen looking like Yetis', in all their attire.

'Gentlemen,' Lord David announced. 'Merry Christmas to you and congratulations on a job well done, so far. Now, we three kings here,' he paused and chuckled at his joke. 'We are going to start digging a path along the front drive of the house. Perhaps you could leave this one for now, call in to the kitchen for a hot beverage and some dry clothes and join us there. Best bring more buckets and shovels with you. We'll take these for now.'

Jameson and Parker both nodded in reply and headed towards

the inviting warmth of the kitchen.

'Pardon me, Sir?' Milroy addressed Lord David. 'Thought I might just go down and check on the horses. Top up their feed and maybe change their blankets.'

Lord David looked around him. 'And just how do you propose to get there, man?' he asked him.

'Well, Sir, I reckon I could use a pair of skis from the front steps and ski down to the stables.'

'Yes, I see. Very well,' Lord David replied. 'But you won't be able to come back that way, will you? What about your Christmas dinner?'

'I shall have to forego it, Sir, but I'd never forgive myself if something happened to them 'orses.'

'Alright, Milroy. Get cook to pack you up a bag of tasty morsels to take with you.'

'Yes, Sir. Thank you, Sir.'

The three remaining men stood at the end of the cleared path and looked up towards the front of the house. The falling snow had drifted up the steps to the entrance and right up to the large front door.

'Right, Gentlemen,' Lord David announced. 'I propose that we go back through the kitchen and start clearing from the front door and down the steps. After Milroy has launched himself from them of course. So, let's just take a wee tot of whisky for fortitude and warmth.'

He removed a flask and three glasses from the large pockets in his overcoat, poured generous measures in each one before passing a glass each to Doctor Hollis and Mr Rochester. Neither gentleman was accustomed to taking a tot, especially as much as Lord David had poured for them, so early in the day. However, they both felt that the occasion clearly warranted it.

They were all just finishing the last few drops when the front door opened, and Milroy appeared. A large canvas bag hung across his body, and he carried a pair of skis and ski poles in one hand. The men looked on in fascination as Milroy attached the skis to his boots and then launched himself down the steps and towards the stables at some speed.

'Goodness me. How completely fearless,' Mr Rochester remarked. Lord David chuckled. 'Not a skier then, Mr Rochester?'

'Oh no,' George replied. 'Bank managers don't have time for that sort of thing. What about you, Doctor Hollis?'

'Sadly not,' the doctor replied. 'I'm afraid I am rather too familiar with the agony of broken bones to risk getting any myself. Anyway, how did Milroy become so accomplished?' he asked Lord David.

'Well, obviously, he drove the family through Europe for our skiing holidays and took himself off to the slopes whilst we were there. Turns out not to be wasted time, eh? Right then, shall we get to it? Build up a good appetite for a spiffing Christmas lunch.'

With that, the three men returned back through the kitchen, collecting Jameson and Parker on the way.

The ladies had lingered a little longer in the dining room, taking extra cups of tea. Alice appeared in the room at her normal time to clear the breakfast things away.

'Sorry, Milady,' she gushed, bobbing a curtsey. 'Should I come back?'

'No, Alice, that's fine.' Lady Serena told her. 'We will go through to the drawing room now and take our morning coffee at the usual time. If any of the others appear for a late breakfast, they will have to ring through. But tell them from me that only tea and toast is available. It's too late now for a cooked breakfast what with the Christmas lunch in a few hours and cook will have enough to do.'

With that statement made, Lady Serena rose and positively flounced out of the room, the remaining ladies following in her wake, once again.

The drawing room was extremely warm and cosy as the ladies entered. Once again, the flames from the glorious fire were reflecting in the glass ornaments that were hanging from the branches of the Christmas tree making them sparkle and shine like they were the Crown Jewels.

The ladies took their seats and Sonia picked up the knitting bag that sat discreetly at the side of her favourite armchair. She extracted her current project which appeared to be a multi coloured striped scarf.

'Oh, how splendid,' Lady Eliza told her. 'I do so wish I could knit. It seems such a marvellous past time.'

'Indeed, it is,' was Sonia's reply. 'And extremely useful also. The Great War taught us not to waste anything. Any old jumpers, scarves, waistcoats or cardigans are unpicked and knitted up again. Even the small scraps of wool can be turned into multi coloured scarves like this one. I keep the whole family warm in winter and donate a few to charity as well. You really should learn Eliza and I will teach you.'

Reaching down into her knitting bag, she extracted a shapeless brown jumper with a massive hole visible in one elbow. 'Now then, you set about unpicking this, and it can be your first project. I was going to use it to knit a waistcoat for Lord David. Imagine how thrilled he would be if you knitted it for him.'

Eliza smiled and set about unravelling the knitted jumper. The contented look of knowing she would knit something for Lord David did not escape Serena. However, for the sake of peace and harmony on Christmas Day, she let it slide. Instead, she reached for her own bag at the side of her chair and extracted her needlepoint.

Turning to Clarissa who was seated on the sofa next to her, she asked, 'Do you needlepoint or knit at all, Clarissa? It would be a marvellous way of passing the time on all your long journeys.'

'Oh no, absolutely not, darling,' Clarissa responded. 'Journeys are a wonderful time for contemplation and catching up on one's sleep. The rest of the time is simply too busy for words.'

'Oh, it must be simply too thrilling,' Serena gushed. 'How I envy your exotic lifestyle. Seeing the world. Never in one place for too long and all the marvellous people you must meet.'

'You are so right, darling,' Clarissa nodded enthusiastically. 'One really should experience New York, Paris and Rome.

Although, and of course I speak from experience, there is no city in the world quite like London. I really would like to spend a lot more time there from now on.'

'Oh, darling that would be too marvellous,' Serena replied. 'We could see so much more of you then.'

Sonia appeared to be engrossed in her knitting and not paying any attention to the conversation taking place between Serena and Clarissa, whilst she had, in fact, been listening intently to every word. Sonia might be old, but she was very shrewd and instinctive. She knew that Clarissa was bluffing. She suspected that Serena's friend was stating how she wanted to stay in London by choice but probably that the roles in the rest of the world were no longer there for her and that Clarissa was now nothing more than a dried-up old diva. Best have the servants check the silver before she leaves, Sonia thought to herself.

Susan Ross was the first of the late risers to make it downstairs. She headed straight for the dining room, in need of food and drink. Not surprised at finding the room empty, she rang the bell and waited patiently for one of the servants to arrive. It was Alice who appeared a few minutes later.

'Ah, Alice. Happy Christmas to you. Where is everyone?'

'Happy Christmas, Miss Susan. Well now, Lady Serena, Lady Eliza, Mrs Ferguson and Miss Llewellyn-Jones are in the drawing room. Lord David, Doctor Hollis and Mr Rochester are out the front with Mr Jameson and Mr Parker, clearing some of the snow. Then there's Mr Stephen, Reverend Smith, Colonel James and Miss Amelia. They haven't come down yet.'

'Right, thank you, Alice. Any chance of some breakfast?'

'Yes, Miss, but Lady Serena says just tea and toast, what with a big Christmas lunch coming later.'

'Fair enough, Alice. That will do nicely.'

'Yes, Miss Susan,' Alice confirmed and left the room to see to the order.

Susan sat down to await her breakfast, enjoying the peace and quiet before the chaos of the Christmas Day celebrations began.

Of Course, she would have much preferred to have stayed in London with all her gay young friends and, for the life of her, could not figure out why her mother remained stuck down here when she could be having the time of her life as a wealthy widow in London.

Susan determined to attempt some more subtle persuasion on her mother during this festive period. Of course, she didn't want her close enough to cramp her own style. Just close enough that she herself didn't have to keep making these tedious, annual Christmas trips.

The door to the dining room opened and Susan looked up expectantly. However, instead of the much-anticipated Alice, carrying a tray of tea and toast, it was Stephen who appeared.

'Oh, good morning, Stephen, Happy Christmas,' she greeted him.

'Happy Christmas, Susan. You sound disappointed to see me.'

'Oh no, not at all. It's just that I'd hoped you were my tea and toast arriving as I am rather peckish.'

'Yes, me too,' Stephen agreed. 'I just hope there is enough for two.'

Right on cue, Alice appeared carrying a large tray bearing a giant teapot, milk jug, sugar bowl, four cups and saucers, plates and knives. Plus, a pile of toast, butter dish and a jar of cook's rather splendid marmalade.

'Oh, excellent and Merry Christmas,' Stephen told her.

'Merry Christmas, Mr Stephen. I did think that the others might be down shortly too, so made extra tea and toast.' Alice said as she placed the tray on the sideboard.

'Thank you, Alice,' Susan acknowledged as Alice turned and left the room, almost bumping into Colonel James as he charged through the door.

'Did you smell the toast, James?' Susan joked as he came into the room. Stephen gave a small scowl, disappointed that he no longer had Susan to himself.

'House seems very quiet,' James commented. 'What is everyone up to then?'

Susan answered him as she poured them all cups of tea. 'Well, according to Alice, Lady Serena, Sonia, Clarissa and my mother are all in the drawing room. Amelia and the vicar are yet to descend. Lord David, Mr Rochester and Doctor Hollis are assisting Jameson and Parker in clearing the driveway of snow.'

'I'm surprised the vicar made it upstairs at all,' Stephen commented. 'Practically passed out in the drawing room he was.'

'Well, I'm sure he's not there now,' Susan responded. 'Unless Clarissa sat on him, and nobody noticed.'

Stephen looked slightly shocked at Susan's words. James however, burst out laughing.

'Oh, how very droll. Stephen, my boy. I suggest we down this tea and toast pronto and go to assist the others. Susan, I suggest you join the ladies in the drawing room and learn some decorum.'

'Rubbish,' announced Susan. 'Why on earth would I want to spend the morning with the old biddies. I'm as strong as any man. Hand me a shovel, Colonel and we'll soon have this drive cleared.'

'My, what a splendid young filly,' Colonel James said to himself. 'Perhaps I should forget about the mother and focus on the daughter.' Chuckling silently, he followed Susan out of the dining room, leaving Stephen to bring up the rear.

Amelia had slept fitfully, troubled by her conversation with Robert Milroy and what Reverend Smith might really know. She had finally dropped off just before dawn and woken with a blinding headache. She took a little medication waiting for the pain to ease, before dressing. She then decided to head below stairs to the kitchen to speak with Robert again, on the pretext of establishing if he had been able to see to the horses.

She did not meet with anyone on the way down, which she was mightily pleased about, as she did not wish to have to explain herself. The house did seem eerily quiet though for Christmas morning. Perhaps, it was all the snow outside that had a way of creating a silent white world that had somehow penetrated to the inside.

As expected, the kitchen was an absolute flurry of activity in preparation for the big feast. Jane was the first to spot Amelia standing at the foot of the stairs.

'Why, Miss Amelia,' she started. 'Happy Christmas. What are you wanting below stairs this morning, Miss?'

'Oh, Jane. Happy Christmas. Happy Christmas to everyone. I was wanting to see Robert; I mean Mr Milroy. Just to check about the horses. I am quite worried about them you know.'

Agnes closed the oven door from where she had been checking the contents and turned to face Amelia. 'Why, Miss Amelia, Mr Milroy has gone down to be with the 'orses and check they are alright. Went racing off on them skis from the front steps by all accounts. He won't be able to make it back up once he's down there I've heard, so he'll miss his Christmas dinner. I've packed him up with some vittles though, Miss, so he'll be alright. I've included a few treats for them 'orses as well.'

Amelia smiled. 'Thank you, Agnes. That is most kind. Enjoy your Christmas feast, won't you?' Amelia turned and hurriedly left the kitchen, chewing on her trembling bottom lip. She realised that she had no way of discovering if Robert had indeed spoken to Reverend Smith or not unless she asked the vicar herself and that would never do. No, on the contrary, she rather wanted to avoid Reverend Smith altogether. There was nothing for it but to hide in her bedroom until lunch on the pretext of a bad headache. By choice, she would miss lunch altogether, but mummy would never allow that to happen. She would drag Amelia, kicking and screaming by the ears, if it came to it. Feeling the tears beginning to gather in her eyes, she entered her room and threw herself face down on the bed.

The gentlemen had successfully managed to clear the steps and were starting to shift snow from the main driveway by the time James, Stephen and Susan joined them.

'My goodness, have you ever seen so much snow!' Susan exclaimed.

'Right. Well best get stuck in then,' said James adding, 'You know what would help here, gentlemen? Let's sing some Christmas carols to compensate for the fact that we are not in church this morning. Let's start with 'Hark the Herald'. Susan, you can sing the descant when we get to it.'

And so it was, that they sang their way through every carol they knew at least once while they worked. Shovelling in time to the music their voices were producing, almost made them work faster. George thought that if there was no more snow and they all came out again tomorrow morning, he might just get back to the bank in time after all.

'What on earth is that?' asked Clarissa, as the sound of the gentlemen and Susan's carol singing penetrated the Manor House walls.

'Why, it sounds like carol singers,' Lady Eliza replied. 'Although it can't be. There is no possible way they could have got through the snow to the house.'

Lady Serena rose and made her way to the window. 'Oh, my goodness. Would you just come and look at this?'

Everyone arose and walked over to the window to gaze upon the seven gentlemen singing at the tops of their voices whilst shovelling and removing snow.

'They put me in mind of the brothers Grimm and their seven dwarves,' Sonia commented.

'Does that make you Snow White, Mummy?' Serena bit back. 'Or more likely, the evil queen,' she thought to herself.

Eliza gave a loud sigh having just spotted her daughter as she appeared from behind a large pile of snow. 'Goodness me, what on earth is Susan doing out there with them? I am never going to make a lady out of her, am I?'

'Now, now,' Sonia comforted her. 'Times have changed since the war when women of all ages just had to get stuck in and get things done. Some liked it and didn't want to go back to the old ways. You should be very proud of her, Eliza. She is shovelling snow as good as any man, whilst my own granddaughter is still in bed.'

Serena despised the dig at her own daughter but bit her tongue as she had to quietly agree with her mother. Where was Amelia for goodness' sake? On Christmas Day of all days, why couldn't she just be a little bit normal for once?

Turning away from the window, she declared, 'Well, ladies, perhaps it is time we went and prepared ourselves for luncheon. You all go up and I'll just ring for Alice to tell Susan and the men to come inside now.'

Once they had left the drawing room and she was alone, Lady Serena rang the servant's bell. Whilst she waited, she went across to the large dresser that stood at the rear of the room and opening the door, pulled out a large sack. As lady of the manor, Serena took care of all the gifts that were to be handed around after the Christmas lunch. This was merely a token, as every year the ladies would receive either gloves or embroidered handkerchiefs and the gentlemen either socks or scarves knitted by Sonia. Even her own family received these gifts and would have to wait until their birthdays to receive a gift of any value.

Serena set about arranging the gifts under the Christmas tree when Alice appeared. 'Ah, Alice. Would you please inform Lord David and the others, that they must come in now and ready themselves for Christmas lunch?'

'Yes, M'lady.' Alice bobbed and turned out of the room and towards the front door.

Lady Serena sniffed. Really that tree was giving off a bit of an odour. It really was a beauty this year, wide as well as tall. This probably meant that the maids hadn't been able to get behind it to clean there properly, hence the odour. Oh well. It was only Lord David who needed to get close to it as he handed out the gifts. With that final thought, Serena rose and left the room.

CHAPTER TEN

Alexander Jameson, now suitably attired in his Christmas finery and having been nicely warmed up by the kitchen hearth, sounded the first gong at the time appointed by Lady Serena. This marked the official start of the day's festivities, as everyone gathered in the drawing room for pre-lunch drinks.

They had all dressed in their finest clothes. So, the gentlemen were looking splendid in their dinner suits. The ladies were shiny and sequined with a plethora of jewels on display.

Dressing in one's finest for Christmas lunch was a prerequisite of Christmas at the Manor House. Glasses were clinked and season's greetings exchanged. There was much hilarity and mirth as James and David recanted their mornings activities. Who had shifted the most snow? Who was responsible for the mini avalanche? And how much they had completely cleared? There was also much praise for Susan, who they considered as good as any man.

Amelia was looking around the room anxiously, wanting to avoid Reverend Smith, if at all possible. But she couldn't see him anywhere. How odd. Surely, he must be up and about by now. She sidled over to her mother who was deep in conversation with Clarissa, tapped her on the arm to get her attention and said, 'Mummy, Reverend Smith isn't here.'

'Isn't he?' Lady Serena looked around the room. 'Goodness me, you are quite right, Amelia. Has anyone seen the vicar this morning?' She asked the assembled guests.

'No,' came general murmurs and shakes of heads, just as the second gong sounded.

'No matter,' she continued. 'I shall have Jameson go up to his room and check. Please go through everyone. David dear, please ask Jameson to go and check on Reverend Smith?'

'Yes, dear, of course,' David replied meekly and went out to the hallway to try and catch Jameson before he entered the dining room or returned to the kitchen.

The remainder of the family and their guests made their way through to the dining room and took their designated places. Alice, Jane, Mary, Betty and Rose were all present, ready to serve the sumptuous luncheon. All that was required was for Jameson to return with Reverend Smith.

Jameson, as was the tradition, would open and serve champagne, enabling Lord David to make the required toasts before they tucked in. However, Jameson returned to the dining room alone.

'Excuse me, Milord,' he addressed Lord David. 'Reverend Smith is not in his room.'

'Did you check the bathroom?' David asked him.

'Yes, Sir and the bed is made. Hard to say if he slept in it at all, Sir.'

'Well really!' Serena exclaimed. 'Was there a note at all, Jameson?'

'Not that I could see, Milady,' Jameson replied.

'Well let's not worry about that now. I expect at some point during the night or early hours of this morning, he decided to get back for the church service. Probably went on skis like Milroy. But very rude of him not to leave a note though and my table is all thrown out now. Whatever next? Jameson, pour the champagne please and let the celebrations commence.' Lady Serena looked around the table challenging anyone to dare make a comment.

Amelia suddenly felt very sick and wondered how she could possibly swallow even one tiny
morsel.

George Rochester did not believe for one moment that the vicar had gone skiing cross country to get back to the vicarage and parish church but knew that this was not the correct time to voice that opinion. His attention turned back to Lord David at the top of the table who was clearing his throat ready for his speech.

'Right then, ladies and gentlemen,' he announced. 'If you could all be upstanding and raise your glasses. My wife, the lovely Lady Serena and I would like to welcome you all and to thank you for sharing this repast with us. There are a few people I would like to include in our toasts this year.

'Firstly, to our King, King George V, ruling us all admirably in these difficult times.

'Secondly, the Prime Minister who has become the very first Prime Minister of the newly formed Labour party. Time will teach us how successful they are to become.

'Thirdly, to our cook and all the servants for this magnificent feast we are about to enjoy.

'Last, but not least to us and all our families and friends. God bless us, everyone.'

'God bless us, everyone,' they all repeated before taking a drink from their champagne glasses.

'Most amusing,' thought Sonia. 'Quoting Charles Dickens in a Christmas toast.'

Everyone took their seats again which was the signal for the maids to start serving. This was carried out with the speed and skill that only comes with lots of experience. Once everyone had full plates and wine glasses had also been filled, Lady Serena addressed her husband.

'You will have to say 'Grace', David seeing as we have been so badly let down by Reverend Smith.'

'Certainly, my dear.' Lord David cleared his throat again and said commandingly, 'For what we are about to receive, may the Lord make us truly thankful.'

'Amen,' was the quiet response from around the table.

'Short and sweet, dear,' commented Serena.

'But to the point,' Eliza added smiling benignly at Lord David. A smile that was returned by him.

Serena decided at that moment that something would have to

be done about Lady Eliza Ross in the New Year. Perhaps she could discover some charitable cause that would require the use of the Gate House and therefore have her evicted. It was about time the woman found her own property. She would have to persuade Lord David but that really shouldn't be too much of a problem.

George Rochester had also noted the little scene and wondered.

'I say,' James began. 'What about the horses in this weather, Amelia. Has anyone seen to them?'

'Oh yes,' Amelia replied. 'Mr Milroy went down to the stables on skis this morning to see to
them. Of course, he wouldn't be able to come back up, so he's forsaken his Christmas dinner to look after them.'

'Not come back up, of course he could,' James snorted. 'Why, there is barely an incline on the way back up to the house from the stables and a young fit man like Milroy, who I might add is a competent skier, could easily have made it. If you ask me, seems as if he'd rather be with the horses than people on Christmas Day.'

A few rather embarrassed chuckles could be heard around the table as they were all aware that the very people who were currently serving them their delicious lunch from huge platters heaped with goose and vegetables, were the same ones that Milroy appeared to wish to avoid.

Lord David was delighted to receive a huge leg onto his plate as the morning's exertions and fresh air had left him extremely hungry. As Lord of the Manor, he would have liked the whole show of carving the geese in front of his guests but, quite frankly, could not be bothered with all the mess and therefore, left it to Jameson to undertake and make a much better job of it than he could have done anyway.

All the plates were filled quickly and efficiently and so they all started tucking in. Like Lord David, the snow clearers had all worked up an appetite and ate heartily.

Only Amelia picked up her fork and started moving her food around her plate without actually eating anything. Why hadn't

Robert come back to the house? He knew that she needed to know what he had said to Reverend Smith. It really was too frightful of him and now Reverend Smith wasn't here either. She raised her eyes and saw her mother glaring at her, so she speared a parsnip and placed it in her mouth, sincerely hoping that she did not choke on it.

'I wonder where Reverend Smith is for his Christmas dinner then,' Susan commented. 'Really thought he might have telephoned to excuse himself or something.'

'Oh, we don't have telephones in the Manor House, dear,' Serena retorted. 'Nasty things, invading your privacy.'

'Really?' Susan questioned. 'I know Mummy refuses to have one, which is really a frightful bore as I do so hate writing letters. But I would have thought a telephone would have been most useful for estate business and indeed your charity work, Lady Mountjoy. My goodness, they are so popular in London now one barely needs to write letters anymore.'

'Well perhaps I will have one installed in the New Year,' Eliza told her daughter. 'It would be lovely to talk to you more often and, as you say, could be most useful for charity work.'

Serena, not to be outdone, was about to agree that they really must see about a telephone next year as well when an idea struck her. Let the phone go into the Gate House and that could become her new charitable headquarters. She could run everything from there and put Eliza firmly in her place. She smiled inwardly at her marvellous plan.

'The world is certainly moving forward, is it not?' commented Doctor Hollis, joining the conversation. 'Who would have believed that three years ago Charles Lindbergh could make a non-stop flight in an aeroplane from New York to Paris?'

'The Spirit of St Louis, his plane,' added George, finally involving himself in a general conversation. 'I imagine it won't be too long before an engine is developed that can power a plane carrying passengers all over the world.'

'Oh my,' Clarissa commented. 'Even as a well-travelled person as I am, George, I am not sure that I would ever care to travel on something like that, would you?'

'Oh yes indeed, Clarissa,' George told her. 'I actually harbour ambitions to become a pilot one day.'

'Pity you're not one now,' Lord David joked. 'You could fly yourself out of here the day after tomorrow.'

George laughed politely and had just decided to raise the subject of Reverend Smith again when Lady Serena announced loudly, 'I think we are all finished now. Alice, Jane you may clear and serve the Christmas pudding.'

For the benefit of Mr Rochester, Doctor Hollis and Clarissa, Lord David explained. 'Now this is rather fun as Jameson will set the pudding alight. I do hope you have plenty of room left as cook will have placed plenty of sixpenny pieces into the pudding mix. We shall have to see who can collect the most.'

Jameson set to pouring the heated brandy over the pudding on the sideboard behind them, before holding it aloft so that everyone could observe as Alice handed him the lit taper and he set it alight. Everyone applauded and cheered until the flame burned out.

'Excellent, Jameson,' stated Lord David. 'Now a generous slice for us all please.'

The pudding had various sauces to accompany it and once again everyone commenced eating, even Amelia who really did love cook's Christmas pudding.

'Oh my!' Clarissa exclaimed. 'I really did think that I was too full after that splendid dinner to eat another morsel, but this really is too delicious.'

'Cook really does excel herself at Christmas,' Serena told her. 'Just wait until you try her mince pies later. The pastry will simply melt in your mouth.'

'Oh, I simply can't wait,' Clarissa admitted.

'I bet you can't,' Sonia thought to herself. 'Eat us out of house and home you will, given half a chance.'

'Oh,' said George suddenly. 'It would appear that I have found the first sixpence.' He extracted it from his mouth and placed it on his side plate.

'Well, how about that?' commented James. 'The first sixpence going to the bank manager.'

Everyone appeared to find that highly amusing, but George suspected that was a result of how much wine had been consumed as opposed to the quality of the joke made by Colonel James.

The consumption of the delicious pudding continued, mostly in a contented silence until yet another sixpence was discovered, and the recipient congratulated. In the end it appeared that only James had not been on the receiving end of a sixpence, whilst Clarissa had found two.

'Oh James, would you care for one of my sixpences?' she cooed at him.

'No, no thank you, Clarissa. All's fair in love and war and Christmas puddings. Besides, it was so delicious, I really don't need to be paid to eat it.'

'Not to worry, James,' Serena added. 'Cook has made a second pudding for tomorrow. I'll make sure that you are served with the biggest piece and perhaps you'll get lucky.'

'Why thank you, Serena. I am looking forward to that already.' James gave his sister-in-law a wink which she thoroughly disapproved of and simply raised her eyebrows in response.

'Right, everyone,' she continued. 'Let's move into the drawing room for our coffee and brandy. We will be much more comfortable there after such a large lunch and I have a splendid treat this year before the gift giving. Some Tom Smith Christmas crackers. So much fun.'

Lady Serena rose and left the room with the assumed expectation that everyone would follow her. Which of course they did, albeit some more eagerly than others.

'Now then, don't take your seats yet,' Serena cautioned. 'We must all be in a large circle to pull our crackers together. Gather round now.' She handed each of them a colourful cracker and they all stood dutifully in a circle, crossing arms ready to pull when instructed.

Serena joined the circle and counted down, 'three, two, one.' Everyone pulled and as always seems to happen on these occasions, some people were left with two ends and contents had spilled out on to the carpeted floor. Lady Serena spoke again, 'Make sure to wear your paper hats everyone. You will also find a little love poem in each one. I suggest you save those and read them in the privacy of your rooms later. There are also some little trinkets. Silver whistles for the gentlemen and fans for the ladies. Please do swap around if you have the incorrect gift.'

So, hats were donned, fans and whistles exchanged, and love poems secreted away with much mirth and glee. How often is it that the simplest of pleasures bring the most happiness?

Clarissa held the fully extended fan in front of her face. 'What do you think, Serena, does it make me a femme fatale?'

'Oh yes definitely, darling,' Serena agreed.

Sonia just thought it was a huge improvement as half of Clarissa's garish face was now hidden.

Various toots broke out as the gentlemen each tried out their whistles.

'That's quite enough of that,' Serena shouted. 'That should prove to be quite useful for you, David dear. You might use it to keep your dog under control.'

'Yes, dear,' Lord David replied solemnly. 'Shall I see to the gifts now?'

'Yes please. Time has really flown, hasn't it? Bless me if it isn't early evening already.'

Everyone took a seat as Lord David wandered over to the Christmas tree and the gifts that were placed beneath it. One by one he delivered the packages to their recipients who placed them in their laps, patiently waiting for Lady Serena to give the order that they could be unwrapped.

Eventually, everyone was in receipt of a gift and Lady Serena spoke, 'Happy Christmas to one and all. Please unwrap your gifts.'

There was much 'oohing' and 'aahing' as the gifts were

revealed and admired. The handkerchiefs for the ladies had been embroidered by Serena herself with initials and flowers. She was really very skilled with an embroidery needle, and they were all quite beautiful.

'My, these are exquisite,' Lady Eliza remarked, and the other ladies nodded in agreement.

'Thank you, my dear. I have always enjoyed needlework,' Serena told her.

'Well, you are very talented, darling,' Clarissa added. 'I'm sure I could never do anything like this.'

'Oh, we all have different talents,' Serena commented. 'We should just make sure we use them to the best of our ability.'

'I think Lady Serena's talent must be inherited from her mother what?' Colonel James commented, holding his knitted scarf aloft. 'Your work if I'm not mistaken, Sonia?'

'Indeed, they all are,' Sonia told him as the gentlemen uttered words such as 'spiffing', 'marvellous' and 'splendid'. Truthfully, Sonia was indeed a skilled knitter, and each scarf had a unique and detailed pattern knitted into it.

'We all could have done with these this morning,' Doctor Hollis commented. 'They would have helped keep us warm whilst we were shovelling that snow.'

'Oh, I am sure we will get to try them out tomorrow for that very purpose,' Lord David replied. 'Plenty more shovelling to be done. Now then, Serena dear, what should I do with the gift for Reverend Smith?'

'Just leave it under the tree for now,' Serena told him.

'Righto then. I'll just move it to the back though, so it doesn't look all sad and alone.' Lord David bent down and moved the lower branches of the tree towards the rear when he suddenly exclaimed 'Goodness me! What's this?'

'What on earth is it, David? Do come along,' Serena retorted somewhat impatiently.

'It's the Reverend. I think he's dead.'

Time appeared to stand still as the people in the room tried to comprehend what Lord David had just told them.

George Rochester glanced quickly around the room, taking in the various expressions displayed on all the faces before him.

Doctor Hollis was the first to react and he quickly sprang into action. 'Quick, out of the way, Lord David. Let me see.' The doctor replaced Lord David and knelt down, attempting to find the pulse in the neck of Reverend Smith. After a short while he stood and addressed the room. 'I'm afraid there can be no doubt, the Reverend is most definitely dead.' Taking charge he commanded, 'Colonel James, help me move this tree so we can lift him out,'

'No.' George declared loudly. 'Things must be left exactly as they are until we can get the police here. The poor man has died in highly suspicious circumstances.'

'Oh, surely you can't think that' Lord David argued. 'Isn't it obvious? The man was so drunk last night that he couldn't manage to get up the stairs. So, what does he do instead? Curls up behind the tree and falls asleep. Probably had a heart attack during the night.'

'I hope you are right, Lord David,' George continued. 'But just look how tight he is in the corner with the tree pushed against him. I do not believe that there is a big enough space for him to have crawled into without the tree being pulled out and pushed back in again. Of course, I may be wrong but that really is for the police to decide, isn't it?'

There was a heavy silence as no one spoke to either agree or disagree with him, so George continued.

'All the doors into this room are lockable, aren't they? So, we must all leave this room now and lock all the doors. None of you must touch anything. It's too dark and dangerous to try to get to the police station tonight but perhaps Colonel James and you, Stephen could ski across there tomorrow.'

'Yes, thank you, George,' Lord David interceded. 'That sounds like the best way forward. Let's all go into the morning room. I'll ring for Jameson from there.'

Everyone stood up, still looking dazed and confused. All apart from Sonia who stood tall, puffed out her chest and addressed George.

'Young man, are you really trying to suggest that someone in this household might have murdered Reverend Smith?'

'Yes, Mrs Ferguson. I believe it might be a distinct possibility,' George told her.

A sudden crash distracted them as Amelia crumbled in a dead faint, taking an occasional table with her.

CHAPTER ELEVEN

A short time later, Lord David, Colonel James, Doctor Hollis, Stephen and George Rochester were alone in the morning room. Doctor Hollis had been the one to lift Amelia from the floor and carry her up the stairs to her bedroom. He had suggested that she take a sedative but was unable to supply one as he had not brought his medical bag with him. Sonia suggested that Amelia be given one of her own sleeping tablets, prescribed to her by Doctor Hollis, to which he readily agreed. Sonia said that she would sit with her granddaughter for a while until she was soundly asleep. Amelia had not yet spoken a word since she had come round. Lady Serena and Clarissa had retired together to the former's room and Lady Eliza had persuaded Susan to spend the night with her in her room. Susan was more spooked than she cared to admit so wholeheartedly agreed. Lord David was currently pacing the floor and running his hands through his hair so that it was now standing on end.

'Do sit down, David. All this constant pacing is not going to solve anything,' Colonel James urged his brother. 'I'll ring for Jameson to bring some cigars and brandy. He'll need to let the rest of the servants know anyway.'

'Yes, you're right, James. Good idea.' Lord David plopped down onto a sofa. 'I am starting to understand the benefit a telephone would be right now,' he admitted.

'Yes well, let's not worry about that now.' James tried to comfort his older brother.

'Ah, Jameson,' he addressed the butler as he entered the morning room, looking slightly confused to see all the gentlemen gathered there. 'Unfortunately, Reverend Smith has had some sort of accident last night and we have just recently discovered him in the drawing room behind the Christmas tree. The room has been locked up and myself and Stephen will take the skis across to the police station as soon as it is light tomorrow morning. Sorry to be the bearer of bad news on Christmas Day but if you could just explain the situation to the rest of the servants and bring us some brandy and cigars. The ladies have retired but best inform the maids that they will ring down if they require anything.'

'Certainly, Sir.' Jameson remained stoic despite what he had just been told. 'Everyone is in the kitchen for their Christmas meal, apart from Mr Milroy who is still down at the stables.

'If I may, Sir, I wanted to inform you that there is a silver candlestick missing from the drawing room. I only noticed it this afternoon when I drew the curtains and went to light the candles. I didn't want to mention it today with it a being a celebration and all, but under the circumstances perhaps it is connected to the Reverend.'

'Thank you, Jameson. Now the brandy and cigars if you please,' Colonel James prompted. Jameson served them all and then made a swift exit to return below stairs.

'Well, what do you make of that?' Colonel James asked nobody in particular. 'Doctor Hollis, you pronounced him dead, could you tell anything about how he might have died?'

'No,' Doctor Hollis replied. 'To be quite honest with you, he is that wedged in behind the tree, it was all I could do to check for the pulse in his neck. So, if you're asking if he might have been hit over the head with a candlestick, I really couldn't say. But there certainly could be a candlestick behind the tree with him. At this point, I am more intrigued by the actions of Milroy. You said Colonel that he could have returned to the house for dinner and yet he chose not to. That could be seen as suspicious in my book.'

'What possible reason could he have for killing Reverend Smith?' Stephen asked.

'None, Stephen,' Lord David told his son.

'Gentlemen, I don't think all this speculation is achieving anything at all,' George commented.

'I really feel that once we have taken the edge off the shock by drinking these brandies, we should all retire and try to get some sleep. We need to continue shovelling the snow at first light if the police are going to be able to get up the driveway.'

The others all nodded in agreement. They finished their drinks in a silence which continued as they left the morning room and retired to their rooms.

As soon as Amelia was sleeping soundly and knowing that she wouldn't awaken until the morning, Sonia left her granddaughter and returned to her own room. She was not a hypocrite and would therefore not pretend that she was saddened, shocked or even surprised that Reverend Smith was dead. In fact, she thought he had it coming. Not one for fancy though, she would wait for the police to confirm that it was in fact murder. Then, she thought, she might rather enjoy employing the wisdom that only comes with age to figure out which of the miscreants currently residing in this household might have done it. She smiled to herself and entered her bedroom, deciding on this occasion to lock the bedroom door.

Lady Serena was adamant that Reverend Smith had drunkenly climbed behind the Christmas tree and died during the night. 'There simply isn't any other explanation, darling,' she explained to Clarissa. 'Who in this household could possibly want to kill the silly little man? No, I simply allowed Mr Rochester to take charge as it seemed the correct thing to do at the time. It will be all be sorted tomorrow when the police get here. You mark my words.'

Clarissa really didn't care about any of it, as long as Serena allowed her to continue sipping this rather fine brandy.

Lady Eliza and Susan, although still quite in shock, were more inclined to agree with George Rochester that Reverend Smith had indeed died in suspicious circumstances and could not have crawled behind the tree on his own.

'Do you think there's any way someone from outside could have got into the house, like a burglar perhaps and come upon the Reverend by mistake?' Lady Eliza asked her daughter.

'No. I would say that was pretty much impossible,' Susan told her. 'There would have been some kind of tracks evident this morning but there weren't even any animal or bird prints when I went out to dig this morning.'

'Well surely it can't have been any of the family or guests!' Lady Eliza exclaimed.

'But he did tell some pretty wild stories about people, didn't he?' Susan replied. 'What if one of those tales was really about someone here? That would give them a pretty good motive, wouldn't it?'

'You don't really believe that do you, Susan?'

'No, actually I don't. However, I do find it quite interesting that Milroy disappeared down to the stables this morning and never came back up to the house, especially after Sonia pulled Amelia aside for fraternising with him. Plus, the way Amelia fainted when Reverend Smith's body was discovered, makes me wonder if she suspected him of something too.'

'Yes, yes indeed. I think you must be quite right about that. That does make me feel a lot better, Susan. I think I may perhaps be able to get some sleep tonight after all.'

With that, Lady Eliza rose and started making preparations for going to bed. Susan, however, remained seated, staring into the flames of the fire in the hearth with a puzzled expression on her face.

Steadfast as ever, Jameson had returned to the kitchen.

'Oh, there you are,' Agnes greeted him. 'Are they all sorted for the night above stairs now? Our own feast is ready for dishing up.'

Jameson looked around to check that everyone was present in the kitchen before speaking.

'Well, yes, they are all settled for the night now. But if you could all just come and sit down at the table for a moment. I'm afraid I have some rather disturbing news.'

They all took a seat as requested and waited expectantly for Jameson to speak.

'I'm afraid that Reverend Smith has been discovered dead in the drawing room behind the Christmas tree.'

Everyone stared at him in a silent disbelief.

'How on earth did that happen?' Agnes finally asked.

'We don't know,' he told his wife. 'The drawing room has been locked up and Colonel James and Master Stephen will go across on skis to the police station in the morning. The ladies have all retired for the night to their rooms and will ring down if they need anything. The gentlemen are just partaking of some brandy in the morning room. Now I suggest we eat the feast you ladies have spent so much time preparing in order to keep our strength up and remember the Reverend as we give thanks.'

Everyone nodded in agreement but their appetites, which had been huge a few minutes ago, had suddenly vanished.

CHAPTER TWELVE

Boxing Day dawned and it was once again a very white vista that was still visible through the windows of the Manor House. Luckily, no more snow had fallen during the night so that the headway that had been made in clearing the drives and pathways yesterday still remained in place today.

The servants rose early and set about their normal duties, albeit slightly more subdued than usual. Apart from Clarissa, who had got completely sozzled on brandy and was consequently still asleep and snoring rather loudly, the rest of the household had awoken earlier than was usual. Most had managed a few hours of restless sleep fuelled by the brandies they had themselves consumed. But now in the cold light of day, the harsh reality of a dead Reverend Smith lying in the drawing room hit them all.

As the first streaks of light had penetrated a small gap in the curtains, Lady Serena awoke with the feeling one often had upon awakening, that everything was normal. Of course, a moment later, reality kicked in and she remembered the ghastly situation they had found themselves in. However, as Lady of the Manor, Serena felt that one must simply get on with things and make sure the morning room was ready for them all to wait in before the police could arrive and sort the whole thing out. Yes, she would keep all the ladies calm and composed. Lord David could take care of the gentlemen, who must resume their digging she supposed. For that, they must eat a hearty breakfast so one had best check on the servants as well. Make sure they hadn't fallen completely to pieces. With a determined manner Serena rose and set about preparing herself to face the day.

Lord David, however, was currently lying upon his bed wondering how all this was to be faced. In his heart of hearts, he knew that what had happened to Reverend Smith was no accident. Which could only mean that someone inside of his home last night had killed the man. He forced himself to rise, reluctantly realising the expectations on him as Lord of the Manor and prayed to a God he was no longer sure he believed in, that his instincts were in fact incorrect.

Colonel James was the first one down to the dining room that morning and was piling his plate high with eggs, bacon and sausages when Lady Serena entered the room.

'Ah morning, Serena,' he greeted her. 'I hope you don't mind but I told Jameson not to sound the gongs this morning. A few restless nights I suspect. Thought it best not to disturb. People will come down when they are ready to.'

'Yes, thank you, James. That was most thoughtful of you, and I am pleased to see that you are partaking in a hearty breakfast before your trek to the police station. Is Stephen up and about yet do you know?'

'I knocked on his bedroom door on the way past and received a muffled reply, so I expect he'll be down shortly. Will you stay and have some breakfast?'

'No. I really don't think I could eat anything yet. You tuck in. I am going to see to the morning room as we will all need to be in there to meet the police later. I'll make sure that there is tea and coffee and perhaps some cake and bread and butter for the ladies to nibble on to keep their strength up. I'm really not at all sure that any of them will be able to face breakfast this morning.'

'Yes, perhaps you are right,' Colonel James told her as she left the room.

Shortly after Lady Serena had departed the dining room, Stephen and George Rochester entered it.

'Ah, Stephen good. Good morning, Mr Rochester.' James greeted them with a mouthful of
egg and bacon. 'Get a good breakfast inside of you, Stephen. We've a long hard trek ahead of us lad.'

'Yes, Uncle James. That's just what I intend.'

'What about you, Mr Rochester?' James turned his attention to George.

'I intend to start clearing the snow again,' George told him. 'If we can clear, at the very least, a narrow path down the drive it will give access on foot up to the house. I'll go to the kitchen and rally Jameson and Parker as soon as I've eaten. I'm sure Lord Mountjoy, Doctor Hollis and even Miss Ross will join us when they are ready.'

'Yes, jolly good. That sounds like a plan,' remarked Colonel James whilst George and Stephen nodded in agreement.

Sergeant Neville Bailey was currently finishing a much simpler breakfast of toast and marmalade before he made his way next door to the police station. His wife and their two children were at his mother-in-law's house in the next town over, where they had spent Christmas Eve and Christmas Day. Neville had been on duty both days but had been looking forward to joining his family in the early evening. Unfortunately, the snow had scuppered his plans.

However, most of the village had appeared on Christmas Day afternoon to try and clear some of the snow from the paths and the road and he had joined them. Quite a jolly time they had all had as well singing Christmas carols while they worked. His baritone voice had really shone through in Good King Wenceslas, even if he said so himself. He had had to admonish some of the younger folk for being a bit too vicious with their snowballs. But all in all, it had gone very well, and pathways were cleared. It was especially gratifying when old Mrs Willis and her husband had invited him into their warm cottage for a bite of supper. Plus, there had been no emergencies so he really couldn't complain.

Today was supposed to be his day off but, as his cover would not be able to reach the village, he had prepared himself to work another day. No need to rush though so he poured himself another cup of tea and picked up *The Times* crossword puzzle that had been tormenting him for a few days now. New to the newspaper since February of that year, Neville had embraced the puzzles since then and enjoyed the challenge they gave his analytical mind. He never gave up on an uncompleted puzzle and sometimes had the newspapers on his desk at work for days at a time. His only frustration was when his wife revealed the answer to a clue that he had been puzzling over for ages.

Neville finished his tea and glanced at the clock on the wall before deciding to take a couple of newspapers with him. He was expecting a quiet day after all. Just as he was unlocking the heavy oak door of the station house, he heard a surprising whooshing sound behind him. Turning around, Neville was greeted by the sight of two men on skis.

'Why, Colonel Mountjoy, Mr Mountjoy. What are you doing here? Have you skied all the way from the Manor House? Has Something happened?'

James was the first to catch his breath. 'It's Reverend Smith. I'm afraid he's dead.'

'Dead! What? How?' Neville spluttered. 'Look,' he continued, 'Come in and get warm. I'll make some tea and you can tell me exactly what has happened.'

James and Stephen removed their skis and followed Sergeant Bailey inside the station. Once they were seated with mugs of hot tea in hand, the Colonel began to explain how the Reverend had last been seen in the drawing room late on Christmas Eve until he was found behind the Christmas tree in that same room late in the afternoon on Christmas Day. He went on to explain that Mr George Rochester, the bank manager had insisted that nothing be moved so that Doctor Hollis had only been able to get near enough to check for a pulse in the neck of the Reverend.

'So, Mr Rochester suspects foul play, does he?' Neville asked.

'Well of course he doesn't know that,' James told him. 'It's just that the Reverend appears to be wedged in so tightly that Mr Rochester doesn't think he could have crawled into the space and so the tree must have been pulled out by someone else and pushed back in again. The man was intoxicated. Absolutely no doubt about that. So, he might have done it himself. But it's a bit odd wouldn't you say?'

'Indeed, I would, Colonel Mountjoy,' Sergeant Bailey replied sternly and after picking up the telephone receiver on the desk he started to dial.

'Who are you calling?' Stephen asked him.

'It just so happens that Inspector Thomas Stewart from Scotland Yard is spending Christmas with his sister and her family in the cottage next door to the vicarage. He popped in on Christmas Eve to offer his assistance if anything came up in the next few days. What with the snow and all. I'm sure this will be of interest to him. Plus, he can get up to the Manor House quicker than we can, over the fields, if he has suitable snow gear.'

The telephone on the other end was answered. 'Ah Good Morning to you, Mrs Travers. It's Sergeant Neville Bailey here. So sorry to disturb you on this Boxing Day morning but could I possibly speak to Inspector Stewart please? Yes, thank you so much.'

Inspector Stewart promptly came to the phone and Neville quickly recounted all that he had been told. Then followed a long silence where the Inspector was quite clearly giving the Sergeant some instructions before he said, 'Yes, Sir' and hung up the phone.

'Right, Gentlemen. The Inspector will don some snowshoes and make his way over the fields to the Manor House. If you set off on your skis now you might just get back there before him and let the household know what's happening. I'll just phone it into Headquarters and follow along.'

Colonel James and Stephen thanked Sergeant Bailey and left the station.

Neville looked longingly at *The Times* crossword by his side as he once again picked up the phone, this time to ring Headquarters, before following along.

Inspector Thomas Stewart of Scotland Yard had been enjoying the Christmas break with his sister, brother-in-law and their young family. He had hardly taken a day off in months but finally, with great determination and diligence, he and his team had finally captured a serial killer in the East End of London. Being in the countryside with his niece Martha and his nephew William, who he absolutely adored, had been just the tonic he needed after some gruelling months. The icing on the cake had been Christmas Day afternoon when the whole family had built a gigantic snowman in the rear garden, culminating in a not too friendly snowball fight. Quite invigorating and much better than nodding off in a chair after a huge Christmas Day lunch.

When he had realised how bad the snowfall was likely to be early on Christmas Eve, he had called in at the local station to offer any support, if needed. The very last thing he had expected in this sleepy little village was a call on Boxing Day morning reporting a suspicious death at the Manor House.

He didn't know the Mountjoy family personally but had come across them a few times at various events when he had visited his sister in the summertime. Having changed into a suit, he put on the thick waterproofs that his brother-in-law had lent him and set out on snowshoes for the Manor House. At the age of thirty-four, he was fit and strong and took up as fast a pace as walking in snowshoes allowed.

Back at the Manor House, George, Jameson and Parker had been joined by Doctor Hollis, Lord David and Susan in working as hard as they could to remove the driveway of snow. The mood was sombre as they worked in silence. The buoyancy and singing of Christmas carols, only yesterday, seemed like a lifetime ago.

Lady Serena had waited alone in the morning room for the rest of the ladies to descend. Lady Eliza was the first to arrive, having been woken by Susan who, after a restless night, was eager to get to work on snow clearance. They bid each other a polite 'Good Morning' as Lady Eliza took a seat on the sofa opposite the lady of the house. There had never been an easy camaraderie between them, but Lady Serena did feel obliged to say something to her guest.

'Did you manage any rest last night?' she finally asked her.

'A little. Susan stayed with me for comfort, and I think we both tossed and turned for quite a while. I would probably still be dozing fitfully now if Susan hadn't awoken me in her eagerness to get outside and start clearing more snow with the gentlemen.'

'Yes indeed,' Lady Serena commented. 'They are all out there now working away. Apart that is from James and Stephen who have gone to the police station on their skis. All the gentlemen and Susan have had a hearty breakfast to keep their strength up, but it will have been cleared by now and I didn't think the ladies would have much appetite after such a disturbed night. If you are happy to wait for the other ladies to descend, then I have arranged for tea, coffee, bread and butter and cake to be served. We need to keep our strength up as well you know.'

'Yes absolutely. Thank you, Lady Serena. I shall simply continue with my knitting until then. Best to keep busy, isn't it?'

'Indeed,' Serena retorted taking out her own embroidery.

They worked in silence for a short time until the door to the morning room opened and Amelia appeared with Sonia on her arm. Amelia looked absolutely dreadful. Despite being given a sleeping draught that had knocked her out for hours, she looked like she hadn't slept for days, so pale and haggard looking was she. Sonia, on the other hand looked calm and rested.

'Ah, Mummy, Amelia,' Lady Serena greeted them. 'Come, sit. We shall take tea and coffee shortly. Now did you manage any sleep?'

'Of course,' Sonia snapped at her. 'I took my sleeping draught as always and Amelia had one too. Your daughter would have stayed in bed if I hadn't forced her to get up. One simply must get on with things. Stiff upper lip and all that. We must be ready for when the police arrive.

'Indeed, we must,' her daughter agreed. 'I will call the servants now for refreshment and not wait for Clarissa to join us. The poor darling has probably had a very disturbed night with the shock of it all.'

Sonia tutted quietly under her breath thinking that that diva would probably have slept like a baby, totally unconcerned with the current events and would only emerge when she wanted to be fed and watered. Secretly, she hoped it would be a few hours before her daughter's friend emerged and demanded to be the centre of attention again. She noted that Amelia was sat staring down at her hands, lifelessly. Sonia sighed before taking out her own knitting and joining the others in silence.

Stephen and Colonel James were the first to make it back to the Manor House across the fields on their skis. On arrival at the steps to the front entrance, they could see that good progress had been made in clearing the driveway. George had taken the lead in attempting to clear a single file footpath. The others following behind in order to dig wider and compact the snow to avoid a mini avalanche.

'It looks like Mr Rochester will get to the end by the time Sergeant Bailey arrives.' Colonel James commented to his nephew. 'Why don't you wait here for the Detective Inspector chappie, and I'll go and update the others.'

Stephen nodded in agreement as the Colonel removed his skis and started walking gingerly down the drive.

Lord David who was bringing up the rear of the snow shovelling party, spotted his younger brother first. 'James, my boy, you're back. How did you get on?'

'We got through ok,' James told him. 'Met up with Sergeant Bailey just as he was opening the station. He is on his way up here through the village so will be able to walk up the drive now thanks to all your hard work.'

'Excellent. Well, we'll keep on clearing until he arrives then.'

'One more thing,' James added. 'Sergeant Bailey told us that there is a Detective Inspector from Scotland Yard staying with his sister in the village over the Christmas holidays. I believe he will be coming across the fields, from the direction of the Vicarage, in his snowshoes. Stephen is waiting for him at the front steps.'

'Think I might have come across the chap, vaguely in passing. Scotland Yard, eh? Jolly good. He'll have seen a thing or two in his time, have this matter resolved in a flash, certainly quicker than the village plod what?' Lord David let out a slight chuckle. 'Why don't you go and wait with Stephen? Give the correct impression for when that Inspector chap arrives? Show him into the library. I'll bring Sergeant Bailey in when he gets here.'

James nodded, turned on his heel and walked slowly up the drive from whence he came. Lord David frowned and returned to his shovelling.

Although he had been injured quite badly during the war, Tom Stewart had worked hard at his rehabilitation and quickly rose up the ranks on his return to the force after the war had ended. He was incredibly fit and after the previous few days' indulgences, was very much enjoying the fresh air and hearty exercise that the walk across the fields in snowshoes was giving him. As his sister's house was at the same end of the village as the Manor House, he made good progress and arrived at the house only a short while after the Colonel and Stephen had returned, following in their tracks for the last few hundred feet.

Colonel James was the first one to spot his approach. 'I say are you the chap from Scotland Yard?' he asked.

'Yes, Sir. Detective Inspector Thomas Stewart. Are you Lord Mountjoy?'

James laughed before responding. 'No, I am Colonel James Mountjoy, Lord David's younger brother.' Turning towards his nephew, he continued. 'This is his son, Stephen Mountjoy. Lord David is with the snow clearing party in the driveway. They are clearing enough for Sergeant Bailey to get through. Lord David advised me that he will wait for the Sergeant and then they will all return to the house. In the meantime, I am to bring you into the library. There is a good fire burning there. Perhaps you would care for some coffee, and I can bring you up to date with events so far.'

'Yes, thank you, Colonel Mountjoy. That will be most

satisfactory.' Removing his snowshoes, the Inspector followed James and Stephen up the steps and into the house.

CHAPTER THIRTEEN

Once he had removed all his outdoor gear, the Inspector was shown into a modest sized library, two walls of which were floor to ceiling with books. The third wall contained a large hearth with a blazing log fire, either side of which were more floor to ceiling shelves of books. The room was extremely light due to the fourth wall being entirely made of glass, looking out to the gardens beyond which were still lying deep with snow, causing extra reflective light to flood into the room. In front of this window was a large leatherbound desk with a comfortable looking leather chair behind it. Placed in front of the hearth were two large armchairs with a table between them and it was to these that Tom turned his attention before turning to Stephen.

'Mr Mountjoy, I feel it would be appropriate if you joined the rest of the family and guests and let them know that I will be in to see them all once Sergeant Bailey has arrived. Thank you. In the meantime, the Colonel can update me as to who is currently in the household.'

'Perhaps you could ring for some coffee to be brought to the library as well,' James suggested to his nephew.

Stephen appeared reluctant to leave but did as he was asked.

Tom waited until the sullen young man had left the room before speaking further. 'Perhaps we should sit down here by the fire,' he suggested and once they were seated, he started to speak. 'Colonel, could you begin by listing all the members of the family please?' He took a small notebook and pen from his top pocket.

James cleared his throat and began. 'Yes well of course the head of the household is my older brother, Lord David Mountjoy.

He has lived at the Manor House for all of his life. Inherited the title from our father, obviously. He is married to Lady Serena, nee Ferguson. Big into charity. Quite the matriarch of the village by all accounts and if you ask me, the one that wears the trousers in this house.'

Tom felt his lip twitch. He had judged the Colonel correctly as someone who was happy to add a few personal characteristics as opposed to the list of names he would probably have received from Stephen Mountjoy. He listened as James continued.

'Now they have two children, Stephen and a daughter, Amelia. Stephen, of course you have just met. He does most of the running of the estate these days, I believe. He's not married but, between you and me, I think that he is hopelessly in love with Susan Ross. But perhaps I shouldn't speculate about that.'

Tom raised an eyebrow but remained silent.

'Amelia is the younger. Mrs Cavendish is her married name. Unfortunately, her husband was reported MIA during the war. Still hasn't accepted that, poor love. Thinks he'll be back one day, just come walking right through that door. Jumpy as a kitten most of the time. I'm just telling you this Inspector so that you don't get the incorrect impression of her and mistake her nerves for something else. Only time she comes alive is when she's with horses. Lord David keeps a couple in the stables. Probably just for his daughter's benefit.

'Anyway, last one of the family living here is Lady Serena's mother, Mrs Sonia Ferguson. Cantankerous old goat if ever there was one. She will tell you exactly what she thinks about everybody, in no uncertain terms and none of it will be good. I don't think the woman has a good word to say about anybody.'

'What about you, Colonel?' Tom interrupted. 'Do you not reside here?'

'Oh no. Far too dull in the country for me. I have a little place in London. Of course, this place was my family home as well and I still have my old room here. Always come down for a family Christmas and a few other times during the year when I fancy a break from city life. No invitation needed. The family are always delighted to welcome me.

'So would you like to hear about the guests next or the servants?'

'The servants, if you would please, Colonel?'

'Right. Not so many as in the old days back in the Pater's time and before the war. I think for the sake of economy Lord David would like to do with even less, but my sister-in-law does like to keep up appearances as Lady of the Manor, and my brother hasn't the heart to dismiss anyone or incur the wrath of his wife. She can be a wild filly once stirred. I'm sure if any of them were to leave though, he would put his foot down and not let her replace them.

'Anyway, so firstly there is Alexander Jameson. Butler and sometimes manservant to Lord David. Been with the family for years. Was my father's butler originally. Trusted implicitly by my brother and an all-round splendid fellow. Outside shovelling now. He is married to the Manor cook, Agnes Trelawney. Don't ask me why she is not Agnes Jameson because I do not know. She is, however, a splendid cook which I am sure you will get to sample later.

'There are two kitchen maids, Alice and Jane. They are sisters I believe and from a local family. Both been here a few years. Then there are three housemaids. Do you know Inspector that I don't even know their names? Only ever seen them occasionally in passing. Might not even have seen them all. Never mind, Lady Serena can fill you in on them, I dare say.

'Now who else is there? Oh yes, Nathaniel Parker the gardener. He's outside shovelling snow as well. Doesn't live in but has stayed over in the servant's quarters for the last couple of nights. He normally potters around the estate six days a week. Too much for one man really but I've never enquired whether funds don't stretch to a second man or it's just too hard to find someone in this part of the country since the war.'

Probably the former, Tom thought. And the second time the Colonel had alluded to a potential lack of funds in the household.

'Finally, there is the chauffeur, Robert Milroy,' James

continued. ‘Although I believe he spends more time chauffeuring Lady Serena between charity functions than he does driving Lord David anywhere. I bet she just loves the impression she creates arriving everywhere in the Rolls. Milroy is groom to the horses as well and lives over the garage next to the stables. That’s where he is right now. Went down there early yesterday morning on skis to see to the horses saying that he wouldn’t be able to make it back up to the Christmas meal with the rest of the servants. That was just an excuse though as it was perfectly doable. Perhaps he just prefers the company of horses.’

‘I see,’ Tom commented. ‘Perhaps you would be so kind as to telephone and get him to come back to the house.’

‘Oh, there are no telephones here. Lady Serena simply would not have it. One must call on her to get her attention, if she decides to be available of course. But not to summon her with the clanging ring of a mechanical device.’

‘Right well perhaps after I have seen the body in the drawing room Colonel, you would be kind enough to once more don your skis and fetch Mr Milroy back to the house. Now what about the guests?’

James could tell that the Inspector was a no-nonsense sort of a man which as an ex-army Colonel he could appreciate. But like it or not he was now expected to ski down to the stables to collect the missing chauffeur. However, putting that small inconvenience aside, he carried on.

‘Now then, Ladies first I suppose. Lady Eliza Ross and her lovely daughter, Susan Ross join the family for Christmas every year. Lady Ross is the widow of Lord David’s best friend, Lord Duncan Ross and she lives at the Gate House, the cottage at the bottom of the drive. My brother is very fond of Lady Eliza and sees himself as some sort of protector since Lord Duncan’s passing.

‘Not that Lady Serena cares for her much, mind you. Eliza competes with Serena in her charity work but between you and me, I think the ladies of the village prefer dealing with Eliza. She really is quite charming and delightful. Susan doesn’t live with her mother. She has her father's trust fund and amuses herself in London. A very headstrong girl, she has been outside shovelling the snow alongside the men these past two days. The world has certainly changed since the war hasn't it, Inspector? Not all young women wish to sit at home demurely embroidering handkerchiefs now, do they?' James gave a chortle whilst Tom remained silent.

'The other lady in the house is Lady Serena's oldest school friend, the operatic singer Clarissa Llewellyn-Jones. Larger than life she is. Perhaps you have heard of her, Inspector?'

Tom nodded before James continued. 'I remembered her from once or twice before when she visited here but I can't say that I know her very well. She does like to be the centre of attention, but apart from my sister-in-law, no one seems to have paid much attention to her at all. She is certainly enjoying her food and drink though, I must say.

'Now to the gentlemen. Two of them are first time Christmas guests at the Manor House. Doctor Hollis only arrived in the village to take over the surgery earlier this year. The previous doctor retired and went to live with his spinster sister, somewhere in Dorset, I think. Can't think what his name was but he always came here for Christmas lunch too. Never stayed over though. Probably why I can't remember his name. Expect I was half cut by the time he arrived. Anyway, this doctor was staying. Believe Sonia, Mrs Ferguson, has taken a particular shine towards him. Quite modern in his thinking I've been told and trying some new ways to treat all her ailments. Must be having some success too if that cantankerous old bat likes him. Came from Harley Street. Why? Don't ask me. Don't know the fellow at all. He's pitched in quite happily with the snow shovelling and made a fair stab at shooting on Christmas Eve but that's about all I can say really.

'The second newcomer is the local bank manager, George Rochester.'

On hearing this name Tom briefly looked up from his note taking.

'Can't think why my brother wanted a bank manager for the festivities. He normally avoids them like the plague. Must have something up his sleeve. Pleasant enough young chap, this Rochester. Seems to spend more time observing than speaking but springs into action when required. He was the first one up and out yesterday and today to start clearing snow,
although I suppose there is a self-interest there as he has stated that he needs to be able to open the bank tomorrow. It was he however, who quickly stopped any of us from doing anything or touching anything and further advised we lock the door to the drawing room and contact the police.'

'Quite right,' Tom commented. 'So, am I correct in assuming that just leaves Reverend Smith then? Tell me about him and his behaviour on Christmas Eve.'

'Yes, well it has always been a long-standing tradition of the Manor House, even before my father's time, that the village Reverend would attend Christmas Eve luncheon, shoot with the gentlemen in the afternoon and perhaps even play a round of Bridge or two in the evening, before leading all the family, their guests and all the servants across the fields and into the church for the midnight service. It is a rather fun procession with candles and lanterns to light the way.

'The Reverend would always return to the Manor House with the family and lead them back over the fields on Christmas morning for the Christmas Day service. The Lords and Ladies of the Manor House have always enjoyed making their entrance towards the front pews in this way. The Reverends would always return for Christmas lunch and stay over until Boxing Day morning as no one expected them to walk home alone in the dark and cold. Plus, there were probably Bridge rubbers to be completed.

'Normally, in my experience, Reverend Smith would not imbibe on Christmas Eve, in the knowledge that he had an important sermon to deliver later on. Don't know if it was because he knew so much snow was expected or some other reason, but he took a pre-lunch sherry then carried on with wine throughout lunch and brandy afterwards at the shoot. By the time we had all descended for pre-dinner drinks, it was pretty obvious that nobody would be attending the midnight service, so he carried on imbibing.

'Don't think he was really used to the old demon drink though. He appeared pretty tipsy after just a couple. Slurred his words a bit during his delivery of 'Grace' at lunch. If looks could kill, he would have dropped down dead then and there from the daggers Lady Serena shot at him. He kept getting muddled up as well. Saying things that had to be corrected. I can't remember exactly what as I wasn't paying that much attention, but someone else will know. I mixed some pre-dinner cocktails that by my own admission were very strong, so I'll hold my hands up now and say that I egged him on a bit at dinner.'

'What do you mean by that?' Tom asked curiously.

'I suggested that he must have heard a few juicy things in confession. Of course, not being Roman Catholic, he didn't hear confession but did admit to being confided in and sought out for advice. I encouraged him to tell a few tales, not naming any names of course and he came out with all sorts – married servants who were living in sin, a doctor murdering his wife, infidelity, the forging of a will. Goodness knows if any of this is to be believed or if it was simply the drink talking and he was enjoying his moment in the spotlight.'

'Yes, very insightful.' Tom acknowledged. 'Now tell me about the events after dinner, if you would, please?'

Before the Colonel could answer, there was a knock at the door and Lord David entered with Sergeant Bailey.

'Not accustomed to knocking on my own door,' the former announced as he entered the room. 'You must be Inspector Stewart from the Yard. You look familiar. Must have seen you knocking around the village previously. I am Lord David Mountjoy, owner of the Manor House. I hope my brother has been accommodating in my absence.'

Tom rose and shook Lord David's outstretched right hand. 'Lord Mountjoy, thank you for letting us use your library. Your brother has just been bringing me up to date with the members of your household and guests. Now that Sergeant Bailey has arrived, I would like a few words with everyone before the two of us go into the drawing room.'

'Yes, the family and guests are all gathered in the morning room. Unless you want the servants as well that is?'

'No, I'll go down and talk to them later, if necessary.'

'Right you are. Come this way then, Inspector.'

Lord David led them into the morning room where everyone was assembled. He and his brother took the only remaining seats in the room whilst the Inspector and Sergeant took up positions near to the door which allowed them to view everyone. Tom's eyes quickly scanned the room. The Colonel's descriptions had been quite accurate, and he could easily tell who was who. The only difficulty he might have faced would have been distinguishing the bank manager from the doctor if he had not previously encountered the former but this fact he did not acknowledge, instead starting on his planned speech.

'Good morning, ladies and gentlemen, and thank you for waiting for us here,'

Sonia gave a snort as if about to make some comment, but her daughter gave her such a look that for once she decided to toe the line.

Tom ignored the small interruption and continued. 'I am Detective Inspector Thomas Stewart from Scotland Yard. It just so happens that I was in the village spending Christmas with my sister and her family, but I will now be leading this investigation. This is Sergeant Bailey who of course many of you already know. The Sergeant and I will proceed to the drawing room now and commence our investigation. If you could all please remain in this room and we will be back to update you as soon as possible. The key, Lord Mountjoy, please?'

Lord David reached into the pocket of his waistcoat and handed over the key to the drawing room that he had concealed there.

'Thank you, Sir. Sergeant Bailey?'

Neville nodded and followed the superior officer out of the morning room along the grand hallway to the drawing room.

The room was dark as they entered, the curtains at the windows still drawn from the previous evening.

'Pull those drapes back would you please, Sergeant? Let's get some daylight on the subject.'

Neville obliged and suddenly the room was filled with light reflected from the snow that was piled high outside the window. Tom turned towards the Christmas tree. As with Lord David before him, it was only when he moved aside the luxurious fronds at the base that he could see the head of the late Reverend Smith.

'Well, what do you make of that, Sergeant? Think the man could have got in here by himself?'

'I would say no way that was possible, Sir. The Reverend wasn't a young or strong man and why would he even want to pull the tree out, clamber in behind it and pull it back in again, even if he was able? Surely some of the ornaments would have fallen off as well?'

'Yes, well we can check that with the maid who saw to this room yesterday morning if needs be. You are correct though. Plus, according to Colonel Mountjoy, the Reverend was intoxicated which would have hampered his ability even further.

'Right, Sergeant lets you and me pull this thing out. Let the dog see the rabbit so to speak. Easy does it mind. We don't want it falling over.'

'Oh no, Sir. I wouldn't wish the wrath of Lady Mountjoy on anyone.'

'Oh, I'm sure her bark is worse than her bite. I'm more concerned about it falling on top of us, it's a monster, isn't it? Let's get down on our knees and take a hold either side of the tub. We should be able to shuffle it forward from there.'

In all his years as an officer of the law, Thomas Stewart could not remember ever having been in such a bizarre situation. He would have laughed out loud if not for the fact that a man lay dead behind the tree. Shuffling the pot and heavy tree inch by inch was hard going and only served to convince the two of them further that Reverend Smith could not possibly have performed this task.

'Must have been someone quite strong to shift this, wouldn't you say, Sir?'

'Yes, I agree, Sergeant. Unless there was an accomplice. There we are now. I think that's far enough.' With some effort they had managed to move the tree to the centre of the room.

'Dust that tub for prints later, would you, Sergeant? Probably find too many to be of use but best to be thorough. Now let's take a look at our corpse here. Ah see here, Sergeant Bailey. A blow to the back of the head. Curious that there is not much blood near the wound at all. What do you make of that?'

Sergeant Bailey looked down at the gaping hole at the back of Reverend Smith's head. 'Well, I've not seen many victims of murder, Sir, but I agree that I would have expected more blood.'

'Indeed. Obvious answer of course is that he was already dead when the blow struck him,
but let's not speculate on that. Reverend Smith has been struck on the back of the head and then moved behind the Christmas tree in a desperate attempt to hide the body. That's murder in my book.

'Right, Sergeant. Best not keep the Mountjoy family and their guests waiting. Let's go and update them now.'

'Yes, Sir.' Neville silently wished the Inspector good luck in having to relay this terrible news to the occupants of the Manor House.

CHAPTER FOURTEEN

The family and their guests were sitting mostly in silence waiting for Inspector Stewart and Sergeant Bailey to return to the morning room. Various emotions were being hidden just under the surface. Anger; shock; annoyance; boredom; disbelief; suspicion. Shamefully, no one appeared to be saddened by the sudden death of Reverend Smith. They all looked up however, as the two men re-entered the morning room noting that the Inspector was very solemn as he spoke.

'Lord and Lady Mountjoy, ladies and gentlemen. I am extremely sorry to have to inform you that Reverend Smith has indeed been murdered. There is a heavy blow to the back of his head, indicating that he was struck down and then hidden behind the Christmas tree. We will move the body to one of the outhouses later until the snow has cleared sufficiently for the coroner's wagon to get through. In the meantime, Sergeant Bailey and I will set up in the library to interview you one by one and take your fingerprints for elimination purposes. Colonel Mountjoy, if you would kindly go down to the stables now as agreed and ask Milroy to return to the house. Thank you.'

The Colonel rose silently and left the room.

Lord David turned towards Tom. 'Excuse me, Inspector. I think you should be made aware that a silver candlestick is missing from the drawing room. Jameson reported it to me yesterday evening after I had advised him of the Reverend's demise.'

'Thank you, Lord Mountjoy. That is indeed most useful. That candlestick could well be our murder weapon. We will need to search the house immediately to see if it is hidden anywhere.

Sergeant, you start in this room and the rest of this floor. I'll start upstairs. Again, I must ask you all to remain in this room whilst Sergeant Bailey and I carry out the search.'

'May we at least ring the servants for some refreshments?' Lady Serena asked crossly, not at all happy at the way they were being confined to one room and now the indignity of having their own rooms searched for a candlestick as well.

'By all means. You might even care to update them on the current situation. Right, Sergeant. Let's get to it.'

Tom left the room, leaving Sergeant Bailey with the disgruntled folk. However, he remained stoic and steadfast and set to carrying out his orders.

Sonia felt like telling him to go and search Clarissa's room first. Not that she thought her a
murderer of course, but definitely thought her capable of stealing the silver. However, she decided to save this thought for future reference.

'Well, this really is too dreadful!' Lady Serena exclaimed. 'Amelia, ring the bell, would you? We will have some sandwiches and drinks sent up. It looks like we are going to be here for some time, so a civilised Boxing Day lunch is probably out of the question, and I am in need of a strong drink.'

George was astounded that despite the fact that Reverend Smith had spent multiple Christmases with the family, and they attended his service every Sunday, his horrific murder appeared to be nothing more than a dreadful inconvenience. But he had also noticed that no one had challenged her cavalier attitude. Then again, perhaps they were all just in denial. He had seen plenty of that in his time on the frontline. Everyone else remained extremely quiet, probably attempting to process the dreadful news. He wondered who would be the first to say out loud what he himself was already thinking. Someone inside this household was a murderer with a motive for wanting Reverend Smith dead. His thoughts were interrupted by Jameson's entrance into the morning room.

'Ah Jameson,' Lord David started commandingly. 'It would

seem that the Reverend was killed by a blow to the back of the head. The Inspector from Scotland Yard and Sergeant Bailey are currently looking for the missing candlestick. If you would be so kind as to inform the rest of downstairs, as I am sure the police will wish to speak with you all at some point. Now, as we are all confined to this room for the time being, Boxing Day lunch will not take place in the dining room. So please arrange to have some sandwiches sent up and serve some drinks straight away, would you? Some brandy for the shock I think, unless the ladies prefer sherry?'

'Thank goodness for that,' Clarissa thought. She'd only got to nibble on some bread and butter this morning and was, consequently, absolutely starving. A large brandy would go down rather well also. She wasn't shocked or appalled that the Reverend had been killed. Indeed, she was rather bemused by the whole thing, and also intrigued as to who might have done it as she fully realised that it had to be someone in the Manor House. No, she would be able to dine out on this one for years and was actually quite looking forward to being around to see how things played out. Of course, she would be here to support her lifelong friend as well. Poor Serena. Imagine the gossip in the village after this.

Her thoughts were interrupted by the return of Inspector Stewart who walked into the room holding the missing candlestick in his gloved left hand.

There were audible exclamations, but it was Lady Serena who quickly asked, 'Where did you find it, Inspector?'

'The very first room I looked in, Lady Mountjoy. The small attic room at the very top of the house.'

Lady Serena looked puzzled.

Jameson looked up from the sideboard where he had been pouring the drinks. 'If I may, Sir? That room is normally empty, being the smallest room in the house. However, because of the snow on Christmas Eve, it was allocated to Mr Milroy and Mr Parker. Indeed, Mr Parker was in there again last night.'

If anyone had turned to look at Amelia at this stage, they

would have noticed that she had turned very pale and was ardently chewing on her bottom lip. However, all eyes were fixed on either Jameson or Inspector Stewart. That was until the Colonel suddenly burst into the room.

'Milroy's gone,' he declared. 'There's no sign of him anywhere.'

Once again, Amelia fainted.

Doctor Hollis leapt to his feet and went over to where Amelia had passed out in her armchair. He began gently slapping her cheeks and repeating her name. She came round and looked into the doctor's kindly eyes.

'Some brandy please, Jameson?' he requested.

Tom stared at the scene before him. Once Jameson had handed the glass of brandy to Doctor Hollis, Tom addressed him.

'Mr Jameson, if you would be so kind as to fetch Mr Parker up into the library for me. Sergeant Bailey and I will interview him first. Doctor Hollis, if you would please calm Mrs Cavendish, we will speak to her next.'

'Can't that wait?' Lady Serena asked insistently. 'My daughter is clearly extremely upset and surely not fit to talk to anyone right now.'

'No, Lady Mountjoy I'm afraid that it can't wait. This is a murder investigation and Mrs Cavendish is clearly hiding something.'

Without waiting for a further response from Lady Serena, Tom turned and left the room, Sergeant Bailey hot on his heels, eager to escape the scene in the morning room. Once they had reached the empty library, Tom placed the candlestick on the desk.

'Dust that for prints, would you, Sergeant? I expect it to be clean, but you never know. If you'd like to stay at the desk and take notes during these interviews, I'll sit down with them in the chairs by the hearth. Try to make them more relaxed. Make it feel more like a conversation than an interrogation. In my experience that can encourage people to open up more. You know this crowd better than I do, Sergeant. What do you make of it all?'

'Hard to imagine any of them committing murder, Sir, especially seeing as it was Reverend Smith. What possible motive could anyone have?'

'That is what I hope we are about to find out.'

There was a knock on the door and without waiting for a reply, Jameson entered with the gardener, Nathaniel Parker. Tom greeted them both.

'Ah, Mr Jameson, thank you. Mr Parker, please come in and take a seat.' Jameson left the room and Parker sat down in one of the chairs by the hearth.

'Now then, Mr Parker. I am Detective Inspector Stewart from Scotland Yard. Sergeant Bailey, I assume you know.'

Parker nodded and acknowledged the Sergeant.

'I also assume that you have been informed of the tragic death of Reverend Smith?'

'Yes, Sir but I don't know nothing about it.'

'How well did you know him?'

'Hardly at all, Sir. I mean I went to the service every Sunday. Lady Mountjoy always insisted on that. I would say 'Good morning' and occasionally pass the time of day about the weather and the gardens and suchlike.'

'And did you see him on Christmas Eve at all?'

'Just in passing when all the gentlemen came out in the afternoon to shoot. I had just been raking some leaves not too far away from them, but I went to my shed soon after.'

'Right, and then what did you do?'

'Well, I cleaned all my tools in the shed and then went round to the kitchen for my tea at the normal time. The snow was proper coming down by then. I stayed for Christmas Eve supper with the other servants in the kitchen. That's what we always do on Christmas Eve before attending the midnight service. But by then it was decided and agreed that Mr Milroy and I should spend the night here. One of the young lasses made up the beds in the attic room for us.'

'And what time did you retire for the night?'

'It weren't too late. Around eleven, I think. We all knew we had a busy day the next day and that was without the snow shovelling we all ended up doing.'

'Did Mr Milroy come with you?'

'No, he was in a chair by the fire when I came up. Never saw him. I was asleep before he came up and he weren't there in the morning when I woke up. Bed looked like it hadn't been slept in if you ask me.'

Tom nodded. 'Do you see that candlestick on the desk there, Mr Parker?'

Parker nodded.

'Have you seen that before?'

'No, Sir. But then I never comes into the house, only the kitchen.'

'So, what would you say if I told you that we believe that candlestick was used to hit Reverend Smith over the head, and it was found under your bed in the attic room?'

'But I never put it there. Did Milroy put it there? You won't find my fingerprints on it, coz I never done it.'

'Are there any fingerprints on the candlestick, Sergeant Bailey?'

'No, none, Sir.'

'Why did you ask if Milroy had put it there?' Tom continued.

'Well only coz he was sharing the room. I don't think he did it or anything like that. Anyone could have come up yesterday and put it there. Some folk probably didn't even know that me and Milroy was staying there. They might have thought they was leaving it in an empty room.'

'Yes of course. Just one more thing. Does your shed have a lock on the door?'

'Yes, Sir, it does.'

'And who has the keys?'

'Just me, Sir. Nobody else has cause to use any of the tools.'

'Thank you, Parker. If you could just hand over the key to me, please? We will need to keep Reverend Smith's body there in a cold place until it can be collected.'

'Certainly, Sir. Anything I can do to help. You'll find it

spotlessly clean Sir. A fitting place for him to rest.'

Handing the keys over to Tom, Parker rose and left the room.

'Do you believe him, Sir?' Sergeant Bailey asked Tom.

'For now, yes, I do, Sergeant. Even if he did have a motive, which isn't clear to us at the moment, why take the murder weapon and hide it in your own room? Much better to wipe it clean and put it back in place. Much harder to establish that it was the actual weapon used. Especially as I bet all the silver is polished, on a daily basis, by the glove wearing butler, Jameson, so no prints would ever be on the thing. No, this says to me that someone wanted to incriminate either Parker or Milroy, unless the missing Milroy is responsible. No, although I suspect Parker might be hiding something, I don't see him as a suspect at this point. But we'll take his prints for elimination later. Ring for Jameson would you, Sergeant? We'll get something to cover the Reverend up and move the poor man to Parker's shed.'

And so it was, with Jameson's assistance, that Reverend Smith was duly wrapped and carried outside to Parker's shed, the equivalent of cold storage, until the corpse could be collected by the coroner. The three men stood respectfully in a minute of silence before leaving the shed and locking the door.

'Sergeant, if you would now dust the Christmas tree tub for prints as soon as we get back, then return to the library. Mr Jameson, we will have finished in the drawing room then.'

'Very good, Sir. I'll send the housemaids to see to it,'

'Thank you, Jameson. I'll go now and update the family.'

Once back in the house the men separated with the Inspector returning to the morning room where anxious faces looked up at him.

'Just to let you know that Reverend Smith has been moved outside into Parker's shed.' A few shocked faces appeared before him. 'Please do not be alarmed. Parker's shed is not only extremely clean but also extremely cold which are the best conditions we can hope for before removal. Jameson will be informing the housemaids so that the drawing room will be serviced and returned for your use in no time at all. Now, I realise how much of a shock this must have been for all of you, especially now as your minds begin to process the facts and the reality sinks in. Therefore, what I propose is this. Doctor Hollis and Mr Rochester. I assume you were planning to return to your homes today for a return to your duties tomorrow?'

Both men nodded in response.

'Well, please feel free to leave at any time. Sergeant Bailey and I will wish to speak to you either later today or tomorrow. Lady Ross, Miss Ross, the driveway is clear, and I suggest you return to the Gate House. Miss Ross, I take it you have no immediate plans to return to London?'

'No, I am here until the New Year.'

'Splendid. Colonel Mountjoy and Miss Llewellyn-Jones are staying with the family, yes?'

'Oh yes, they are both here until the New Year.' Lady Serena replied on their behalf.

'Good. Well please remain at the Manor House so Sergeant Bailey and I may speak to you, but you are no longer confined to this room.'

Turning to Amelia, Tom addressed her directly. 'Mrs Cavendish. I trust you are sufficiently recovered. If you would come with me to the library, please?'

Amelia rose having now resigned herself to facing the inevitable. Tom led her to a seat by the hearth and noted that Sergeant Bailey was already seated behind the desk.

'Now then, Mrs Cavendish. It is very apparent to me that something is troubling you in connection with Mr Milroy. Now is the time to tell me the absolute truth. The truth will set you free, and please believe me when I tell you that there isn't anything you tell me that can't be fixed. Sergeant Bailey and I wish to help you, don't we, Sergeant?'

'Indeed, we do, Sir,' Neville replied.

Amelia dabbed her eyes with her lace handkerchief and took a deep breath. 'I suppose you could say, Inspector that Mr Milroy and I were friends. Nothing improper you understand but we bonded over our love of horses. When my husband didn't return from the war, it made me very unsettled. Being around the horses was the only thing that helped. That was until Mr Milroy told me that he could get me some tablets that would help with my nerves and everything. Mummy would never allow me to see a doctor for something like that, so I bought some pills from Mr Milroy. They really helped steady my nerves and I've been taking them on and off ever since. Just when things get a bit on top of me.'

Tom looked into Amelia's eyes and saw that the pupils were dilated. Opiates he suspected. If so, he hoped that Amelia would not have too tough a time of it now that her supplier had disappeared. He determined to have a quiet word with a doctor friend to see if anything could be done to help the poor girl, angered by a mother to whom appearances were so important, that she could not see what was happening to her own daughter. 'Please continue,' he gently encouraged her.

'Well, on Christmas Eve, Milroy collected Clarissa from the station in the Rolls and dropped her off just as I was going down to the stables to check the horses before the Christmas Eve drinks and lunch. So, he gave me a lift down as the garage is next to the stables. I hopped into the front seat of the Rolls, but grandmother saw me and told me off in front of everyone at the pre-lunch drinks party. From that point on, Reverend Smith kept staring at me at every opportunity, especially during meals when he was seated opposite me, and I thought, 'he knows. He knows about me and Robert.''

He probably didn't Tom thought. But the potential for paranoia in someone high on opiates could quite easily presume that.

'Anyway, I thought that I had better warn Milroy so went down to the kitchen to see if he was still there before I went to bed. He was sitting by the hearth in the kitchen. He said that he was going to fall asleep in the chair because they had put him in a room with Parker, who apparently snores. I told him that I thought the Reverend knew about the pills and he said that he would have a quiet word with him.'

'So now you are worried that perhaps that quiet word turned into an argument and Milroy killed him and left?'

'Yes.' Amelia dabbed her eyes again. 'Reverend Smith was alone in the drawing room and Milroy has gone.'

'Yes, Mrs Cavendish. It is indeed very damning, and we will be searching for Mr Milroy. But you really must not blame yourself.'

'Are you going to tell my mother and father about me?'

'No, that's not my place. It will be up to you to tell them, if and when the time is right. You might wish to see Doctor Hollis in a few days though. Perhaps he could prescribe you a tonic that would help. Lady Mountjoy needn't find out. You fainted because you were overcome with the shock of it all, nothing more than that.'

'Thank you, Inspector.'

The door to the library burst open and Sonia came striding into the room. 'Inspector Stewart, I must insist that you cease this interview with my granddaughter now. She has been in here for far too long and needs to rest.'

'Certainly, Mrs Ferguson. We are quite finished. Mrs Cavendish, please go and get some rest.'

Amelia rose and left the room.

'I'd like to speak to you now, Inspector before I go and take my own rest.'

'Certainly, Mrs Ferguson. Please come and take a seat.'

Sonia had barely sat down before she started speaking. 'I think you should know, Inspector that I shall not be shedding any tears for that dreadful little man.'

Tom raised an eyebrow, somewhat surprised at this outburst of Mrs Ferguson's.

'It's of no surprise to me that someone decided to murder the man. Took to the drink the very moment he stepped into this house. Then, the showing off. Repeating things that had been told to a holy man in confidence, even if he didn't name any names. Well, I did not care to listen to such talk. But I will tell you one thing, Inspector. That man was no Christian.'

'And what brings you to that conclusion, Mrs Ferguson?'

'Hold your horses. I'm just drawing breath and I'll tell you. A very good lady friend of mine, who shall remain nameless, told me this in confidence. It was many years ago now in a parish in the North of England. A young and unmarried housemaid became in the family way. There were even rumours that Reverend Smith himself might have been responsible. But did he do his Christian duty and help the young lady? No, he did not. Threw her out of the house and onto the streets. Poor lass ended up in the poorhouse, sick with a fever. Both mother and baby died. That's the sort of man he was. Never waited for an invitation to come to the Manor House for Christmas. Just turned up anyway. Would I have liked to kill him? Yes certainly. But it wasn't worth the effort of dragging around a Christmas tree or climbing the stairs up to the attic room to hide a candlestick. I'd simply have given him a few of my sleeping potions. Looks like Milroy's your man anyway. Never did take to him. Far too familiar with my granddaughter. Well, that's all I have to say, Inspector. I shall go and take my rest now.'

Without waiting for a response, Sonia Ferguson rose and left the room.

'Well, that's us well and truly told,' Tom commented.

'Yes, that's Mrs Ferguson I'm afraid. Direct and to the point.'

'I rather admire that, Sergeant. One very smart lady. I don't believe for a minute that she is physically capable of shifting that big old Christmas tree or dragging Reverend Smith behind it. But she may well have fed him some of her sleeping draughts and had an accomplice who did the rest. She was certainly very quick to accuse Milroy but that would be very convenient wouldn't it, not to have the family involved? No, until we know exactly how Reverend Smith died, nobody can be ruled out.'

At that point there was a knock on the door and Jameson appeared. 'Pardon me, Inspector, but Parker was wondering if he could return to his own house now, seeing as a path has been cleared and you have already spoken with him?'

'Yes, yes that's fine thank you, Mr Jameson. Sergeant Bailey and I will be leaving now for the day. We'll see ourselves out.

Perhaps you could let Lord Mountjoy know that he can have his library back for now and we will return tomorrow to talk to the family and servants. We'll be taking this candlestick with us.'

'Certainly, Sir.' Jameson clicked his heels, turned and left the room.

'Right, Sergeant. Lots of ground to cover so let's prioritise. Any prints on that tub by the way?'

'Nothing, Sir. Clean as a whistle.'

'My, the housemaids are worth their salt. Killer probably wore gloves then. Means we can leave collecting prints for elimination for the time being – nothing to compare them to, yet. Go back to the station, Sergeant and set the wheels in motion for tracking down Milroy. See when we can expect the coroner and have a good look at that candlestick with a magnifying glass.
Might find a trace of something. I'll try and join you later but in case I get waylaid, let's meet back here tomorrow morning at ten.'

'What are you going to do, Sir, if I'm allowed to ask?'

'Of course, Sergeant. Well, luckily, I have my battery-operated torchlight with me, and the sun is also out, as I propose to go and take a very close look at Reverend Smith's body for any further evidence.'

'Right, Sir. Good luck. I hope you find something.'

The two parted outside the front door. Sergeant Bailey started the long walk down the Manor drive and through the village as Tom donned his snowshoes for a shortcut across the garden to Parker's shed. Once inside, he peeled back the white sheet and gazed at the face of Reverend Smith, strangely calm and serene. Then again that's what death did, took away all your cares and worries. Simply left them all behind. Heaving a big sigh, Tom set about his task. Sometime later, he left the shed and locked the door, satisfied with the conclusions he had drawn. The sun had set, and dusk was just arriving. He decided to pay one more visit and found his way back to the drive for the walk into the village.

George Rochester had been mightily relieved to be able to leave the Manor House and return home. Even though he had initially found the characters at the Manor House quite fascinating, the subsequent events had made things very awkward. He had just settled himself down in his big comfortable armchair, by the fire with a pot of tea, when he heard his front doorbell ring. Rising reluctantly, he left his sitting room and went to answer it.

'Inspector Stewart. Please come in. I've just this minute made tea.'

The Inspector followed George into the sitting room, sat and waited while he brought another cup and saucer and poured tea into it.

'I think Tom will be appropriate, don't you? It's good to see you, old friend.'

'Yes, indeed,' George acknowledged. 'I am only sorry that we finally meet again under such trying circumstances. Congratulations on attaining the rank of Detective Inspector at Scotland Yard by the way. Quite the accomplishment.'

'As is becoming the Bank Manager,' Tom responded. 'The Great War certainly left plenty of opportunities for young men who were prepared to work hard. Of course, some of us only got that opportunity because of men like you, willing to risk their own lives to save others.'

George blushed slightly. 'You would have done the same for me, I'm sure. The fuss and the medal, although gratefully received, were not necessary. How's the leg by the way? I didn't notice a limp.'

'No. When you and life gave me a second chance, I grabbed it with both hands. Worked hard at rehabilitation. Slight ache now and again when I overdo things but can't complain.'

Tom paused and took a sip of tea. 'Excellent cup of tea, George. Good and strong, just as it should be. Now then, I trust that you didn't let on to anybody up at the Manor House that you knew me?'

'No, absolutely not. Although I can't say I wasn't shocked when I saw you.'

'Well, you didn't give anything away. Not that anyone would

have been looking at you at the time, I suppose. Colonel Mountjoy had mentioned your name as being one of the guests and I wondered then if it might be you. Hence my neutral expression when I saw you. So, what do you make of it all, George? You're an observant fellow. See or hear anything that would make someone want to kill the Reverend?'

'Potentially, I would say yes. He was extremely inebriated and said things that upset people. But what about Milroy, our missing chauffeur?'

'Yes. Turns out he's been supplying Amelia Cavendish with drugs. Now Mrs Cavendish got it into her drug addled brain that Reverend Smith knew all about it. So, she in her infinite wisdom asked Robert Milroy to have a quiet word with the Reverend and now believes that that quiet word turned into an argument and Milroy killed him.'

'You don't sound so sure.'

'I'm not. I see Milroy as someone who enjoyed quite a cushy life, driving a Rolls, looking after horses and earning a bit extra by supplying drugs to Amelia Cavendish and goodness only knows who else? Then, all of a sudden, he's got a paranoid addict on his hands. Doesn't need the hassle. Can easily start again with his network, so just takes off. Doesn't even bother to talk to the Reverend let alone kill him.'

'I do see your point,' George agreed.

'I do think however, that it could prove very beneficial to let everyone think that he is the main suspect. People will talk more openly if they think they are in the clear. George, I will be straight with you. I would like your assistance with this. You are a very observant man with an obsessive attention to detail and a great memory to boot. You are also a very honest and noble man. I need you to tell me every little last thing that occurred on Christmas Eve. Who said what to who and when?'

'I'd be delighted,' George told him. 'I assume you've already ruled me out as a suspect then?'

'George Rochester, you could not so much as hurt the proverbial fly. I'd stake my career on it.' George smiled at his old friend.

'Now then, George. I think that there are a couple of things you would find it useful to know. Firstly, Reverend Smith did not die from the blow to the back of his head made by the silver candlestick.'

'Really?' George questioned. Completely taken aback by Tom's statement.

'Yes, the base of the candlestick made quite a dent in the Reverend's head but there was very little blood around the wound, indicating that he was already deceased. When I left the family this afternoon, I went to have a closer look at the body. I found a pin prick on the side of the neck with some faint bruising around it. I believe he was injected with something and that's what killed him.'

'Then why bludgeon him and go to the trouble of hiding him behind the Christmas tree? Surely, if he'd just been found in the drawing room, seated as he had been last seen on Christmas Eve, no foul play would have been suspected? I would have suspected a heart attack, brought on by all the alcohol he had consumed.'

'Exactly. Which at this stage leads me to believe there are two people with strong enough motives to want to kill. The second simply not realising that the Reverend was already dead. Interesting you say that he would simply have been found in the drawing room. I take it he had not retired for the evening then?'

'No, he hadn't. Amelia, Stephen, Reverend Smith and myself were the last ones in the room. Amelia departed first. She told us that she was going down to the kitchens to see if Milroy was still there. She wanted to have a word with him about the horses. See that he would be able to get down to the stables the next morning to check on them.

'I quickly smoked one last cigarette and chatted to the Reverend. He was asking why I wasn't with family this Christmas. Just for the record, Tom, my fiancée, Sophie Westchester and her parents are with relatives in Yorkshire. My role at the bank would not permit me to travel with them. Anyway, I rose to retire, and Reverend Smith said he would come too but Stephen delayed him saying that he needed a quick word. It was late by this time so what was so important that it couldn't have waited until morning, I do not know.'

'So as far as you are aware then, Stephen was the last one to see the Reverend alive?'

'I would say so, yes.'

'Right. I will make Stephen top of my list for tomorrow.

'The other thing I wanted to mention to you was something that Sonia Ferguson said to me. She accused him of abandoning a maid that had become pregnant whilst in his service many years ago. Said that he threw her out of his house and the girl, and her unborn child subsequently died in the poorhouse. Apparently, there were even rumours that he had fathered the child.'

George nodded. 'If that were true it would show a very dark side to his character. It might even indicate a vindictiveness to some of the tales he was regaling us with throughout the evening.'

'Indeed. Look, George, it's just occurred to me that no one will have informed the curate what has happened. Perhaps I could leave you to gather your thoughts and we can talk some more tomorrow.'

'Yes of course. I have to be at the bank all day but why don't you come for dinner tomorrow evening? I'll make some notes this evening, provide some clarity to what actually happened.'

'Splendid. I shall look forward to it, George and by the way, congratulations on your engagement. I really must do that myself someday.'

George showed the Inspector out and returned to the fireside to place his thoughts in order.

Tom was grateful for the walk to the vicarage in order to clarify his own thoughts. There was a lot more here than met the eye and a lot of patience would be required to get to the truth of the matter. He felt blessed that he had an ally such as George Rochester, who had been there amongst it all, to assist him. The man who had once so unselfishly saved Tom's life. He might well owe him another favour at the end of all this.

Actually, what he owed George, Tom felt could never be repaid. But it was because of men like George that he had become a policeman in the first place. With his mind once again at ease, he approached the door to the vicarage and rang the bell.

The door was opened by the curate himself. Thomas Mason's eyes were bloodshot, and he gave the appearance of a man in great distress.

'Mr Mason? You may not remember me. I have occasionally attended services here with my sister, Mrs Emily Travers and her family. I am Detective Inspector Stewart of Scotland Yard. Am I correct in assuming that you have heard the sad news about Reverend Smith?'

'Yes, Inspector. Please do come in. Sergeant Bailey was good enough to telephone me from the police station with there not being a phone at the Manor House. I can't understand it at all, Inspector. Who would want to kill Reverend Smith? A more Christian and pious man you could not wish to meet.'

'Indeed, Mr Mason and that's exactly what I intend to find out.'

The curate had led them to a small but comfortable sitting room and indicated for the Inspector to sit in the large armchair closest to the fire, whilst he seated himself on the sofa opposite.

'I apologise, Mr Mason, but I do have to ask this. Did Reverend Smith have any enemies or anyone with a grudge against him that you know about?'

'No, not at all. He was loved in this village. In fact, he was the very heart of it.'

'And did you live here alone with the Reverend?'

'Yes. It is only a small dwelling but big enough for our humble requirements. Mrs Wainwright comes in daily to keep house, so to speak. Cleaning, washing and cooking.'

'I see. And tell me did Reverend Smith drink much alcohol at all?'

'Oh no, Inspector. I've only ever known him to take a small glass of wine with Christmas lunch and again on Easter Sunday, after the two big services of the year. Apart from taking the wine during communion of course.'

'So, what would account for him taking a pre-lunch sherry and drinking wine at Christmas Eve lunch then?'

'I really don't know, Sir. I know that we both thought there could be heavy snow coming and he had given me his sermon in case he couldn't get back for the midnight service. It was a good one too. One of his best. Pity that no one got to hear it. But it hadn't started snowing at lunch so it couldn't be for that reason. Unless.......'

'Go on, Mr Mason,' Tom urged him.

'Dutch courage, Inspector. There was something that he needed to talk to Lord Mountjoy about and I know that he was quite anxious over the matter. It was concerning the large plot of land that lies between the church and the Manor House. Originally the land was part of the Manor estate. But then the current Lord Mountjoy's grandfather or great grandfather needed to raise some capital and sold it to the church. The church at the time thought it would require the extra land in order to extend the current cemetery. However, the village has never grown to that extent, not helped by the Great War of course, and most of the plots in the current cemetery are family plots.

'During the Great War, the land was lent back to the Manor estate who co-ordinated the land girls that worked upon it. Since the war however, the land has just been left, the Reverend, correctly presuming, because it had now returned to the church. Although, down through the years, the Reverend has often reported to me that he had overheard the Mountjoy's talk of needing to do something with the land. He never challenged it at the time as he didn't wish to create any issues and the matter never went any further.

'However, just recently, the Reverend decided that it would be years before the land might ever be needed as a burial site and what with people really feeling the pinch in this great depression, he would turn it over to the village. He proposed that all the people of the village could come together to plant all manner of vegetables and fruit. Maybe even keep some hens or some pigs. He wanted to announce his grand scheme from the pulpit in his first sermon of the new year. Nobody knew a thing about it yet, but he fully intended to let the family know of his plan whilst he was there over Christmas, as it is still land that belongs to the church even if the family think differently.'

'I see,' said Tom thoughtfully. 'Will you be able to carry out his wishes?'

'I hope so, Sir. He had cleared it with the church, and I shall be staying on and holding the fort for the time being.'

'Very good. One last thing, Mr Mason. Did the Reverend have any family?'

'None that I know of Sir.'

'Very well. Please let me know if you think of anything else?'

The curate nodded in silence and with that Tom took his leave, once more processing the information he had just received. It was getting late now, and he hadn't eaten anything since breakfast that morning. Hungry and just a little weary, Tom decided to head back to his sister's cottage and enjoy some family time. He often found that by simply relaxing and putting a case out of his mind completely, clarity of thought could be achieved. He would telephone Sergeant Bailey from the cottage and insist that he also went home and got some rest before what promised to be a very busy day tomorrow.

Nathaniel Parker had felt very relieved when he had been allowed to return home. He was very confused as to why the silver candlestick had been placed under his bed. Was it literally just to hide it in what was believed to be an empty room or had someone deliberately tried to frame him? The latter made him feel extremely angry. He hoped and prayed that the police investigation led them to Robert Milroy.

Nathaniel Parker was not a murderer, but he did indeed have a little secret that he truly hoped would not have to be revealed. If he had been Milroy's age, he might have considered making a run for it. But, then again, that would only cast suspicion on himself. No, he must wait it out. Act normal and hope it would all just go away.

The Manor House had been extremely subdued since the guests had left. Lord David had taken himself off to the library with his beloved dog, Chester and found solace in his books. He had informed Jameson that he did not wish to be disturbed and would ring if he needed anything.

Amelia and Sonia had not returned from their afternoon rest, although Sonia had rung down and asked that a light supper be delivered to her room.

Colonel James had returned to the drawing room once the house maids had completed their servicing of it. He sat reading magazines and drinking brandy as a distraction until Stephen joined him late in the afternoon.

Stephen, himself had been outside pottering here and there. Anything to keep moving and keep himself busy, until his fingers grew numb, and he was forced to come inside. He gave his uncle a simple nod before picking up a magazine and pouring himself a brandy.

Lady Serena, like her son, had also felt the need to be doing something and so had spent the last few hours keeping her hands busy with her embroidery in the morning room.

Clarissa, on the other hand, was quite content being idle and lounged on a sofa, occasionally flicking forward the page of the current magazine she was perusing.

'I'm so glad you are here,' Lady Serena told her friend. 'I know this is all just too awful but where the devil would I be without you? David is hiding away in the library. Goodness only knows when he will emerge. James and Stephen have returned to the very room where a dead body was laying just a few hours ago. Too sordid. Then Amelia and Mummy have taken to their beds. I'd be facing this all on my own if not for you.'

'Well, that's exactly it, darling. I shall be your rock, and this will all be over in no time. The snow has melted a tad today and once the roads are clear and they catch that Milroy fellow, everything will return to normal, you'll see. In the meantime, I shall stay here with you for as long as you need me. Now what are we going to do about dinner? Life does go on you know.'

'You are so right, darling and if one looks on the bright side, at least all those frightful guests have left.'

'Yes, they were rather an odd bunch. How on earth do you tolerate that Lady Eliza Ross? Could she make it any clearer that she is sweet on your husband?'

'Oh, I know, darling. But her late husband, Lord Duncan was David's oldest and dearest friend. I think the silly man feels obliged to look after and protect his best friend's widow and is flattered by her attention. I always thought that it kept him from being a grump. Unfortunately for her though, she will not find it so easy to flirt in the New Year as I am going to need the Gate House for my charity work, and she will have to move. Let her daughter have her in London with her for a time. With a bit of luck, she might even get her married off again.'

'In London Colonel James might woo her. She has funds I take it?'

'Oh yes, her husband left her a very wealthy woman. But don't joke, darling. I do not wish her for a sister-in-law.'

'No. He'd probably prefer the daughter anyway. Now what about that bank manager fellow? Strange chap he is. Barely said two words.'

'Oh, I know, darling. I think David only invited him to get him onside. Looking for some funding for his antiques business. Every time I have encountered him, he is the same. Just stands and stares, observing and taking everything in. Makes one most uncomfortable.'

'Yes, one does like to know what someone is thinking. I wonder what he thought of us lot. Didn't really fit in did he? Mind you, that doctor didn't say too much either.'

'No, he is new to the village this year. Mummy adores him for the new modern treatments that he is prescribing for her various ailments. At least if he doesn't say much, he smiles and nods during conversations appearing to be interested.'

'Is he treating Amelia also?'

'No, of course not, darling there is nothing wrong with Amelia. Why do you ask?'

'Oh, no reason, just curious. Now what about dinner? Should we eat in the dining room to keep up appearances?'

'Yes, we shall, darling. I shall ring through now. It's up to the others if they want to join us or not but you and I shall continue with a stiff upper lip and enjoy some good food and wine and talk about our schooldays.'

Clarissa laughed. 'Don't even get me started on that battle axe of a headmistress. What was she called again?'

'Miss Lucie. More commonly known as Lucifer.' Both ladies laughed and settled into reminiscing, setting aside all other cares and worries for the time being.

CHAPTER FIFTEEN

December the twenty-seventh dawned with a slight rise in temperature, so that by the time Tom was ready to depart for the Manor House, melting snow could be both seen and heard falling from the branches of the trees that grew all around the village. Before departing, he had telephoned Sergeant Bailey and requested that he meet him round by the kitchen. Tom wanted to have a quick chat with the servants and as he was going to take the longer route via the road through the village, he was also hoping that a cup of tea and a slice of cake would be forthcoming.

He had heard that Agnes Trelawney was an excellent cook and whilst his sister did create some very tasty meals, baking was really not her forte. Now he wouldn't have claimed to be able to bake a cake to save his own life, but how she could produce a Victoria sponge that was burnt on the outside and yet uncooked in the middle, Tom simply could not fathom.

The sun was shining, and he had to admit that he was enjoying the peace and solitude the walk was affording him. So totally different from his life in London. Not that he would want to change that life. Oh no. The hustle and bustle of the city was the place for him. But as the saying went, 'a change is as good as a rest' and even though he had a murder to solve, he could at least enjoy the change of scenery.

As he walked down the driveway of the Manor House, he noticed that some of the drapes in the upper windows were still pulled to. More restless nights, he imagined. Not being able to drop off until early dawn. He took the footpath to the side of the house that led him to the kitchen, knocked on the door and walked in.

To his great surprise all the servants were sat at the kitchen table, apart from Jameson who was in a comfortable chair by the hearth. It was Jameson however, that rose to greet him.

'Why, Inspector Stewart, good morning. Do come in and take a seat. Have you walked from the village? You must be cold, Sir. Jane, pour the Inspector a mug of tea. Mrs Trelawney, how about one of your delicious homemade scones for the Inspector, after that long walk?'

'Of course, Mr Jameson and you must try it with my blackberry and apple jam, Inspector. Won first prize at the autumn fete it did.'

'Thank you very much, Mrs Trelawney. The family not up and about yet then?'

'No, Sir,' Jameson replied. 'The girls have already seen to all the downstairs rooms. But Lady Mountjoy said yesterday evening not to adhere to breakfast time as folk would sleep in. Not even heard a bell for a tray of tea for anyone so far. Everything appears to be at sixes and sevens.'

'Quite so,' Tom agreed. 'I am sure things will get back to normal soon. Now I just wanted to ask you all about Reverend Smith on Christmas Eve. Did he seem quite normal to you? And I must stress that you mustn't worry about speaking ill of the dead or gossiping. Every little detail, no matter how small, could be hugely important in helping us to find our killer.'

'But isn't it Mr Milroy who's scarpered?' Agnes asked.

'Well yes, Mrs Trelawney, it certainly looks that way. But we do need to gather more
evidence which is why every little thing is so important.'

'Well in that case,' Jameson began. 'No, he was definitely not normal. He never touches a drop of drink until Christmas lunch when his Christmas Day duties are complete and then only the smallest glass of wine. This year he took sherry at the pre-Christmas Eve lunch drinks. More than one, fair knocked them back he did. Slurred a bit over the giving of thanks which Lady Mountjoy was most displeased about.

'But he didn't stop there, Sir. He took a glass of wine and knocked that back as well. Now Lord Mountjoy always insists upon me to keep my eye on the table and never leave a guest with an empty glass. So, I kept filling, and he kept drinking.'

'He kept getting things wrong as well, Sir,' one of the kitchen maids interjected. Jane or Alice, Tom didn't know which, but he knew they were sisters.

'Normally he would sit quiet as a mouse, not speaking until he was spoken to but they was all talking about the garden and what a good job gardener does and the Reverend called him Nathan Parkes when his name is Nathaniel Parker.'

Tom raised one eyebrow in surprise.

'Yes,' the other sister joined in. 'Then he told Lord Mountjoy that he had seen one of his antique statues in the village antique shop and it almost looked like the real thing. You should have seen Lord Mountjoy's face. He told him good and proper that it couldn't be one of his because he didn't deal in statues.'

Jameson took up the thread again. 'There was an incident after luncheon as well, Sir, during the afternoon shoot. I attend to the gentlemen there. Reverend Smith was asking Doctor Hollis if he was from Yorkshire or had lived in Yorkshire at any time. Well, Doctor Hollis told him no, but the Reverend insisted that the doctor had a trace of a Yorkshire accent. Doctor Hollis looked a bit put out about it. My understanding was that he came from Harley Street.'

'Right. Well, thank you all very much for your help. This has all been most useful.'

The kitchen door opened, and Sergeant Bailey appeared. 'Ah Sergeant, we've just been having a little chat about the Reverend, but we'd better get on now. Mr Jameson, we'll take the library again and if you would be so kind and ask Mr Stephen Mountjoy to join us there, thank you. And to you, Mrs Trelawney, the scone and jam were delicious.'

Agnes Blushed.

Inspector Stewart rose and took the stairs up to the main house, Sergeant Bailey following in his wake. Luckily, the

Sergeant did not believe in accepting a morsel to eat or drink whilst on duty and so was not at all put out by not being offered a mug of tea or a home baked scone with award winning jam.

Once they were both settled in the library, Tom asked Sergeant Bailey for an update.

'I had a good look at the candlestick under the magnifying glass, Sir, and there appears to be just a trace of blood at the base. Should be just enough for a match and confirmation that the candlestick is indeed the murder weapon.'

'Excellent, Sergeant. Any news on the missing chauffeur?'

'Not yet, Sir. But he can't have got far with the snow and everything.'

'No, that's true. We'll don some snowshoes and take a look at his place later. See if he left us any clue to his whereabouts. Thank you for contacting Thomas Mason by the way. I called in to see him on my way home yesterday evening. Now he thinks that Reverend Smith may have been imbibing for Dutch courage, in order to inform the Mountjoy family that the church intended to reclaim the land that had been lent to the estate during the Great War. The family appear to have presumed that it was theirs to keep.

'Called on George Rochester as well. Solid fellow. We served together you know, Sergeant. He informed me that Stephen Mountjoy may well have been the last person to see the Reverend alive. Hence why I wish to speak to him first this morning. Ah, I think I hear his footsteps now.

'There are a couple of other items to update you on, Sergeant. So, I will fill you in on our way to the stables later.'

The door to the library opened and Stephen Mountjoy entered the room. He had the look of a man who had slept badly, grey in pallor and seemingly aged overnight.

'Mr Mountjoy. Thank you for coming to speak with us. I apologise if we have disturbed your rest. Do you need to ring for some tea or coffee before we begin?'

'No, no that's fine. You've done me a favour really as I need to get on. It occurred to me that no one saw to the horses yesterday and my sister is certainly in no fit state to do so. Plus, the estate won't run itself. Going to rally Daddy, Uncle James and hopefully Susan, Miss Ross for a bit more snow clearance now it appears to be starting to thaw. Best to keep active. That's the way to get through this.'

'Quite right, Mr Mountjoy. Your attitude is to be commended. I won't keep you too long, but I did want to ask you about Christmas Eve night. I believe that after your sister and Mr Rochester left the drawing room, you detained Reverend Smith from also retiring. May I ask what you wished to speak with him about?'

Stephen gave a big sigh and began chewing his bottom lip. 'Well, I suppose it's all going to come out now anyway.

'I propose to sell the land that was originally owned by the church but given to the Manor estate during the war. Nothing was ever signed but it was agreed by my father and Reverend Smith's predecessor with a gentlemen's handshake. The church no longer required the land, and it was believed that the Manor could put it to much better use.

'However, now that I wish to sell the land, a legal document is required. I approached the Reverend during pre-dinner drinks for his signature on behalf of the church and he told me no. He said that the church was taking the land back for some sort of village project. He also said that even if his predecessor had agreed that transfer of land on a handshake, he had not had the legal right to do so.

'I will not deny that I was extremely angry, but it was not the time and place to get into it then and there. When I detained him, I simply wanted the name of someone higher in the church that I could talk to, but he would not help me. The matter is not over as far as I am concerned, and I fully intend to take it further. Morally, that land belongs to the Manor estate, and I am convinced that the church will see that. He was alive when I left him, still sitting on the sofa. Doctor Hollis will vouch for that. I was just leaving the room when he came back downstairs to pick up some magazines. I believe he even spoke to the Reverend. I remember he caught up with me on the stairs and said that he wouldn't be surprised if the Reverend was still on the sofa on Christmas morning, as he was nodding off then and there.'

'I see. Well, thank you, Mr Mountjoy. Sergeant Bailey and I would like to take a look at Mr Milroy's residence now. Do you have a key please, Mr Mountjoy and some snowshoes we could borrow?'

'No need for a key, the place will be unlocked. Over the garage it is, steps to the side. I'll be down to the stables myself once I've had some breakfast. There are several pairs of snowshoes just outside the front door. Help yourselves.'

Tom and Sergeant Bailey donned their outside gear, as Stephen headed for the dining room, before exiting via the front door in search of snowshoes.

'Well, at least it's not uphill, Sergeant.'

'No, Sir. We must be grateful for small mercies.'

'Right then, Sergeant, the other items I must tell you about. When I looked closely at the Reverend Smith's body yesterday, I found the site of a small injection mark in one side of his neck.'

'So, you think that's what killed him, Sir, an injection of something lethal?'

'Yes, Sergeant, I do. What's more, I do not believe that he was then struck on the head by the same person. According to the servants, the Reverend upset a few people yesterday by some of the things he said.'

Tom filled Neville in with what had been told to him in the kitchen, concluding with his planned visit to George Rochester's house that evening to build a further picture.

They finally reached the garage and stables, with Neville slightly red in the face, and climbed the steps to the space over the garage where Milroy resided. Although the area was small, the room had been laid out to give the appearance of space. It was very neat and tidy with no personal effects scattered about and very little evidence that anyone lived there at all. Consequently, the search did not take very long, and it appeared that Milroy had taken very little with him.

'Anything strike you at all here Sergeant?' Tom asked.

'Lived very simply didn't he, Sir? Not put down any roots. In fact, he lived like a man that was ready to take off at any time.'

'Yes, I thought that too.' Tom agreed wholeheartedly with Neville's assessment of the situation.

'Well, I think we've seen all we need to see here. I'd like to talk to Doctor Hollis next as potentially he is now the last person to see the Reverend alive.'

'Yes, Sir.'

Tom and Neville were just descending the steps when Stephen arrived at the stables.

'All done here, Inspector?' he asked as he opened the stable door.

'Yes, Mr Mountjoy. We will leave you for the time being and head back to the village.'

Stephen bowed his head in acknowledgement and entered the stable.

Tom and Neville once again put on their snowshoes for the walk back up to the Manor House when they heard a loud scream and Stephen came running out of the stable door.

'Inspector, it's Milroy. I think he's dead,'

'What?' Tom abandoned the snowshoes and ran into the stable. The first two stalls he passed were occupied by horses. Stephen indicated towards the third stall.

'I just came in here for some fresh hay and saw him.'

Robert Milroy was seated on a bale of hay and although his body had fallen to the left, more bales of hay had kept him upright. Tom approached him and checked for a pulse, knowing full well that it was in vain. He spotted an empty glass bottle at Milroy's feet.

'Mr Mountjoy, take that bale of hay nearest to the door please and just do the minimum required to make sure that the horses are comfortable. After that please return to the Manor and gather the household, including Jameson, in the morning room. I will be there as soon as I can to speak to you all.'

Stephen moved like a man in deep shock as he collected the

hay and began to see to the horses.

Tom turned to Neville. 'See that bottle at his feet, Sergeant? Collect that and dust for prints. Take Milroy's prints as well.'

'Yes, Sir. Look there's a few bottles the same on that shelf behind you.'

Tom turned and saw five of the same type of bottle filled with a cloudy liquid standing on a small shelf.

'Best print them as well, Sergeant. We will need to establish where they came from.'

Neville, having already put on his gloves, picked up the empty bottle and sniffed inside it.

'Smells like lemonade, Sir. Can't make out anything else.'

'So, Sergeant. Have we got Milroy all wrong then? He comes down here on Christmas morning on skis and comes straight into the stables to see to the horses. But his trek had made him thirsty so, the first thing he does is come in here, take a bottle from the shelf, sit down on this bale and drink. Yes, Sergeant. There is a dust ring on this shelf indicating that the bottle was here until recently.'

'There's his bag and skis behind those bales over there, Sir,' Neville indicated to the far corner of the stall as Stephen popped his head around the door.

'Excuse me, Inspector. I've done enough to a make sure the horses will be alright until tomorrow. I'll go up to the house now.'

'Yes, thank you, Mr Mountjoy. Just one thing. Could you tell from the state of their stalls if Milroy actually saw to them on Christmas Day?'

'Hard to say, Inspector. He left them well provided on Christmas Eve, but their water and feed were pretty low now.'

'Alright. Thank you, you can go up now, Mr Mountjoy.'

Stephen had left them before Tom spoke again. 'Sergeant, could you go back up to Milroy's space please and fetch a sheet to cover the body? I don't think he'd mind being here for a while longer with the horses.'

'Yes, Sir. Right away.'

Tom took a seat on the nearest bale of hay and looked around him, frowning as he did so. This was indeed most curious and not at all what he had expected. Waiting for Sergeant Bailey to return, he went over in his mind everything that he had discovered so far, hoping to find some clarity in the death of Robert Milroy.

Stephen made his way back up to the house, aware that he should probably quicken his pace yet strangely hardly able to place one foot in front of the other. What on earth was happening? He felt the weight of the whole world on his shoulders as he contemplated having to tell the family about this latest occurrence. He made his way to the morning room and found all the ladies gathered there.

'Stephen. My goodness what on earth has happened, you look terrible?' Lady Serena greeted him.

'Where's Daddy and Uncle James?' Stephen asked, completely avoiding his mother's question.

'Why they are in the dining room, having a late breakfast. I believe they intend to go outside and clear some more snow shortly.'

'Right, I'll go and fetch them. Could you ring for Jameson please, Mummy? The Inspector will be here shortly to talk to us all.'

Without waiting for a response, he turned on his heel and left the room.

'What on earth has happened now?' Lady Serena muttered, mostly to herself as she went to ring the bell. Turning towards her friend she added, 'There's been more drama in this house than in one of your Italian opera's hasn't there, darling?'

Clarissa smiled and returned to the magazine article featuring the film star, Gary Cooper, which she had been very much enjoying.

Stephen burst into the dining room. 'Sorry to interrupt your breakfasts, Daddy, Uncle James but there's been a development. Inspector Stewart wishes to speak to us all in the morning room.'

'A development, eh?' Lord David remarked. 'Well, we're just about done here. James, bring your coffee through.'

The men entered the hallway to be joined by Jameson.

'You've been summoned too have you, Jameson?' Colonel James asked him. 'Well let's hope it's good news.'

Upon entering the drawing room, Lord David looked for Inspector Stewart and found that he was not present. 'Where is he then?' he asked.

'On the way from the stables,' Stephen told them all. 'I met the Inspector and Sergeant Bailey down there. They had gone to search Milroy's room.'

'Oh, have you seen to the horses?' Amelia asked her brother.

'Yes, and they're fine,' Stephen told her.

'Oh good. I've been so worried about them.'

All that could then be heard was the ticking of the clock on the mantle, while they all waited in silence for the Inspector to arrive.

After what felt like hours, but in reality, was only a few minutes, Tom entered the morning room alone, having left Neville to finish collecting prints in the stables.

'Good morning, Lord Mountjoy, Lady Mountjoy. Is everyone here? Yes, well I'm afraid that I have some more rather bad news to impart. Robert Milroy has just been found dead in the third stall of the stables.'

'Good grief. Was he killed as well?' Lord David asked, appearing most shocked at the news.

'It's too early to say, Sir. However, there was an empty bottle of what appeared to have been lemonade at his feet, removed from the shelf behind him. Does anyone know about those?'

Tom looked slowly around the room, allowing his gaze to rest on each of them, searching for any change of expression in a society that was used to maintaining a stiff upper lip.

'Permit me, Sir?' It was Jameson who finally spoke. 'That would be Mrs Trelawney's homemade lemonade, Sir. He always took some bottles down to the stables after a batch was made. Said it was the best thirst quencher he'd ever had. He fair drank gallons in the summer when he got really warm from the mucking out. Not so much in the winter months though. Those bottles must have been there a while now. Mrs Trelawney hasn't made any lemonade since September, but then Milroy always mucked out the horses after his breakfast, so he'd have had several cups of tea. Wouldn't need any more to drink unless it was warm, Sir.'

'I see, and did anyone else ever share these bottles? Mrs Cavendish, you spend a lot of time at the stables. Did you ever partake of this lemonade?'

Amelia glanced up. She appeared so completely out of it with this latest news that Tom doubted whether she had even heard or understood the question.

'What? No,' she stumbled.

Sonia interrupted. 'Inspector, I can quite categorically inform you that my granddaughter did not drink any of those bottles of lemonade because she does not like the stuff. Finds it too sour. It's pretty clear what happened here, isn't it Inspector? The man kills the Reverend for some sordid reason or another then in the cold light of day on Christmas morning, had a fit of remorse and kills himself.'

'Yes, well that is certainly one line of inquiry we will be following,'

'It is the only line of inquiry, that much is obvious, Inspector.'

'Yes, Mrs Ferguson. We will get on to that straightaway.'

With a curt bow, Tom left the room and met Sergeant Bailey in the hallway.

'All finished with the printing, Sir. How did it go with the family?'

Tom filled him in with what had transpired in the drawing room.

'So where to now, Sir?'

'Let's just wait a minute for Jameson to appear. I have a few more questions I'd like to ask Mrs Trelawney about that lemonade.'

'What about what Mrs Ferguson said? Do you think she could

be right?'

'It's certainly the right solution for them, isn't it, Sergeant? Cut and dried. All nicely packaged up. Nothing to do with the family and we leave them to get on with their lives. No, my mind is like a parachute, Sergeant. Works best when it's open. For now, I will let them think that we are in agreement, whilst we carry on with our inquiries.

'Ah, Jameson,' he greeted the butler as he emerged from the morning room.

'We'll follow you down to the kitchen if we may? Just a couple of questions for Mrs Trelawney about her lemonade.'

'Certainly, Inspector.' Jameson snapped his heels and led the way down to the kitchen.

The room was a hive of activity when the three men entered.

'Inspector,' Agnes greeted him. 'Come back for another of my scones, have you?'

'Unfortunately, not, Mrs Trelawney. But I would like to ask you about your lemonade, if I may?'

Agnes looked slightly puzzled and called over to Alice. 'Take over the soup please, Alice? Seems like appetites have returned, Inspector. Her Ladyship has requested a full lunch today.'

'Indeed.' Tom looked over to Jameson and met his eye. 'Mr Jameson has some news about Mr Milroy that he will share with you all shortly. I just need to know how he received the bottles of lemonade from you?'

Agnes knew her place not to question the Inspector no matter how curious she might be, so simply told him what he wanted to know. 'He had a little bottle carrier. Carried six bottles, it did. Once he'd drunk all six, he would bring the carrier up to the kitchen to be refilled.'

'And who did the refilling, was it anyone or just you?'

'Just me, Inspector. I makes the lemonade in a big pitcher. It's too heavy and awkward for the girls to do without spilling. It's too precious to be spilled, that's what Milroy told me. So, I would remove the bottles from the carrier, he had already rinsed them you see, pop in the funnel, fill them up and place them back in the carrier for him. Then he would carry it back to the stables.'

'I see and the last batch you made was in September?'

'Yes, that's right. Later than I normally makes it, but after that we had a chilly autumn. There're still some bottles left in the pantry that no one's felt like drinking. Best on a hot summer's day my lemonade is.'

'Thank you, Mrs Trelawney. I really must come back next summer and try some. If it is anywhere near as good as your jam, then I am sure I will find it delicious.'

Agnes was still blushing a few moments later as Tom and Neville took their leave. They exited via the front of the house and saw Lord Mountjoy, Colonel Mountjoy and Stephen clearing snow from the driveway down to the garages.

'Fancy joining us, Inspector?' Lord David asked. 'Many hands making light work now you've tied up the case?'

'Plenty of loose ends still to tie up I'm afraid. My superiors insist on all *I*'s being dotted and *T's* crossed. I am going to call on Lady Ross and Miss Ross at the Gate House now. I'll mention it to Miss Ross, she might care to join you.'

'Right, you are, Inspector,' Lord David retorted.

Tom left them to it and carried on down the drive to the Gate House, Sergeant Bailey carrying on back to the station with the evidence he had gathered from the stables. The door was opened by Susan Ross who did not look at all surprised to see him.

'Ah, Inspector Stewart. I wondered when you would get to us. Sergeant Bailey not with you? Never mind come through to the sitting room, Mummy is there.'

Lady Ross was sitting by the hearth, her knitting in her hands. 'Ah, Inspector Stewart,' she greeted Tom cheerfully. 'Do come in and sit by the fire? Will you take tea, or perhaps you would prefer coffee?'

'No, thank you, Lady Ross. This is just a brief update for the time being. I'm sorry to have to inform you that Mr Milroy has been found dead this morning in the stables.'

'What, trampled by one of the horses was he?' Susan interjected.

'No, Miss Ross. He was found in the third stall where the bales of hay are kept. It appears that he headed straight there when he left the Manor House on Christmas morning, took a bottle of lemonade from the shelf behind him and died after he had drunk it.'

'Are you saying that he killed himself, Inspector?' Susan asked.

'That could be one explanation, Miss Ross.'

'And the most obvious one I would have thought, Inspector. He kills the Reverend and then kills himself,' Susan continued, haughtily.

'Yes, well one must be sure about these things. Ladies, thank you for your time. I must take my leave now. By the way, Miss Ross, the gentlemen are outside clearing more snow, in case you would care to join them.'

'Do you know, Inspector, I think I will. I'll just see you out then go and change. Be back a bit later, Mummy, ok?'

With that, Susan positively hustled Tom out of the Gate House and on his way. Not that he minded. There was plenty to be getting on with after all. Far too many unanswered questions and his gut feeling was not allowing him to jump to the same conclusions that Sonia Ferguson and Susan Ross had immediately jumped to.

He decided that his next port of call should be Doctor Hollis as, up to this point, he was still the last person known to have seen Reverend Smith alive. Tom had not met this doctor before. His sister had informed him that the village's previous doctor had finally retired and how good the new chap was with the children, not set in his ways like the old chap.

The waiting room was empty when he arrived but the Doctor's receptionist, Darlene, was seated behind the desk.

'May I help you?' She asked him in a clipped tone.

'I'm Inspector Stewart of Scotland Yard. I'd like to speak with Doctor Hollis please?'

'Oh yes of course, Inspector. Doctor Hollis has told me all about it. The poor Reverend. Such a shock as I cannot tell you.

Anyway, Doctor Hollis has seen his last patient before lunch, so I can take you right through.'

Darlene tapped on the door to the left and entered without waiting for a response. Doctor Hollis looked up from where he was seated behind a desk updating case notes.

'Ah, Inspector Stewart, isn't it? Please come in. Darlene, you may take your lunch now. I'll see you this afternoon.'

Darlene closed the door and left them to it.

'I was just about to make a sandwich for lunch. The kitchen is just along the hallway. Would you care to join me, Inspector? I do have a nice bit of Cheddar in.'

'That sounds very nice, Doctor Hollis. I'd be delighted, thank you.'

The Doctor led the way and busied himself making the sandwiches whilst Tom took a seat at the kitchen table.

'How's the investigation going, Inspector?'

'Moving forward slowly, as the wheels of justice do grind. I did want to ask you about late Christmas Eve. Stephen Mountjoy tells me that as he was leaving the drawing room, where Reverend Smith sat alone on the sofa, you came back downstairs to pick up some magazines.'

'Yes, that is correct, Inspector. The Reverend was beginning to nod off. Don't suppose he even saw me. I just picked up some magazines from the coffee table and joined Stephen out in the hallway, then we continued upstairs together. I suppose that makes me the last one to see him alive. Apart from the killer, that is. Quite honestly, Inspector, with the amount of alcohol the man had consumed, he would have been quite comatose. Easy enough for anyone to bash him over the head. Probably wouldn't have felt a thing.'

'Did he have any underlying health issues that you were aware of?'

'He certainly never consulted me, if that's what you are asking. I didn't know the man at all well, but he appeared to be as fit as a fiddle to me.'

'What about Robert Milroy, was he a patient of yours?'

'No, I've never treated him either. First time I met him was when we were shovelling snow on Christmas morning. Have you found him yet?'

'Unfortunately, yes. Milroy was discovered in the stables this morning, dead.'

'What? How?' Doctor Hollis appeared genuinely shocked to hear this news.

'That's still to be determined but suicide can't be ruled out.'

'Remorse, eh? Can even strike people who don't appear to have any conscience whatsoever. That must be some relief to Lord and Lady Mountjoy. How is your sandwich, Inspector?'

'Very good thank you, Doctor Hollis. It really is a very tasty Cheddar. So, what brought you down to the West Country then? Didn't I hear that you came down from Harley Street?'

'Yes, that's quite correct. It was just for a change of pace really. I'd always worked in and around the city and thought I'd like to try the countryside for a change. Get some good clean air into the old lungs.'

'And how are you finding life in the country?'

'Very good, so far. I took over a thriving, well run practice which continues to tick over quite nicely.'

'Excellent, that is good news. Now can I just confirm that you didn't have your medical bag with you up at the Manor House?'

'Yes, that's quite correct, Inspector. I'd seen all the patients that needed treatment, administered all the necessary drugs and there were no imminent births or deaths to see to, so I didn't see the need for it. Plus, there was a notice on the front door advising that I was up at the Manor House. So, I could have been found if there had been an emergency, and we hadn't been snowed in of course.'

'I see. Just one more thing if I may? Have any drugs gone missing from your supplies at all?'

'No, most definitely not, Inspector. I am the only one with a key to the drugs cabinet which I always keep about my person. Plus, I took inventory as soon as I returned. That's something I do daily. It is vital that one keeps accurate records.'

'Indeed, it is. Well, thank you for your time and hospitality, Doctor Hollis. Have you ever had any discrepancies in your records?' Tom asked as an afterthought.

'Just once with a patient who is prescribed morphine. They were adamant that I had given them one less box of sachets than usual, which was not the case. That little mystery was never cleared up.'

'I don't suppose you can tell me who that was, Doctor Hollis?'

'No, no I can't. But if you think it's really important, I could ask the patient's permission.'

'No, that's alright for now. I'll let you know if that situation changes. Anyway, I've taken up enough of your time. Your receptionist will be back soon. So, once again, Doctor Hollis, I thank you for your hospitality. I'll see myself out.'

Taking his leave, Tom pondered just how important that missing box of morphine might turn out to be. He decided to return to the station and catch up with Sergeant Bailey. However, as he walked along the High Street, he passed the village antique's shop and seeing that it was open, decided to call in.

A Mr Arthur Pentelow was the proprietor of said antique shop and Tom found him polishing a beautiful grandfather clock as he entered the premises.

'Mr Pentelow?' Tom enquired.

'Yes, indeed. That's my good self, Sir. How may I be of service to you today?'

'I'm Inspector Stewart of Scotland Yard.'

'Oh, you must be here about the deaths up at the Manor House.' Noting the Inspector's look of surprise he added, 'News travels fast in a village such as this one.'

'Indeed, it does. Tell me, Mr Pentelow, do you do much business with the Manor House?'

'Now and again. They all pop in looking for birthday presents for family members but nothing too valuable. The little shop keeps a fair turnover with inexpensive items like that but most of my trade comes from specific customer orders, like this grandfather clock for example. I hold them in the shop until they can be collected with a 'sold' label on and that looks attractive to customers as well.'

'I see. Do you trade with Lord Mountjoy specifically?'

'I do have a little arrangement with Lord David that started recently. His Lordship is trying to dip a toe into the antiques business, just starting really. He's brought me a couple of items to display in the shop. I don't buy them from him you understand just display them at the price he's decided and if they sell, which they won't I hasten to add, I will take ten percent of the profit. He has also asked me to put the word out amongst other dealers but between you and me, Inspector, no one I know will have any interest in what he's selling.'

'And why is that Mr Pentelow?'

'Why they are fakes, copies and the poor deluded man thinks they are the real thing. Now see this little statue here. Reverend Smith came in before Christmas to take a look at this. He thought it might make a nice Christmas gift for his housekeeper. Couldn't believe it when I told him the price, until I explained it was one of Lord David's. The penny will drop for his Lordship eventually.'

'Thank you, Mr Pentelow. Just out of interest, how much would a grandfather clock like this one sell for?'

On hearing the amount, the clock had been sold for, Tom took his leave fully realising that Detective Inspectors were not destined to own beautiful antique grandfather clocks.

Sergeant Bailey was busy typing up a report when Tom walked in. He quickly brought the Sergeant up to date whilst Neville poured him a good strong cup of tea from the pot on his desk. His wife had knitted a tea cosy in the shape of a policeman's helmet, which had caused Neville much amusement. He listened intently before commenting.

'Could be interesting about the morphine, Sir, depending on what the post-mortems reveal. The coroner will be here tomorrow morning to pick up the bodies, Sir. They believe they will be able to get through by then.'

'Very good, Sergeant. Did the fingerprints from the bottles of lemonade tell us anything?'

'Yes, Sir and something quite interesting, I must add, bearing in mind what you have just told me. The five bottles of lemonade that were on the shelf in the stables, all had two sets of prints on them, one of which was Milroy's. I'll go back to the Manor House tomorrow and take Mrs Trelawney's prints for elimination purposes. Now the bottle that Milroy drank from has only one set of prints on it and that's his.'

'Well, that is most interesting,' Tom commented. 'But also, extremely puzzling. We'll have the contents of the other bottles tested just to be sure. Have you finished typing up your report?'

'Yes, Sir, I was just finishing it as you walked in.'

'Very good. Get yourself off home then, Sergeant and I'll meet you here at eight o'clock tomorrow morning. I'm off to see George Rochester this evening. He has an excellent memory along with top class observation skills. He should provide us with a lot more insight that we will be able to follow up on.'

'That will be most useful, Sir. I'm off home to have a good tidy up. The wife and kids are coming back home tomorrow.'

'Oh, that's nice, Sergeant. I expect you've missed them. Best have everything spick and span then.'

Neville nodded and hurriedly left the station. Tom moved to the chair that the Sergeant had vacated and read through his report. He had given an excellent account of events so far and Tom felt a swell of pride towards the man who was so obviously dedicated to his role as a police sergeant. His eyes fell on the helmet tea cosy which he suspected the Sergeant's wife had made for him. He would check and then perhaps Mrs Bailey would be kind enough to knit one for himself, although he would prefer a police box.

Turning his attention back to the report, he lifted the phone and made the necessary calls until it was time to keep his appointment at George Rochester's house for dinner.

George had had an interesting day. All the staff had made it into the bank, but the bank itself had been incredibly quiet all day, as was quite usual for the time between Christmas and the New Year. Always a good time for getting to the little unimportant tasks that needed to be completed nonetheless, and his assistant manager had kept them busy all day.

This had left George with the time to stay in his office and go over the events at the Manor House. He also took a long hard look at the Manor accounts which he found quite enlightening. He would invite Lord Mountjoy and his son in for a meeting in the New Year, once the dust had settled. He had no desire to add to their burden at the current time.

George left the bank promptly at five o'clock to prepare for his dinner with Tom. He would never have claimed to be a great cook, but he could turn his hand to a rather tasty Shepherd's pie and intended to make one now.

Said pie was cooking nicely in the oven as Tom rang the bell right at the time agreed. George opened the door and ushered his friend in.

'Come through to the kitchen, Tom. I thought we'd eat there as it's nice and warm. Now how about a drink? I was going to have a beer myself but have some scotch if you would prefer?'

'No, I'll join you in a beer, George, thanks. My, something smells good here.'

'Ah yes. I do make a mean Shepherd's pie even if I do say so myself. Any developments today you can tell me about?'

Once both men were seated at the kitchen table with their beers, Tom began to talk.

'I suppose you've heard about Milroy?'

'What? No, I haven't heard a thing. I've been shut away in my office for most of the day. What's happened?'

'He was found dead this morning in an empty stall down at the stables, by Stephen Mountjoy as he came to see to the horses. Luckily, Sergeant Bailey and I were searching Milroy's living quarters at the time.'

'Oh, my goodness!' George exclaimed. 'How on earth did he die?'

'That is where it gets really interesting. It would appear that when he left the Manor House on Christmas Day, he went straight to the stables into the empty stall where the hay is kept. His bag was on the floor still full of the vittles' Mrs Trelawney had supplied him with. Obviously thirsty when he arrived, he grabbed a bottle of the homemade lemonade he kept on the shelf there, to quench his thirst before seeing to the horses. However, the bottle he drank from was either drugged or poisoned. The family are quite happy to believe that in a fit of remorse, Milroy killed himself.'

'But clearly, you don't believe that.'

'No. For one thing the remaining five bottles on the shelf had two sets of fingerprints, as we would expect knowing what we know. However, only Milroy's prints were found on the bottle that he drank from. That would indicate to me that someone tampered with the bottle and then wiped it clean.'

'So, it was murder. But if it was connected to the killing of Reverend Smith, how could the killer have tampered with the bottle and furthermore how could they guarantee that Milroy would drink a bottle of lemonade that morning and then pick the bottle that contained the poison?'

'Exactly. We'll test the other bottles of course but I'm not expecting to find anything in them. So, the answer is that he or she couldn't guarantee that Milroy would die that day. Now, I have a very vague idea whirling around inside my mind of who might have done it but when, how and why remain very blurry so I'll keep that to myself for now, and I cannot yet link it to the murder of Reverend Smith.'

'I see,' George commented. 'Why don't we take a break and do some justice to the Shepherd's pie? Over coffee I'll begin my recollections and see where that takes us.'

'Splendid idea,' Tom agreed.

George removed the Shepherd's pie from the oven and placed it on the table. Tom's mouth began to water.

Shortly after, replete from three helpings each of what was the best Shepherd's pie that Tom had ever tasted, the two men sat either side of the hearth in the sitting room with coffee and brandy on the small table between them. Tom sighed contentedly.

'OK, George. I'm ready to hear everything that happened on that fateful Christmas Eve.'

'Yes, I've been thinking a lot about that since we spoke yesterday, and I've also made some notes to make sure I've got the sequence of events correct.

'Everyone arrived around the same time into the drawing room, as had been stated by Lady Serena. The last person to enter the room was Mrs Ferguson. All the chat then ceased as Lady Serena acknowledged her mother. Then, the first strange thing occurred in that Sonia laid into Amelia about being pleased to see that she had made it back in time after getting into the Rolls Royce with Milroy and heading towards the garages. Of course, everyone heard this, and Amelia blushed bright red and explained that she had merely wanted to check on the horses before lunch and Robert had kindly given her a lift down to the garages. I mean it might be nothing, but I did find it odd that Amelia used Milroy's Christian name and even odder that her grandmother would chastise her in public like that.'

'Yes, I agree,' Tom commented. 'I've met Mrs Ferguson and she certainly speaks her mind but even so.'

'Well, there was a sort of stunned silence in the room after that but, thankfully, Jameson sounded the gong, and we all went into the dining room. The Reverend walked in with Amelia. I've drawn up the table seating plan as part of my notes.'

George handed the table plan to Tom who noted that Reverend Smith had been directly opposite Amelia. Therefore, constant glances across the table by him just to check that she was alright, could have appeared suspicious to a doped-up Amelia.

'Yes, that is useful. Thank you, George. Please do continue.'

'Once we were seated, Lord David gave a quick welcome speech and Lady Serena asked Reverend Smith to say 'Grace'. I only mention this because the Reverend's speech was already slurred and after his few short words, Mrs Ferguson gave a snort of derision.'

Tom nodded and imagined that he had been present in the room. He could sense an atmosphere not quite as jovial as one would expect for a Christmas Eve.

George continued. 'It was Doctor Hollis who broke the ice after this second awkward silence by commenting to Lady Serena how wonderful he thought the grounds were looking and asking if they had had any success with vegetables this year? Serena replied that they had, and we would indeed be sampling them with our Christmas luncheon. She went on to add that it was extremely difficult now that they had only one groundsman and this is where Reverend Smith interrupted and said, and I use his exact words here, 'Ah yes, Nathan Parkes.' Lady Serena snapped back at him that the groundsman's name was Nathaniel Parker. I don't think she was best pleased at being interrupted in that way either.

'Hearing the name Nathan Parkes took me by surprise because I knew that I had heard it before but simply could not place it. Until, that is, it suddenly came to me last night. I think it was around the time that you were in the army hospital that a communication came listing a group of soldiers who had gone AWOL. Nathan Parkes was one of the names on the list. Could be just a coincidence.'

'Yes, but definitely worth checking,' Tom agreed. 'I absolutely felt that Mr Parker was hiding something, and he would have learned about the Reverend's faux pas as it was joked about in the kitchen in front of everyone. I'll talk to him again tomorrow.'

'Right. Well, it was just after this, during another awkward silence around the table, that I asked Lord David how his venture into the antiques business was going? He told me that he thought it was going well so far, but that it was very early days, and that's when Reverend Smith piped up again by saying that he had seen a couple of Lord David's statues for sale in the local antique store, and that you would almost think that they were the real thing. Lord David told him that he must be mistaken as he did not deal in statues or supply the antique shop in the village.'

'Now that was a lie,' Tom told George. 'I called in to the antique shop this afternoon and the owner, a Mr Arthur Pentelow, told me that two statues were being displayed on behalf of Lord David, who had set the price. If they were sold, Mr Pentelow was to take ten percent of the profit. He believed they never would sell though as they were merely copies, yet Lord David believed them to be the real thing. I think he lied to save himself from embarrassment. How dare a lowly Reverend challenge him in front of his family and guests. His pride would hardly want him to have to admit that he had fallen at the first hurdle. Think I might have to subtly suggest to Lord David that he goes to the antique shop and takes them back. He could always save face by telling Mr Pentelow that he has found a private buyer for them. I just hope your bank hasn't lent him any money to start this business. It would appear the man hasn't got a clue.'

'No, no not so far. Although I've an inkling that's one reason why I was invited up to the Manor House for Christmas, to be softened up, so to speak. But believe me I won't have a problem saying no to the Lord of the Manor.'

'My goodness. So that's three people the Reverend has managed to upset, and you haven't even finished Christmas Eve lunch yet.'

'No and I haven't got to the really good stuff yet either. After the Reverend's comments about the antiques, Lord David quickly changed the subject and advised the gentlemen that we would all be taking part in the traditional Christmas Eve shoot that afternoon. In actual fact he then had Jameson flask up our coffee and brandy so that we could start straight away and before the snow came down. So, we all bundled up and went outside. Stephen Mountjoy shot really well. Lord David and Colonel James seemed to be in competition with each other. Doctor Hollis, Reverend Smith and myself took a few shots and then sort of left the Mountjoys to it.

'I'd managed a couple of kills, which the Reverend commented on and then he asked me if I had done much shooting. I told him that my fiancée's family had an estate in Yorkshire and that I had shot up there from time to time. He replied that he had spent some time in the North himself as a younger man. He then turned to Doctor Hollis and asked if he had spent any time in Yorkshire. Doctor Hollis told him that it was a county he was unfamiliar with. But then the Reverend said that he thought he had detected a slight Yorkshire accent from time to time. Doctor Hollis shrugged that off but did appear to be irritated by it. I thought it was quite an odd thing to say as I certainly haven't detected even a hint of an accent when the Doctor speaks, have you, Tom?'

'Not at all. A perfect example of the King's English if ever there was one.'

'Indeed. However, it might relate to something Reverend Smith said later which is why I mentioned it now.

'The shoot ended soon after that as the snow began to come down. Once we got back inside the Manor House, everyone went up to their rooms to rest before dinner.

'The gong sounded for pre-dinner drinks and that's when everyone descended into the drawing room once again. Colonel James was mixing cocktails, the latest thing from London, apparently. I had something called an 'Old Fashioned' and goodness me it was strong.

'It was Stephen who handed an Old Fashioned to Reverend Smith and then led him away to the corner of the room. They spoke for a few minutes and then the Reverend walked away. I don't know what they were talking about but the look on Stephen's face was a mixture of anger and anguish.'

'Ah, now I believe I can throw some light on the matter there. It's all about the piece of land that the church lent to the Manor House during the Great War. The Reverend wanted it back now to create some sort of community garden. The theory is that that's why he started drinking at lunch. To pluck up the courage to inform the family of the church's intention. As far as Stephen was concerned though, the land had been given to the Manor and he intended to sell it. It would appear that this was the moment when both sides made their intentions clear.'

'I see. Well, that certainly begins to make sense now. By this time, it's becoming pretty clear that no one will be attending the midnight service and the Reverend has just staked his claim over the land. He must have been feeling pretty confident right about then and ready to indulge in some more fine wine. The cocktails had certainly made everyone very jovial as the gong sounded and we all went into dinner. Lord David declared that there would be no attendance at the midnight service for anyone and the Reverend managed to say 'Grace' without slurring his words this time.

'It was Colonel James who stirred things up by mentioning to Reverend Smith how he bet the Reverend had heard a thing or two in his time in confession. The Reverend told him that the confessional was the remit of the Catholic faith but as a spiritual guide he was often sought out. Susan Ross encouraged him to reveal something and added that it didn't need to be about anyone or anything from the village.

'So, what with the drink having loosened his tongue and now being the centre of attention, he started on these stories which I am going to tell you now. The thing is, I've been reflecting on all of the tales he told and each one could apply to a member of the household on that day. That has consequently led me to wonder whether he actually knew something about someone there and was telling a true story, or he simply suspected something and was letting someone know what he suspected. Of course, I might just be letting my own imagination run away with me.'

'No, I think not, George. The man got himself killed after all and with what you suspect, he was playing a very dangerous game. I can't wait to hear what you've got to tell me.'

'Well, he began with a tale of a young maid coming to see him, who worked in a house much like the Manor House, very respectable. Two of the senior staff were married to each other, only the maid's mother had discovered that the male party already had a wife, but nobody knew where she was. At this point there was a clatter as Jameson dropped a knife on the floor.

'Apparently, the Reverend had advised that the maid should be absolutely certain before she said or did anything as it might just be someone with a grudge. Lady Serena, however, was adamant that she would want to know if there was even a hint of impropriety. I formed the distinct impression that she would not tolerate it.'

'No, I would imagine not. So, Jameson, eh? Can't say that he was high on my list of suspects and dropping a knife may be purely a coincidence. Then again, from what I have observed, the man is unflappable, so definitely worthy of a conversation.'

'Yes, well if the family can't put the blame on Milroy, wouldn't it be convenient if the butler, did it?'

'Very droll, George, pray continue.'

'Apologies. Well, Susan continued to egg the Reverend on by saying that she was sure that sort of thing happened all the time, you know, living in sin with a curtain ring on the third finger of your left hand. She then asked him to reveal something juicy from above stairs. So, he then regaled a story of a Lady from a fine estate who a few years earlier had borne a fine son,
the heir her husband had always wanted. According to the Reverend, the Lady had come to him for advice as apparently, she had been somewhat indiscreet and could no longer be certain that the child was in fact her husband's and that one day soon her husband would become suspicious. Susan commented that this was more like it and asked if it was someone they all knew, but Lady Serena chastised her at that point and told her to let the Reverend eat. She then immediately changed the subject to the weather and the falling snow.'

'You don't for one minute think that Reverend Smith was referring to Lady Serena, do you?' Tom asked with a look of amazement.

'Well, yes and no.' George replied as Tom looked at him enquiringly. 'Let me explain what I'm thinking. I don't believe for one second that even if the facts of the matter were correct, that Lady Serena would have confided in the Reverend. Now, Stephen Mountjoy is a lot like his father, Lord David in some ways but there is one characteristic that he shares with his uncle in that they both raise an eyebrow whenever they are asking a question.'

'Yes, you are quite right, George. I recall seeing that now. Lord David doesn't do that does he?'

'No and that doesn't mean anything in itself, but it got me thinking. What if the Reverend was curious or suspicious and made up these tales just to 'poke the bear,' so to speak? But then somewhere amongst these stories is the truth which drives someone to commit murder.'

'Yes, I see. Excellent point, George. Did he tell anymore tales that evening?'

'Oh yes. As soon as the ladies left the dining room and we started on the brandy and cigars, Colonel James urged him to tell us some darker tales now that the ladies had left us. By this time, the amount of wine the Reverend had consumed really loosened his tongue and he boldly stated how surprising it was what some people would reveal to you, especially things that should really have been reported to the police. The Colonel asked him what he meant by that and so the Reverend recounted a time when he had been in a parish in the North of England. A young lady had come to see him because she was terrified that her husband was going to kill her. Apparently, she wasn't from that parish and had travelled to where she was completely unknown. Reverend Smith said that he had told her that she must report her suspicions to the police. But her reply had been that she could not do that as she did not have a shred of evidence and the police would not believe her anyway. Her husband was the local doctor and a pillar of the community. Member of the golf club, extremely popular, charming and courteous to all, including her. To all intents and purposes, there was no reason to believe that he meant her any ill will and yet she remained convinced that he intended to kill her. Colonel James asked Reverend Smith what actions he took, and the Reverend replied that he had done all he felt he could do at the time. He prayed with her and encouraged her to keep praying and eventually a solution would come to her. However, not long after that, the lady died of a gastric condition. So, feeling that it was his duty, the Reverend went to the police but was told that there were no suspicious circumstances as the doctor had been treating his wife for some time. It was believed that the complaint had made her a little depressed and she was prone to all sorts of imaginings. Then he told us that the doctor had left the area soon afterwards for a fresh start, yet the Reverend remained convinced to this day that the doctor had somehow murdered his wife and got away with it.

'Colonel James made a joke to Doctor Hollis about having a chat with him about poisons that could manifest as a stomach complaint as it might prove to be useful one day. The doctor smiled but I can't say that he was overly amused at the suggestion.'

'Now this really is quite interesting, George. Did the Reverend really suspect that Doctor Hollis was the doctor from the North of England?'

'Well, it might explain the jibe suggesting that he had detected a hint of a Yorkshire accent in the doctor.'

'It might well, mightn't it? And if true, a really strong motive for Doctor Hollis to commit murder. I wonder where he practiced before Harley Street. Think I'll make some discreet inquiries there. I can always go and consult him on his expert knowledge of modern practices and poisons.'

'Yes indeed. Although, on the other hand I have a hard time reconciling Doctor Hollis with the charming and popular member of the golf club.'

'I see what you mean, George. However, that persona could have been the act of a man planning to murder his wife. Or indeed this quiet country doctor may be an act. He's moved to the top of my suspect list for the moment anyway, unless you have any more of the Reverend's tales to tell me?'

George smiled. 'I'm afraid I do. As soon as Colonel James

had made his comment to Doctor Hollis, Lord David advised his brother that he needed to make sure, given his own philandering, that some cuckolded husband did not come after him.

'That prompted Reverend Smith to state that the question of the unfaithful wife didn't always end in murder. A gentleman, very near to the end of his life, had once asked him to go and visit as he wanted to confess that he had changed his will so that his wife would not inherit a penny. He had always suspected that his wife had married him for reasons other than love and she was, in fact, in love with his best friend. He believed that the romance had recently been rekindled, despite his best friend being married. It had made him so angry that he had changed his will. However, when the gentleman had died shortly afterwards, it appeared that he hadn't changed his will at all, and the wife inherited everything.'

'Goodness me. You don't suppose that tale refers to Lady Eliza Ross, do you?'

'Well, it would certainly fit. She is a widow. Her husband was Lord David's best friend. Lord David has her living in the Gate House and there was certainly some mild flirting between them. They obviously care deeply for one another. Plus, when we rejoined the ladies in the drawing room, Lady Serena questioned why we had taken so long, so Colonel James recounted the two tales. Lady Serena quite firmly stated that that was quite enough and there was to be no more tale telling.

'However, as I looked around the room, I noticed a look on Lady Eliza's face that was either fear or anger and her daughter Susan was also staring at her with what could only be described as a look of complete puzzlement on her face.'

'Good heavens above. What is it with the landed gentry? So, the oldest motive in the book – money. I'll see if I can track down the solicitor who dealt with Lord Ross's estate.'

'I can help you there, Tom. Call me at the bank tomorrow, it will be in our records.'

'Thank you, George. Now please tell me that there is nothing else that the Reverend came out with?'

'Just one more small thing. Probably nothing but best have every detail no matter how small.'

'Indeed. Please continue?'

'Just after Lady Serena had commented, Reverend Smith turned to Clarissa Llewellyn-Jones and admired the outfit she was wearing. It was a very colourful and quite elaborate kaftan. He then said that he imagined it would be perfect for the shape and size of most female opera singers and asked if that was what made them such good singers. Clarissa was quite obviously offended by this as she assured him that it was not a prerequisite and as a matter of fact in her younger days, she had been extremely slim. But then the Reverend retorted with 'oh but when I saw you,' but he didn't finish the sentence. Just added that it was no matter and had been a long time ago.'

'So, what do you think he meant by that then?'

'The immediate thought I had was that he thought he had seen an expectant Clarissa, even though she has never married or had any children that the world is aware of.'

'Yes, and he never said that he'd actually seen her performing so, he could have bumped into her somewhere else whilst she was waiting to have a child. Yes, that is certainly a possibility. Goodness, is there anyone that the good Reverend didn't upset that day?'

'Well, there's myself. I mean he didn't come up with any stories about suspect bank managers absconding with the contents of the vault, or Colonel James come to mention it. I'm sure it would all have been water off a duck's back to the Colonel anyway and it's certainly no secret what a serial philanderer he is. Can't think of a single reason why he would kill the Reverend though.'

'No, unless he is Stephen Mountjoy's father.'

'Lady Serena and Colonel James? Well, I don't envy you that conversation.'

'George, I can't say that I'm looking forward to any of the conversations that I must have tomorrow but can't thank you

enough for your insight on this. I really had best be taking my leave.
Much to do tomorrow. Thank you for the splendid dinner. I simply must get that recipe from you.'

'You're most welcome, Tom. Any evening you would care to call and shoot the breeze, I'd be glad of the company.'

'I'll bear that in mind. Don't get up now, I'll see myself out. Goodnight, George.'

'Goodnight, Tom.'

Tom left George's house and started off on the short walk back to his sister's. There was not much to be thankful for from the Great War, but he was very grateful that he had had the honour to serve with George Rochester and what a blessing that he was also there at the Manor House. Tom sighed and began planning in his head the conversations he would need to have tomorrow.

CHAPTER SIXTEEN

The weather turned milder again overnight, so that when Tom left the house the following morning, the big thaw had already commenced and the road through to the village was now clearly passable by a motor vehicle. He heaved a sigh of relief knowing that the coroner's wagon would at last be able to remove the bodies of Reverend Smith and Robert Milroy.

Sergeant Bailey was already at the station when Tom arrived, typing away on the old Remington. He looked up from the report he was currently working on as Tom entered.

'Ah Good Morning, Sir. You'll be pleased to hear that His Majesty's Coroner is on his way to the Manor House. Would you like some tea, or should we head up there straight away?'

'Oh, I think I'd like to get up there as soon as possible thank you, Sergeant. In the car today, I think.'

'Certainly, Sir. It's right outside,'

Once they were on their way, Neville asked Tom, 'How did it go with Mr Rochester last night, Sir?'

'Very interesting, Sergeant. It appears that the Reverend told a few tales about supposed past shared confidences. Whether they were true, based on suspicions or just downright made up is unclear. But they certainly could have given more than one person a motive, if they believed he was speaking the truth.'

'Sounds to me like he was playing with fire.'

'Yes, Sergeant and we all know that if you play with fire, you get burnt. I suspect that he was trying to let someone know what he knew, but too much wine loosened his tongue rather.'

'Which of them did it then, Sir?'

'I don't know yet, Sergeant. But let me emphasise the 'yet'. I shall talk to them again and ask them about these stories. One of them will give something away. They always do.'

They arrived at the Manor House and Tom asked Neville to drop him at the front door before the sergeant made his way down to the stables to await the coroner.

'I'll have a word with the family first,' Tom told him. 'And then direct the coroner to Parker's shed to see to the Reverend when he gets here. We'll come down to the stables after that.'

'Right you are, Sir. I'll make sure it's all ship shape and Bristol fashion, ready for his arrival.' With that he drove off leaving Tom staring after him.

Tom decided to enter the Manor House via the kitchen. Although the pathways were now clear, he bumped into Parker shovelling up snow from the gardens into a wheelbarrow.

'Morning, Inspector. Thought I'd use some of this snow to fill the water butts. We've not had that much rain this autumn and they're getting pretty low.'

'Good idea, Mr Parker. Just to let you know that the coroner will be here this morning to collect Reverend Smith and Mr Milroy, so you'll be able to have your shed back.'

'Why thank you, Inspector. It will be good to get all my tools back. Get on with things again after the last couple of days.'

'Indeed. Well, I won't delay you any further, Mr Parker. Keep up the good work.' Tom didn't add that he intended to speak to the man later. He was hoping for the element of surprise.

The kitchen door was open as he approached, and a glorious smell of baking reached his nostrils. Agnes greeted him.

'My, Inspector Stewart. You must have sensed I had a fresh batch of scones in the oven. Due out any minute they are. Plain ones, but they go lovely with this honey. The Manor beehives did very well this year. Everyone else is busy in their duties about the Manor, so do join me in a cup of tea. It's not been brewed long.'

Agnes finally paused for a breath and poured Tom a cup of tea before turning to the oven and removing the scones, which did indeed look delicious.

'So how has everyone been coping with everything that's been happening, Mrs Trelawney?'

'Do call me Agnes, Inspector Stewart please? Well, below stairs we're all still in shock, obviously, but we're all just getting on with things as usual. Doesn't do to dwell on things, does it now? Life has to go on. They tell me that above stairs nobody says a word if there is a servant present in the room. Whether they speak to each other when they're on their own, I don't know, I'm sure. How are you getting on, Inspector? Come to talk to them again 'ave you? 'Ere, take one of them scones now. It will have cooled down a bit.'

'Thank you, Agnes. Well, the coroner will be here this morning to collect Mr Milroy and Reverend Smith and I will get around to talking with everyone, now that they have recovered from the initial shock and had a chance to think things over. This scone and honey are really quite delicious, Agnes.'

'Thank you, Inspector and you'll always find a warm welcome down here should you want to speak with any of us.'

'That is good to know. Anyway. I'd better hurry along now. I'm hoping to catch the family at breakfast.'

'Yes, I think you'll find them all there, Inspector. Mr Jameson, Alice and Jane haven't returned from the dining room yet. Although Jane did come down for a fresh pot of tea. Jameson rang the gong this morning, so formal dining arrangements have returned.'

'Splendid. I will see you later then, Agnes, and thank you again for the delicious scone and honey.'

'You're welcome, Inspector. I'll be making a ginger cake later. You must come down and try some of that.'

'Oh, I will, indeed I will.' Tom blew the cook a kiss which made her blush to her roots as he ascended the stairs from the kitchen.

All were present in the dining room eating breakfast this morning. Twenty-four hours and a good night's sleep had indeed made a difference. They were no longer the silent group that Agnes had described and were in fact discussing their plans for the day.

'Chester needs a jolly good walk this morning,' Lord David declared. 'James what say you and I take a couple of rifles with us? We can see if the snow has caused any damage anywhere and do a bit of shooting as well. Stephen, will you join us?'

'Maybe later, thank you, Daddy. I was going to suggest that Amelia and I go down to the stables. The horses really need to be exercised and the fresh air would do us both the world of good.'

'Yes, I would like that,' Amelia agreed.

'Isn't that ghastly little chauffeur still lying in the stables?' Sonia asked.

'I believe so,' Stephen told her. 'But we really don't have to go anywhere near that. Hopefully, after last night's thaw, someone can get through to remove the bodies.'

Amelia shivered.

'Where is that Inspector?' Lady Serena asked. He really should be keeping us better informed with exactly what is happening.'

'I expect he'll be along shortly.' Lord David attempted to pacify his wife. 'And what are your plans for today dear?'

'I really must go and see the curate. Find out what is happening with the New Year's Eve jumble sale.'

'Do you really think that will go ahead now in light of the circumstances?' Sonia asked her daughter.

'Of course, it must. I'm sure the curate will be running all the church services as usual, and this is an important charity event for the village. I'm sure Reverend Smith would have been mortified if he thought it wasn't going ahead. I shall be expecting you all to go through your wardrobes, as you normally do at this time of year, for things to donate.'

'Especially jumpers and cardigans,' Sonia added. 'I need some more wool to knit up.'

'Yes, Mummy, and I shall see that you get it. Clarissa, you must join me. We can take a stroll through the village and call on the curate. Imagine how thrilled he will be in the presence of an international opera star.'

Clarissa forced a smile, obviously not thrilled at the prospect of either a walk outside or meeting with the curate.

Sonia thought that the curate would be far from thrilled under the current circumstances.

There was a knock on the door which then opened to reveal the Inspector.

'Ah, Inspector Stewart. Good morning,' Lord David greeted him. 'Do you have any updates for us?'

'Good morning to you all and yes I do,' Tom responded. 'The coroner is on his way to collect the bodies of Reverend Smith and Mr Milroy. I will go outside to wait for him shortly. I also have some follow up questions for all of you at some point. You will all be here I assume?'

Lord David took up the mantle. 'Well, Inspector. James and I intend to walk Chester around the grounds and do a spot of shooting. Stephen and Amelia need to get to the stables to exercise the horses and Lady Serena and Clarissa need to go into the village to talk to the curate. There's no reason why we can't all do that is there, surely?'

'No, no that's fine. I'll come and find you when I need you. Right. I will leave you to breakfast in peace.' With that, Tom turned and left the dining room.

'Well really!' Lady Serena exclaimed. 'If he thinks I am going to be at his beck and call, he's got another think coming.'

'Yes, dear,' Lord David tried once again to pacify his wife. 'But looking on the bright side, once he has asked these so called 'follow-up' questions we can be done and dusted with it all and get completely back to normal.'

Lady Serena tutted and started furiously buttering a slice of toast.

Tom let himself out of the front door. As he descended the steps down to the drive, he saw Lady Eliza Ross and her daughter Susan walking up to the Manor House. 'Ladies, good morning. Are you on your way up to see the family?'

'Yes, we are.' Susan replied. 'It really is too tiresome sitting around and waiting for news. It could drive one insane. Mummy wanted to check with Lady Serena about the New Year's Eve jumble sale anyway, you know under the circumstances, and I thought I'd see if Amelia wanted to take the horses for a ride now that the snow had thawed a bit. Get some fresh air and exercise.'

'I do believe Stephen and Amelia are planning to go to the stables.'

'Good. Well, Amelia and I can ride, and Stephen can muck out. That's man's work anyway.' Susan laughed before suddenly remembering. 'Oh, is Milroy still down there?'

'For the moment, but the coroner is on his way. Sergeant Bailey is down there waiting.'

'Right. Come along, Mummy. Let's see if we can scrounge a cup of coffee.' With that, Susan bounded up the steps and rang the doorbell.

Tom nodded a farewell to Lady Eliza and started walking down the driveway to pass the time and hopefully meet the coroner on his arrival before too long.

Lady Eliza and Susan found the family, and Clarissa, still lingering over breakfast in the dining room when they entered. Both Lord David's and Colonel James's eyes lit up in the presence of Lady Eliza whilst Stephen blushed at the sight of Susan Ross, although it was Lady Serena who greeted them first.

'Good morning, Eliza, Susan. And what brings you up to the Manor House at this hour?'

'Thought I might see if Amelia wanted to go for a ride,' Susan told her. 'We could both do with the fresh air and exercise, and Stephen, you could muck out whilst we are on our ride. That Inspector chappie just told us that Sergeant Bailey is down there with the body but that shouldn't concern us.'

'No, indeed,' Amelia agreed, trying to display more courage than she actually felt. 'I'm ready now. Let's go. Stephen, are you coming?'

Stephen nodded in agreement. Much as he would rather be riding than mucking out, he would happily do whatever Susan suggested without question. The three of them eagerly left the dining room without a backward glance.

Lord David addressed Lady Eliza. 'Eliza, my dear, do sit down. There is still some tea in the pot if you would care for a cup.'

Without waiting for a response, he turned to Jane who was dealing with the used plates on the sideboard. 'Jane, a cup of tea for Lady Ross. Eliza, to what do we owe this pleasure?'

'Well, I was rather listless sitting in the Gate House so thought I would come and speak to Serena about the New Year's Eve jumble sale. It would be nice to be getting on with something useful.'

Lady Serena nodded in acknowledgement. 'Funnily enough we have just been talking about that very thing. Clarissa and I are going to take a walk through the village and visit the curate. You may as well come with us. There's safety in numbers and he might need a bit of convincing, but we agree, it must go ahead. I am sure it is what Reverend Smith would have wanted and it is always so popular just after Christmas, even more so this year in such hard times.'

'Yes, thank you. I would like to come and then I can get started on the collections,' Lady Eliza humbly replied.

'And you must let everyone know that a world-famous opera star will be there in person this year, as well. That should draw them in. Have you finished your tea dear? Right then ladies, let's go. The sooner we can talk to the curate, the sooner we can get started. Let's make this the best sale ever as a tribute to Reverend Smith.' With that, Lady Serena rose and fairly flounced out of the dining room, leaving Lady Eliza and Clarissa to meekly follow.

Sonia shook her head. Her daughter really was two faced and neither one was particularly attractive. She rose unsteadily to her feet. 'If you gentlemen will excuse me, I shall retire to the morning room. Perhaps I shall see you for morning coffee?'

'Might still be out and about then, but back for lunch,' Lord David told her. 'Come on, James. Let's you and me get going as well.'

So, they all left the dining room and went on their way leaving Jameson, Alice and Jane to clear away the remnants of their hearty breakfast.

Tom had only needed to walk up and down the long drive twice before the coroner arrived. The Inspector directed him off to the side of the house where Parker's shed was positioned.

The coroner parked up and stepped out of the wagon. He was a tall man with slightly stooped shoulders. His thick dark hair was greying at the sides, and he wore little round glasses. He walked over to Tom with his right arm outstretched.

'Good morning. You must be Detective Inspector Stewart? I'm Hector Wilson, His Majesty's Coroner at your service.'

Tom took the proffered right hand and Hector shook it vigorously. 'Thank you for coming, Mr Wilson. I hope the journey wasn't too demanding?'

'Oh no. The roads are quite clear now and call me Hector, please? Now, what do you have for me today?'

'Well, body number one is in this shed here, Reverend Smith. I believe that he was killed in the very early hours of Christmas morning.' Tom opened the door and showed Hector the sheet covered corpse. 'Now, I know you can't say too much here, but I would just like to point out the lack of blood where his head is caved in at the back, and the small puncture wound, I suspect a needle mark, on the side of the neck.'

Hector extracted a magnifying glass from his top pocket and took a close look at both areas. 'Indeed, Inspector. I can see the point you are making. Right then, help me load him into the wagon. I believe there is a second body, where is that one?'

'That is the chauffeur and groom, Robert Milroy. He is in a stall in the stables. We will need to drive down there.'

'Right you are then, Inspector.'

Once the Reverend was safely aboard, Tom climbed in next to Hector for the drive down to the stables. On the way he filled the coroner in with a brief synopsis of events, to which Hector would give the occasional nod and mutter, 'I see.'

On arrival at the stables, a welcoming party awaited them. Susan and Amelia sat astride horses, ready for the off, as Stephen made some final adjustments to Susan's stirrups. Lord David with his dog Chester and Colonel James were chatting to Sergeant Bailey.

'Thank goodness I left the Sergeant here,' Tom commented. 'I'll send them on their way before we go in.'

'Yes well, sometimes a corpse will draw in as many people as it does flies,' Hector joked as they both stepped out of the wagon. Tom addressed the small assembly.

'Lord Mountjoy, gentlemen, ladies. This is Mr Wilson, His Majesty's Coroner. I'd be grateful if you could all move away from the stables now, so he can get to his work.'

'Absolutely,' Lord David replied. 'Ladies, you have a good long ride. Lord knows the horses need it. James let's be on our way. Stephen don't get in the way.'

As they departed, Stephen turned to Tom. 'Can I at least start mucking out the first stall, Inspector?'

'Yes, I suppose so, but keep the door closed.'

Stephen gave a look of disapproval but remained silent as he entered the first stall. Tom led Hector along to the third, where Robert Milroy's body had been left. As Hector had been brought up to date with the details of the death, the corpse was simply lifted and carried out to the wagon.

'Right, I'll be on my way then. I'll be in touch as soon as I have any information,' Hector told them.

'Thank you, Hector. If you have any questions just contact Sergeant Bailey at the station.'

'Will do. Goodbye Inspector. Goodbye Sergeant.' Hector climbed up into his wagon and drove off with Reverend Smith and Robert Milroy. Tom and Neville removed their hats and bowed their heads as he drove away.

Once he was no longer in sight, Tom addressed Neville. 'Did you manage to keep that lot away from the body, Sergeant?'

'Yes, Sir. They went in to get the horses and the equipment, but I had my eye on them at all times, Sir. None of them went anywhere near the stall.'

'Very good, Sergeant. Well, you'd best go back to the station now. Hold the fort, so to speak and wait to hear from the coroner. Take the car. I can carry out the rest of my inquiries on foot. I'll check in with you later.'

'Yes, Sir. I'll see you later on then, Sir.'

Neville climbed into the car and drove off whilst Tom considered his plan of attack. He decided to call back at the Manor House and speak to Sonia Ferguson about her granddaughter. As he rounded the bend towards the house, he spotted Lady Serena, Lady Eliza and Clarissa walking down the drive on their way to the village and couldn't help feeling a little sympathy for the curate having to face them.

The three ladies had started their journey in silence until Clarissa could stand it no longer. 'So, why is this jumble sale so important?' She asked.

Lady Serena smiled benignly at her best friend. 'Well, for starters it is a huge occasion as it is the only jumble sale that is held in the village all year. Of course, we have a marvellous summer fete in the grounds of the Manor estate with stalls, games and lots of tremendous fun things. But people save up their jumble and their pennies all year long for this one event. The timing is so good you see, dear, being on New Year's Eve. Those who are not so badly off might have been lucky enough to have had some new clothes and toys for the children at Christmas, so are more than happy to donate some of their old things. The less well-off who have not managed much for Christmas can start the New Year off with some new things.

'Nothing gets wasted. Mothers will buy woollens in any size to unpick them then knit them up again. Any clothing can be cut up and made into a multitude of different things. Mummy and I run classes to show people how. It was the war dear. One simply had to do what one could. Eliza helps out as well, don't you, dear?'

'One does what one can. But I really think you will enjoy this, Clarissa. People bring along food left over from Christmas, so it really is quite the New Year celebration.'

Not quite the celebration she herself would have chosen, Clarissa thought to herself. But then again, beggars couldn't be choosers. As the three of them approached the village, they were greeted by the villagers who were going about their daily business. Clarissa noticed that some of them looked embarrassed or averted their eyes really quickly. She supposed by now that it was no secret that there had been two dead bodies up at the Manor House and one of them was their very own Reverend.

Lady Serena however was oblivious to it all and carried on regardless. 'Ah here we are at the vicarage,' she announced. 'Now then, ladies, let me do all the talking and we'll have it sorted in no time.' Serena launched herself down the path and rang the bell with confidence.

Mrs Primrose Wainwright, the housekeeper, had seen the ladies approaching from the scullery window and although she cursed silently, obediently trotted to the front door to allow them entry.

'Ah, Mrs Wainwright. We are here to see the curate. Where is he?' Lady Serena barged past the housekeeper without waiting for an invitation.

'I believe he is in the study, Lady Mountjoy.'

'Excellent, we will go through,' Serena added without a backward glance, meekly followed by Lady Eliza and Clarissa.

'And may God help him,' Primrose muttered under her breath.

Thomas Mason, the curate was indeed in his study trying to find inspiration for the next sermon. Trying to find the appropriate things to say about poor Reverend Smith by balancing the words of celebration for a life well lived with the words of respectful mourning and loss. So far, he was really struggling and would have welcomed just about any distraction, even a headstrong and very determined Lady Serena Mountjoy, who barged straight into the study without knocking.

'Ah, Curate there you are. I've brought Lady Ross with me, and this is my very best friend in the whole world, Clarissa Llewellyn-Jones, who I am sure you will know as the very famous and very talented opera singer. Anyway, we are here to discuss the New Year's Eve jumble sale. Now you are probably thinking that under the circumstances it should not go ahead this year, but that's where you would be so very wrong. Reverend Smith would so have wanted this great event to happen, and it will do so in his name and as a tribute to the great man. Therefore, we must make it the most successful one ever held. Now, I am sure that you have a lot on your mind right now, so you just leave everything to us. All you must do is announce it in all your services between now and then. Couldn't be simpler. I'll just take the keys to the village hall on my way out. Still hanging in the hallway, are they? Very well then, Curate, we'll see ourselves out. Goodbye.'

And so, Lady Serena left in a whirlwind with Eliza and Clarissa in her wake. Thomas Mason sat in stunned silence, not really sure what had just happened, but at least he now had a place to start with his sermon.

Tom had decided that his first conversation would be with Mrs Sonia Ferguson, partly because he knew that she would be somewhere to be found inside the Manor House. He climbed the steps to the front door and rang the bell, which after a few minutes was answered by Jameson.

'Oh, hello again, Inspector. Please come in. Who would you like to speak to?'

'Thank you, Jameson. I'd like to see Mrs Ferguson please?'

'Certainly, Sir. Mrs Ferguson is currently in the morning room. Let me take you through. Would you care for some tea or coffee, Sir?'

'No thank you, Jameson.'

'Very good, Sir. Here we are. I shall be in the dining room polishing the silver if you need me for anything afterwards.'

'Thank you. I will let you know.' Tom waited for Jameson to depart before knocking gently on the door and entering the room.

Sonia Ferguson looked up from her knitting as he walked in. 'Inspector Stewart. Back again so soon. Have those dreadful corpses been removed yet?'

'Yes, indeed they have, Mrs Ferguson.'

'Well thank goodness for small mercies. Now what can I do for you, Inspector? I take it this isn't just a social call?'

'No unfortunately not, Mrs Ferguson. I just wanted to ask you about the drilling down you gave your granddaughter, Amelia, at the pre-lunch drinks on Christmas Eve, in front of everyone. I suppose that I am curious as to why you chose to do it in public instead of pulling her to one side?'

'I really don't see how that is any of your business, Inspector,' Sonia retorted.

'Everything is my business where murder is concerned, Mrs Ferguson.'

Sonia sighed. 'Very well, Inspector. If you really must know that little display was more about trying to capture the attention of my daughter and son-in-law than chastising Amelia. For the last twelve years that girl has been moping, pining and waiting for a husband who is never going to reappear. The only attachment she has formed outside of this family was with Milroy, supposedly over their common love of horses. I am not a fool, Inspector, and I could quite clearly see that my granddaughter was taking something, supplied by Milroy, not that her mother or father would ever have noticed. You see as far as they are concerned, Amelia is simply grieving and needs time to heal but will be absolutely fine as long as she is with her family. Being mollycoddled if you ask me. Look at Susan Ross. She and Amelia used to be friends when they were young girls. I think Amelia is actually terrified of her now. Susan has had her own losses, as we all have Inspector, but has simply got on with things. Living life to the full, a strong and independent, young woman. Look at how she pitched in with all that snow shovelling. Well, I'm not sure I entirely approved of that, but it did display a tremendous spirit.' Sonia paused. 'Look, Inspector. I am a very sick woman and don't have that much time left. I suppose I just needed to draw some attention to the situation, although I don't suppose it matters so much now that Milroy is dead.'

'Well at least she'll have the horses to keep her occupied and your support will be vital. Who knows what sort of withdrawal she might be going through? I'd be happy to have a word with Lord and Lady Mountjoy if you'd like?'

'Oh goodness me no, Inspector. That would never do. I will have to speak to them myself quite frankly about it. I can see that now.'

'Yes, well thank you for your time, Mrs Ferguson. May God bless you.'

'Thank you, Inspector. May He also bless you.'

Sonia returned to her knitting as Tom left the morning room, deep in thought. He decided that as he was already in the Manor House, he might as well speak to the butler and so entered the dining room.

Jameson was sitting at one end of the large dining table. His hands were encased in pristine white gloves and rows of various knives, forks and spoons were laid out in front of him. Tom could see the shine from the butler's excellent polishing skills from where he stood in the doorway.

Jameson looked up and placed down the knife he was currently working on. 'Can I help you, Inspector?'

'Yes, I just wanted a quick word if I may, Mr Jameson?'

Jameson nodded without a hint of curiosity on his face.

'It's about all the things the Reverend was saying. At dinner on Christmas Eve, I believe he spoke about a maid that had once come to consult him because she did not believe that the senior servant in the house could possibly be married as they purported to be. Apparently, the girl's mother had told her that the man was already married to someone else. The telling of this tale caused you to drop an item of cutlery on the floor and I was wondering if you could tell me why that was?'

The normally stoic butler placed his head in his hands.

'I think you had better come clean and tell me the truth, don't you?' Tom asked gently.

Jameson looked up. 'Yes, I will, Inspector. I don't know what is to become of me, but I will tell you what happened.

'Agnes and me, we're from Cornwall originally. Known each other all our lives. Our families lived next door to each other, and we went to school together as well. I have a brother two years younger and Agnes has a sister the same age, Andrew and Agatha. Inseparable we all were. Known as 'The Four A's' to all those that knew us.

'Then as we all grew up, our great friendships turned to love. Only I fell head over heels with Agatha and Andrew fell in love with Agnes. We even had a double wedding and remained inseparable, even after we were married and still living next door to each other. Perhaps that was the problem. That and the fact that we had married so young. Eighteen and sixteen we were but that's what people like us did back then.

'Anyway, we all went into service together. Lovely big house in Cornwall and I thought we were all very happy. Two years later and I wake up one morning to find myself alone with a note on the pillow next to me telling me that she'd run off with my brother, Andrew, like a thief in the night, and not to try and find her as she just didn't love me anymore.

'Agnes found a similar note on the pillow next to her. So, Agnes and me, well we found consolation in each other. It became too painful to stay in Cornwall after that, so we came up here. I know it was wrong to say we were married but we are in-laws, so we are related. We care very deeply for one another and have made our own vows to each other.

'Believe me, Inspector, we would marry if we could. It's just with what her Ladyship said after the Reverend had told the story, I'm scared that she would throw us out onto the street. I just don't know who could have told Reverend Smith. I can't believe it would be any of the Manor girls. But I didn't kill the Reverend, Sir. I swear to you, I did not kill him. I was fast asleep in bed. My Agnes will vouch for that. My snoring kept her awake half the night apparently.'

Tom tried to hide the half smile he felt forming on his lips. 'It's alright, Mr Jameson. I have no intention of telling Lady Mountjoy about your past. It really wouldn't benefit anyone would it? No, least said soonest mended, that's the way to go.'

'Thank you so much, Inspector. But if the Reverend knew, who else might know?'

'I'm not so sure that he did know anything for definite. It would appear that some of his tales were complete fiction. He may have been curious or even slightly suspicious about a few things, but appeared to extract great pleasure from trying to goad people. Perhaps he saw something in some old parish records or heard some rumours, but I really don't think you have anything to worry about.'

'Oh, I'm so relieved, Inspector. I haven't told Agnes what the Reverend said, it would worry her to distraction.'

'And we can't have that now, can we, Mr Jameson? Can't have her distracted from making those delicious scones.'

Jameson finally managed a weak smile. 'Thank you, Inspector. You are a most understanding man.'

Tom nodded in acknowledgement and rose to leave the dining room. He decided to not even try and track down either Lord or Lady Mountjoy and the others in their various activities at this point and so would return to the Manor House after lunch. In the meantime, there were still plenty of inquiries to be made in the village.

He had left the house and begun the walk back down the driveway, when he spotted Nathaniel Parker in the distance and decided to get this potentially tricky conversation over and done with. Parker spotted him as he approached and waved at Tom in acknowledgement.

'Hello again, Inspector, is there anything I can help you with?'

'Yes, Mr Parker. I would like a quick chat with you, if it's not too inconvenient?'

'No, now is a perfect time. I was just going to take a break for my vittles. Why don't you join me? Cook has made me a pile of ham sandwiches, with mustard, from the Boxing Day ham and bread baked fresh this morning. Plus, there's a flask of homemade scotch broth and a thick slice of Christmas cake for afters.'

'Well, that really is too tempting. Thank you, Mr Parker.' Tom followed Parker into his shed where he offered him a crate to sit on.

'Let's enjoy our vittles first, shall we, Inspector? No use chatting on an empty stomach.'

The food was really very good, and they ate mostly in silence apart from chatting casually about what work Parker undertook at this time of year in the Manor House grounds. Once they were finished, Parker looked at Tom inquisitively, prompting him to finally start speaking.

'Mr Parker, it is becoming quite clear that Reverend Smith told a lot of stories during the time leading up to his murder, that were deliberately meant to upset or goad people. At the Christmas Eve lunch when the gardens were the topic of conversation, he referred to you as Nathan Parkes. I know you were made aware of this by one of the maids in the kitchen, later on in the day.

'Now there was a Nathan Parkes who went AWOL during the war, and I need to know if this was in fact you?'

Parker hung his head in silence and Tom waited patiently, allowing him time to gather his thoughts. Finally, he raised his head and looked Tom straight in the eye. 'Yes Sir, I am the Nathan Parkes who went AWOL, and I would like to explain it all now to you please?'

Tom nodded.

'I'd been there, on the frontline, over two years. Proud to be fighting for my King and Country, when I took a bayonet in the shoulder. It missed anything vital, Sir, but it was a nasty wound, and I was sent back here to recuperate. It took six months to heal the physical wounds, Sir, but not the mental ones. They didn't heal.

'When I was told that I was to be sent back, well I just couldn't face it and I thought that nobody would want a nervous ninny fighting alongside them. It'd be dangerous. I might have got someone killed. So, I ran away. I made it from London to a parish near here and the church took me in. The vicar, he was a good man. Prayed with me and for me and got me back on my feet again. Then he got me a place over here working on the land, so I was still doing my bit for the war effort.

'Perhaps he felt he had to tell Reverend Smith the truth as I was now a member of his parish, but he had never mentioned it before. As far as I knew, everyone believed that I had received an honourable discharge. I understand if you have to report me, Sir, but I did not kill the Reverend.'

'Mr Parker, I was there on the frontline also. I took a bullet to the leg and if it had not been for the courage of another soldier, I would not be here today. So, I understand what you went through. Two years was a long time to be in the thick of it all and, understanding the situation as I do, I think that they were very wrong to try and send you back and you should have received that honourable discharge after all. I am not going to report you. As far as I am concerned, Nathan Parkes died in service. Nathaniel Parker however, played his part fully in the war effort.' Tom rose from his crate and saluted Parker, who returned the action with tears in his eyes.

Lady Serena had once again route marched Lady Eliza and Clarissa, this time along to the village hall where they were currently seated at a small table in the corner. Enjoying what she felt was her natural role as a leader, Serena had taken control.

'Right, here's the plan. We'll get everyone involved. Let's all go back to the Manor House for lunch, and I will get Stephen to make up lots of notices for distribution. After lunch, Susan and Amelia can distribute the notices all over the village. We know people will have jumble ready so David, James and Stephen can start to collect it and bring it here. Eliza, you can come back here and start the sorting. Clarissa and I will gather all the Manor House jumble and bring it back here. Stephen can bring us in the Rolls. David and James will just have to use James's silly little sports car. Oh, isn't this exciting?'

Lady Eliza smiled and nodded, knowing from past experience that agreeing with Lady Serena was the easiest and therefore probably the best option.

Clarissa personally felt that pulling all her fingernails out with a pair of pliers would be more exciting than this but refrained from saying so.

The three ladies rose and started back to the Manor House.

Tom decided to call on his good friend George Rochester to obtain the name of the solicitor who had handled the late Lord Duncan Ross's estate. George was alone in his office when he arrived at the bank and was shown straight in by the assistant manager.

'Tom, good to see you.' George rose from behind the desk and shook his friend's hand. 'How is it all going?'

'Making progress I believe, George. I'll bring you up to date later. I did speak to Mr Parker though and it turns out that he is the missing Nathan Parkes.'

'Are you going to report him?' George asked solemnly.

'No and I would ask you not to as well. Sad and all too familiar story during those awful times but believe me that man has played his part in full. Nothing to be gained. More like lessons learned.'

'I see. Well, I trust your judgement, Tom, so will say no more about it.'

'Thank you, George. It's for the best, believe me. Now I wondered if you had the name of the solicitor who dealt with Lord Duncan Ross's estate ready for me?'

'Oh yes. It's a Mr Edward Pendergast who dealt with everything. He's with Pendergast and Wortley, just along the High Street.'

'Excellent. Thank you. I shall pop along and see him now.'

'Very good, Tom. Do come and have a drink with me this evening, if you have time that is,' George added.

'Thanks for the offer. I'll see what I can do. Maybe see you later then.'

Tom departed eager to continue the investigation and speak with Mr Pendergast, the solicitor. He found the premises just where George said they were. Pendergast and Wortley were on the first floor above the bakers, and he wondered for a moment if they were ever distracted in their duties by the aroma of freshly baked bread.

At the top of the stairs, he was greeted by a stern-faced receptionist. Miss Emily Fortescue regarded herself as more of an office manager than merely a receptionist. She was a thin, angular woman of indeterminate age who always wore a tweed skirt and silk blouse, no matter what the season or the weather. Her grey hair was pulled back tightly into a bun, and she wore pince-nez at the end of a rather long nose. Her long fingers had been typing earnestly when Tom walked in.

Emily looked at Tom sternly. As office manager, she kept all the appointment books, and this gentleman certainly did not have an appointment. Drop-ins were simply unacceptable in Emily's mind. One should correspond and request an appointment, that was the proper way.

'Yes, may I help you?' She asked, sounding to Tom like she didn't actually wish to help him at all. He decided that he would need to be at his most formal to make any impression on the woman who guarded the inner sanctum.

'I am Detective Inspector Thomas Stewart of Scotland Yard. I need to speak with Mr Pendergast please?'

Even though the face of Miss Emily Fortescue took on an inquisitive look, her manner immediately altered to gushing and helpful. 'Why of course, Inspector. I will just go and inform him that you are here. May I inform him what it is concerning?'

'I'm afraid I can't say but please tell him that it is extremely urgent.'

Emily trotted off towards the closed door on the left side of the room. She knocked and entered without waiting for a reply. Then, a few minutes later, she returned and with a smile that softened her features quite remarkably and told Tom that Mr Pendergast would see him right away. Tom walked past a row of filing cabinets and entered the office of Mr Edward Pendergast.

The room was dimly lit, having only one small window to

allow any natural light to enter. Mr Pendergast was seated at a large desk in front of that window. The desk was neatly organised with files placed into an inbox and an outbox. There were currently more files in the outbox leading Tom to believe that the solicitor had enjoyed a most productive morning.

Mr Pendergast was a short, middle-aged balding man who was becoming a little plump. He was wearing a pair of large, rimmed spectacles but these did not hide a pair of bright blue eyes.

Edward rose and extended his right hand. 'Ah, Inspector Stewart. Please do come in and take a seat. Is this about the poor Reverend Smith? Such a tragedy, although I can inform you that Pendergast and Wortley are not handling his estate.'

'Well, yes, it is in connection with the death of the Reverend but not his estate. I believe you handled the estate of the late Lord Duncan Ross?'

'Yes, indeed I did, Inspector. Quite straightforward, a few legacies for loyal servants, a trust fund for his daughter Susan and the remainder to his wife, Lady Eliza Ross.'

'I see. Mr Pendergast, If I could ask you this in strictest confidence. Did Lord Ross at any time suggest to you that he wished to alter his will so that Lady Eliza Ross did not inherit anything?'

'Goodness me, whatever gave you that idea? No, absolutely not. Everything was as it should have been, and the estate handled accordingly.'

'Well, that's very good to hear. I suspected that it was all just a nasty rumour but I'm sure you understand that I must investigate all matters that are brought to my attention.'

'Of course, of course. I am happy to be able to clarify that for you, Inspector.'

'Well, thank you for your time, Mr Pendergast.' Tom rose and shook the solicitor's hand warmly before leaving the office.

Edward Pendergast turned and gazed out of the window while he pondered all the unanswered questions in his head.

Tom had been very relieved to hear the solicitor's words. He hadn't wanted to believe for one minute that either Lady Eliza or her daughter could be forgers of a will and thereby committing fraud. It didn't explain the expression George had witnessed on Lady Eliza's face when the Reverend was telling his little tale though, so he would have to speak to her about that.

Tom winced a little as he walked along the High Street. Unfortunately, he had run out of the cream prescribed to him that he applied to the old wound on his leg. He really didn't need the distraction of discomfort whilst continuing with the investigation, so decided to call on Doctor Hollis for an emergency prescription before he went back to his sister's cottage for a nice cup of tea.

The sun was shining down as he walked along, giving the gathered snow an appearance of containing sparkling diamonds.

The reception area of the surgery was free of waiting patients as Tom entered. Darlene, the doctor's receptionist was engrossed in a book, and it was a few moments before she looked up and saw Tom there.

'Ooh sorry, Inspector, totally engrossed in my Dickens there. Got it for Christmas. Doctor Hollis doesn't mind me reading when I'm not busy, says it's educational. Always quiet this time of year it is. Come January I'll be rushed off my feet. Anyway, what can I do for you, Inspector?'

'I'd like to consult with Doctor Hollis if he's available to see me please?'

'Yes, I'm sure that will be fine. I'll just go and ask him. Have a seat a moment.'

Tom sat down in the waiting area and picked up a newsletter from the top of the pile of reading material that was placed neatly on the table in front of him. How interesting he thought to himself and began flicking through.

Darlene returned after a few minutes and said brightly, 'Doctor Hollis can see you straight away, Inspector. Oh, silly me!' She exclaimed. 'That newsletter shouldn't be in the waiting room, that's the doctor's personal copy. Still, no harm done. I'll give it to him later.'

Tom handed Darlene the newsletter and walked into the doctor's office.

'Ah, Inspector,' Doctor Hollis greeted him. 'What can I do for you? Do you have some more questions for me, although I'm not sure what more I can tell you?'

'No, no, Doctor. This is a private matter, if I may?' Tom showed Doctor Hollis the wound on this leg and described the treatment he was using.

'Oh yes, I can give you something for that.' Doctor Hollis unlocked the bottom drawer of his desk and extracted a small tub.

'Do you keep all your drugs in there?' Tom asked him.

'No, only a ready supply of the most commonly prescribed ones and that includes this cream. How's your investigation going by the way, Inspector?'

'Oh, still following up a lot of leads. Probably why the old leg is playing up again.'

'Indeed. Well, this lotion should have you feeling as right as rain in no time at all. You can pay Darlene on your way out.'

'Thank you, Doctor Hollis. I won't take up any more of your time.'

'My pleasure, Inspector, my pleasure.'

Tom took his leave, stopping off to pay Darlene who was once again engrossed in 'Bleak House', not one of his own favourite Dicken's novels, but each to their own he supposed. Now feeling a little peckish again, he hurried along to his sister's, eager to apply his new lotion and enjoy a little late lunch.

Lunch at the Manor House had turned into a strategic planning meeting, with Lady Serena at the helm doing what she liked to do best and that was organising everyone.

'People will have their jumble ready for collection,' she was currently telling them all through the soup course. 'They always do. They just won't know what to do about it under the circumstances, so this is where we all come in. Now what I propose is this. After lunch is over, Lady Eliza will head straight back to the village hall to await the collections. Amelia, Stephen and Susan can walk with you and start collecting from the houses on and off the High Street. Now Clarissa and I will gather together the Manor House jumble and bring it down in the Rolls.'

Lord David cringed inwardly. His wife had insisted on learning to drive in case of another war, and she was needed, but the way she ground the gears on his beloved Rolls made his teeth stand on edge. His wife carried on.

'Once we've offloaded, Amelia, Stephen and Susan can take the Rolls and carry on collecting to the south and west of the High Street. Now David. You and James can have some fun in his nifty little sports car and drive around collecting from the properties that are north and east of the High Street. We might even get them all covered this afternoon if we're smart about it. Now you must stress that this jumble sale is going ahead as a tribute to Reverend Smith. It is what he would have wanted, and we must therefore all strive to raise the largest amount ever.

'However, it is also an opportunity for us all to clear the air about what has happened at the Manor House. We must let people know that Milroy killed the Reverend and then killed himself in a fit of remorse, to quell any rumours that might be already circulating. And, if they should ask, we will not be getting another chauffeur. David, Stephen and I can drive the Rolls. Amelia, you really must learn next year. We might even think about getting a more appropriate car. But that's a discussion for another time.'

Lord David looked momentarily relieved. There was absolutely no way he would be parted from his precious Rolls. Neither would he let his daughter Amelia anywhere near it. Too much of a nervous ninny to be anywhere near such a beautiful machine.

'Yes,' continued Lady Serena. 'It will be good for the people in the village to know that in these hard times, we are also making economies. Now then Mummy, I haven't included you as I thought it might all be too much for you, but you are of course welcome to help.'

Sonia personally thought she was dodging a bullet as she replied, 'No, no I must take my afternoon rest. Doctor's orders. You all keep up the good work.'

'Fair enough,' Lady Serena told her mother. 'Right has everyone finished. Let's get going then.'

Clarissa had hoped for a second helping of sherry trifle but realised this was not to be.

Once everyone had left the dining room, Lady Serena turned to her best friend with glee. 'Darling, this is just the opportunity that I've been waiting for. Traditionally, the family just give me a few items for the jumble a couple of days before. Such hoarders, the lot of them. Today we are going to have a thorough clear out. David has things in his wardrobe that will certainly never fit him again in this lifetime, clothes and shoes. And Amelia still has her dead husband's things in mothballs. How morbid is that darling? Not to mention Stephen. Now he was given a lovely new dressing gown for his birthday, so we can relieve him of his old one.'

Clarissa thought that it actually might be quite entertaining poking about in people's things so this would not be such a wasted afternoon after all.

Lady Eliza, Amelia, Susan and Stephen were ambling along, in no great rush, towards the village High Street.

'So,' Stephen started. 'No replacement for Milroy then. So that means no chauffeur and no groom. How are you going to enjoy mucking out the horses every day come rain or shine?' Stephen teased his sister.

'Actually, I shall relish it,' Amelia was quick to reply. 'Something of my own to focus on and look forward to everyday. I shall look after them and ride them and become much more outdoorsy, just like Susan. I did so admire you Susan, shovelling all that snow, as good as any man.'

'That's the ticket, Amelia,' Susan told her. 'And remember what we talked about?'

'Oh yes,' Amelia replied enthusiastically. 'You know how every year at the summer fete, we give the children horseback rides? Well, I am thinking about starting a little riding school, where children or anyone really can come and learn to ride, and I shall teach them. It will put my own skills to good use and bring some income to the estate. I shall talk to mummy and daddy about it in the New Year.'

Stephen nodded in approval. Goodness knew the estate needed a boost in income from somewhere. 'Good idea Amelia, and I shall give you my full support if there are any objections from mummy and daddy.'

Stephen wondered about the noticeable changes in his sister. Two days after being a fainting hysterical wreck, one horse ride with Susan appeared to have altered her outlook completely.

As they approached the village hall and Lady Eliza unlocked the door, Susan said 'See you later Mummy. Stephen, why don't you take this side of the street, and Amelia and I will take the other?'

After watching them set off, Lady Eliza went inside the village hall and started to get things organised.

At first, Lord David had thought that there could be absolutely nothing worse than driving around the countryside collecting jumble. However, he had already spent a very enjoyable morning walking his beloved dog Chester with his brother James. That had made him aware of how very little time the two of them spent alone together now.

As boys on the Manor estate, they had been great chums, inventing all kinds of games and getting into all sorts of mischief. Their relationship had altered, as it was destined to do, when David had married, raised a family and taken on the Manor estate as it was passed on to him along with the title.

James, on the other hand had taken up a life free of cares and responsibilities. There were certainly times when Lord David envied his brother's carefree lifestyle, but what he was unaware of was that there were also times when James envied his older brother's home and family life. So now there was absolutely no reason why they couldn't have a little fun with the jumble collection and maybe even get into a little mischief.

'Let's start up at Major Birch's place. Some rich pickings to be had there by the way his wife spends in London. I'm sure that there will be the offer of a tot or two whilst we wait as well,' Lord David told his brother.

'Splendid,' James agreed and started singing 'Good King Wenceslas' at the top of his voice to which his older brother eagerly joined in.

The Birch's rambling old property was situated at the top of a hill. The thaw hadn't completely reached there yet and so a few slushy and icy places had to be negotiated by the little sports car and the Colonel. But both gentlemen were in fine humour and laughing merrily as they arrived at the house.

Major Birch had heard the revs of the sports car approaching so had looked out of the window, curious as to who would risk driving to the top of the hill before the snow and ice had completely cleared. Seeing Lord David and Colonel James step out of the car, he went to the front door himself to greet them.

'David, James. What on earth brings you up here? Come in, come in. Expect you could use a snifter couldn't you just, there's still a nip in the air?' Major Birch ushered them into his library where a fire was blazing in the hearth. 'What's it to be whisky, brandy?'

Both men settled for whisky and once they were all seated with drinks in hand, Lord David spoke.

'We've been sent by my good lady wife to collect items for the big jumble sale on New Year's Eve.'

'Oh absolutely. That's all ready for you in a cupboard under the stairs. Every time the wife buys something new, another old thing will come out of her wardrobe and into one of the boxes under the stairs. Has to you see, wardrobe is jam packed full. Won't find any of my things in those boxes though. Made to last mine are. That's what a great tailor will do for you. Maintain your weight and you need never buy a new suit again. Anyway, I must say I'm surprised the jumble sale is going ahead under the circumstances.'

'Oh, you've heard about that have you?' Lord David asked the Major.

'Yes, the wife insisted we get a telephone installed in case of emergencies. No emergencies yet but enough gossip to fill an encyclopaedia. One of her cronies was on the telephone about it yesterday.'

'Well, I don't know what she will have told you but at least now myself and the Colonel are here we can set the record straight.'

'Please do. Quite right too. It's not healthy to have a lot of gossip circulating around the village.'

'Absolutely. So let me tell you that for some reason, as yet not known, our chauffeur and groom, Robert Milroy, killed Reverend Smith and then in a fit of remorse killed himself the very next day.'

'Well, that is good to know,' the Major said sombrely. 'Very trying for you all I should imagine?'

'Indeed, it is. But Lady Serena very stoically feels that life must go on and has agreed with the curate that this New Year's Eve sale must be bigger and better than ever as a tribute to the Reverend. So, she has galvanised us all into action. Speaking of which we really ought to get going. Lots of ground to cover this afternoon.'

'Of course. Follow me, gentlemen, I believe there are several boxes here for you.'

There were in total, six boxes to be loaded into the little sports car which filled it to capacity. Lord David and Colonel James thanked the Major and set off back to the village hall to unload before any further collections could be made.

Major Birch watched them depart before quietly commenting, 'If that man truly expects me to believe that Robert Milroy killed Reverend Smith and then killed himself, he must be dumber than an ox.'

Stephen, Susan and Amelia had already dropped off quite a few things by the time Lord David and Colonel James returned with the collection from Major Birch. They quickly unloaded their boxes and set off again, eager not to bump into Lady Serena lest she should smell the whisky on their breath which would not bode well for them.

This left plenty for Lady Eliza to be carrying on with and she was looking forward to unpacking Mrs Birch's boxes. Eliza herself did not get up to London much, so she was excited to think that she might find a nice fashionable item that would do for herself.

Lady Serena and Clarissa arrived shortly afterwards with numerous bags full of various items of clothing. Lady Serena looked around her.

'My, that's a good start,' she admitted observing all the bags and boxes already piled high.

Amelia, Susan and Stephen entered the village hall, each laden down with more items.

'Right, that's the High Street done,' Susan declared. 'Just the side streets left now.'

'Excellent. Well, you take the Rolls now. Clarissa and I can manage the side streets on foot, can't we darling? So, let's collect as much as we can today, finish off where we don't get to tomorrow and then we still have the day after to pitch in with sorting and pricing. I take it that is satisfactory to you also Eliza?'

'Oh yes, I am quite happy thank you.'

'Jolly good, off we go then.' Lady Serena bustled everyone outside once again.

Lady Eliza could see that she was absolutely in her element, at her bossiest best, and so was more than happy to be left alone in the village hall.

Tom had enjoyed some cold turkey and some pickles for his late lunch and, after applying some cream to his wounded leg, had sat down in a comfortable armchair to rest for a little while before getting back to work.

The warmth of the room had made him drowsy and before he could rouse himself, he had nodded off to sleep and only woke up as the dusk was descending. As he came to, he was initially annoyed that he had allowed himself this momentary lapse. However, common sense prevailed, and he told himself that if he had slept, it was because he was tired, and a tired detective is not an effective detective.

Avoiding his sister and her family, Tom quickly splashed some cold water on his face and left the house, thinking that he had best call at the police station to see Sergeant Bailey before he finished for the day.

As Tom walked past the village hall, he could see a light coming from within and decided to investigate. To his great surprise he came upon Lady Eliza Ross, all alone but completely surrounded by pile upon pile of jumble.

'Goodness me!' he exclaimed.

'Oh, hello, Inspector,' Eliza greeted him. 'As you can see, we have had a very productive afternoon. I'm just finishing up for the day here myself.'

'Oh well I'm glad I caught up with you then, Lady Ross. There was just one more thing that I wanted to check with you. My what a splendid dressing gown.'

Tom's eyes had fallen on a large pile of clothing, the item on the top being a quilted dressing gown, deep maroon in colour with a gold collar and matching cuffs.

'Oh yes, that pile is from the Manor House. I believe the dressing gown belonged to Stephen. I seem to recall that he received a new one on his last birthday and, if I am not mistaken, that one is Royal Blue with a navy-blue collar and cuffs. I'm sure this one would fit you Inspector if you were in the market for a new dressing gown?'

'Why yes, I shall try it on shortly.'

'Oh do, I think these colours would look marvellous on you, Inspector. Anyway, what was it that you wanted to ask me?'

'Just more filling in of details really. It's about all these stories Reverend Smith was telling on Christmas Eve.'

'Oh yes, some proper tales he came out with,' Eliza agreed.

'Quite so. Now I've heard that he told one story about a wife who forged her husband's last will or at least destroyed a new will that would have left her with nothing. I know, of course, that you did no such thing Lady Ross, but your reaction to the story was pointed out to me, and I wondered why that was?'

'How can you be sure I did no such thing, Inspector?' She asked playfully.

'Well, in the interest of dotting all the *I's* and crossing all the *T's*, I spoke with Mr Pendergast, the solicitor who handled Lord Ross's estate.'

'I see,' Eliza responded pensively. 'Well, the explanation is really very simple, Inspector. I really felt that the stories the Reverend was telling were pure fabrication. He was certainly enjoying being the centre of attention and James, Colonel Mountjoy that is, was definitely encouraging him. I felt that he had concocted these tales in such a way that they could have referred to someone at the Manor House, like trying to point an imaginary finger. Complete nonsense to my mind.

'However, in the interest of complete honesty, Inspector, I will tell you this. Towards the end of his life, my husband was a very sick man. He was with fever and drifting in and out of consciousness. I was sitting with him on his very last afternoon before he passed and David, Lord Mountjoy, also came over to visit his best friend for the last time and of course to be of some comfort to me. He was in fact comforting me when my husband opened his eyes, stared straight at us and shouted that he knew I was being unfaithful with his best friend and demanded that we contact Mr Pendergast as he needed to change his will right away. He then took his last breath and died.

'But I really must stress to you, Inspector, that even though Lord Mountjoy and I enjoy each other's company very much, there has never been any impropriety between us.'

'Thank you, Lady Ross for both your honesty and your

opinion of the Reverend Smith. That is most helpful. Now let me try this magnificent dressing gown.'

As Lady Eliza had stated, it really was a marvellous fit and the colours suited him enormously. Tom adjusted the cuffs slightly and frowned, but then quickly adjusted his features into a smile for Lady Eliza's benefit.

'Now that is perfect, Inspector,' she told him.

'Yes, I think so too. How would a shilling be?'

'Oh, that is most generous, Inspector. I was going to price it at sixpence to start with, knowing that I would probably have to settle for threepence at the end of the day.'

'Well, it is all in a good cause,' Tom said whilst handing over two sixpence pieces. 'I will leave you in peace now. Goodbye, Lady Ross.'

'Good evening, Inspector.'

Tom placed the dressing gown over his arm and left the village hall.

Sergeant Bailey glanced at the clock on the wall and wondered how much longer he should wait for Inspector Stewart to appear. His tea would be ready soon and he didn't want the first meal cooked by his wife, since she had returned, to be ruined. Luckily, at that moment the door opened and through it came the Inspector himself.

'Sergeant Bailey. Thank you so much for holding on here. Just give me a very quick update and then you must go home.'

'Thank you, Sir. Well, there's medical reports and another report I've typed up here. Shall I go through them, Sir?'

'No, that's marvellous, Sergeant. I'll read through them once you've gone. Now I'm going to be away for the next couple of days so if anyone asks you don't know where I am, how I can be reached or what I'm doing and that will be the truth.'

'Yes, Sir. Is that a dressing gown, Sir?' Neville had spotted the item over Tom's arm.

'Indeed, it is, Sergeant. Snagged myself a pre jumble sale bargain. Rather splendid, isn't it? I couldn't afford a brand new one of this quality on a Detective Inspector's salary.

'Off you go now, Sergeant and I'll see you bright and early on the thirty first. I will get a message to you with any orders.'

'Right, Sir. I hope your trip turns out to be most profitable.'

'So do I, Sergeant, so do I.'

Neville left the station more delighted that he was not going to be late for his tea than curious about where the Inspector might be going.

Tom sat down and started reading through all the reports Sergeant Bailey had left for him. When he had finished, he sat back in his chair and pondered what he had read. Although there was a lot of information swirling around in his head, he was now fairly certain that what he believed was the truth.

Therefore, the little chats he still wished to have with Lord and Lady Mountjoy and Clarissa Llewellyn-Jones could wait a little longer as must his evening with George Rochester.

Folding up the dressing gown and tucking it inside his coat, he picked up the reports he had been reading and left the police station.

CHAPTER SEVENTEEN

It was still dark on the next morning of December twenty-ninth when Tom left the house. Despite his little siesta the previous afternoon, he had still managed to sleep soundly after an early night. He knew that the next couple of days were likely to be quite trying and require all his energy.

He set off from his sister's cottage and truly hoped that by the time he returned all the pieces of the puzzle would have fallen into place.

Later that morning at the Manor House, the whole family had descended to the dining room at the sound of the breakfast gong. The previous evening everyone had been too exhausted to dress and attend dinner so had taken light suppers in their rooms. Now, fully rested they were all ready to tuck into a hearty breakfast.

Lady Serena was particularly buoyant. She felt she had commanded her jumble sale army well yesterday and therefore all the collecting had been completed. Now, all that remained to be done was to sort everything the way that Lady Serena Mountjoy liked it to be sorted.

Sonia, meanwhile, was delighted to witness how well her granddaughter was looking. Her cheeks were rosy, and she had piled her plate high with eggs and bacon. A quite remarkable turnaround in such a short space of time. Sonia looked forward to having a good chat with her granddaughter later on to discover the truth behind such a rapid transformation. Her attention returned to the table as Amelia spoke.

'By the way, Mummy, did you go through all our wardrobes

yesterday? All of my husband's clothes have gone.'

'Yes, Amelia. These are hard times for everyone and there are plenty of people around who are a lot worse off than ourselves. Those clothes were doing no one any good just hanging in the wardrobe.'

'Yes, you are probably right, Mummy. Someone could make really good use of them now and that's what my darling husband would want, I'm sure. They probably wouldn't fit him now anyway. He's almost certain to be a little fatter or thinner.'

'Did mine as well, did you, dear?' Lord David asked his wife. 'Can't say as I noticed.'

'That's because I took all the stuff that you keep at the back of the wardrobe that no longer fits you,' she replied haughtily.

'Ah yes, the stuff I wore when I was a little tubbier,' Lord David admitted, patting his paunch. 'Shan't be needing those again.'

No one was really sure if he was joking or not at this point, so they all remained silent.

'What did you take of mine, Mummy?' Stephen asked.

'Not very much actually, Stephen. You could probably do with buying a couple of things at the jumble sale.' Lady Serena laughed at her own joke and winked at Clarissa. 'Just your old dressing gown that was screwed up in the bottom of your wardrobe. You had that beautiful new one for your birthday but your old one is still in very good condition. We'll put it on the sixpenny pile.'

'Oh, Mummy I loved that dressing gown and it's always good to have a spare.'

'Well, you had better go and buy it back then, Stephen, if that's the way you feel.'

Lady Serena gave a snort which indicated that as far as she was concerned, that particular conversation was over.

'Right then,' she continued. 'Who's coming to the village hall to help with the sorting this morning? Mummy, do you feel up to helping today?'

'No, no I think I'll stay here. I've done my fair share over the years. Time for the young ones to take over.'

'Very well. David, James what are your plans?'

'No, sorry, dear. There's some estate stuff that must be seen to, isn't there, James?'

'Yes, that's right, David. But perhaps after lunch we might be available.'

'Oh, don't trouble yourselves. You'd probably just get in the way anyway.'

Lord David and Colonel James both tried hard not to smile. It was worth incurring the wrath of Lady Serena if it gave them the day free to do as they pleased.

'Amelia, what about you?' Turning her attention to her daughter.

'Well, I have to see to the horses, then Susan and I intend to ride again this morning. They really do need their exercise after being cooped up for a few days over Christmas. But we can both join you after lunch, I'm sure.'

'Delighted to see how you've taken charge now that Milroy has gone,' Lord David told his daughter.

Amelia blushed slightly. 'Actually, Daddy, Susan and I were talking yesterday, and you know how we always take the horses to the summer fete and give rides to the children of the village? Well, we both think that I should offer horse riding lessons and not just for children but for anyone who wants them really. The fees could cover the horse's costs and hopefully provide a little income for the estate also.'

'I think that is a splendid idea, Amelia,' Lord David said proudly.

'Yes, indeed it is,' Colonel James agreed. 'Bravo, Amelia.'

Lady Serena personally thought her daughter's time would be better spent looking for a husband but, not wishing to be a sourpuss, agreed with the gentlemen. 'That's marvellous, Amelia and of course I shall help you get started in any way I can. Well done, darling.'

Sonia looked on approvingly whilst Clarissa simply carried on buttering her toast.

Amelia was beaming as Stephen turned to her and said,

'I knew they would approve.' He then turned to his mother. 'Mummy, I can assist you this morning for any heavy lifting or what have you. It would be my pleasure.'

'Why thank you, Stephen. Clarissa and I would love your company, wouldn't we, Clarissa?'

'Oh yes,' Clarissa agreed through a mouthful of toast.

They all set off on their separate missions shortly afterwards. Stephen walked with his mother and Clarissa to the village.

Serena was surprised to find Lady Eliza already there. 'Oh, good morning, everyone,' she greeted them. 'Thought I'd come early and finish unpacking all the bags and boxes before we started with the sorting. What a tremendous amount we have collected. Should be the best sale ever.'

'Yes, indeed,' Serena agreed. 'Stephen, if you would just set up the trestle tables all around the walls of the hall, we can let you go back to the Manor House then.'

'Righto, Mummy.'

Stephen got to work whilst Clarissa and Serena joined Eliza in the unpacking. He had soon completed this task but before taking his leave he turned to Eliza.

'Lady Ross, I don't suppose you've seen my old dressing gown amongst this lot, have you?'

'Why yes, Stephen. The Manor House jumble was among the first to arrive. It's already been sold. I actually got a whole shilling for it, and you'll never guess who bought it?'

Stephen looked puzzled.

'It was Inspector Stewart. Is that a problem?' She asked seeing Stephen's crestfallen look.

'Only that I wasn't ready to part with it. I do so like to have a spare. I suppose I will have to ask the Inspector if I can buy it back.'

Lady Serena tutted and shook her head. All this fuss over a dressing gown.

'Ladies, good luck with all your sorting.' Stephen departed and headed for the police station.

Sergeant Bailey was having a very peaceful morning so far. So peaceful in fact that he was feeling quite guilty about it. He could not fathom, as hard as he tried, what the Inspector was up to or even where he might have gone. But there was nothing that he himself could do up at the Manor House for the time being. Meanwhile, all his reports were up to date and the telephone had not rung all morning. This was giving him time to catch up on some of his crosswords, which had been sadly neglected in the last few days.

The station door opened and when Neville looked up, he was actually a little bit surprised to see Stephen Mountjoy standing there.

'Ah, Sergeant Bailey,' Stephen rushed forward. 'Is the Inspector in?'

Neville noticed that Stephen looked quite anxious. 'No, I'm afraid he isn't. He has gone away for a couple of days. I don't know where, but I do know that he won't be back until New Year's Eve. Can I help you at all?'

'Well, it is such a silly thing really, Sergeant, but Mummy, Lady Mountjoy gave away a favourite dressing gown of mine for the jumble sale on New Year's Eve and I believe that Inspector Stewart purchased it from Lady Ross yesterday. I really didn't want to part with it so wish to buy it back from him.'

'Oh, I see,' Sergeant Bailey commented. 'Yes, I do recall him coming into the station with it yesterday afternoon. Rather pleased with it he was. But I'm sure if there's been some kind of mistake, the Inspector would be more than happy to return it to you. You could always ask at his sister's where he is staying. Mrs Emily Travers, her husband Derek runs the village bakers.'

'Yes, yes, I know Mrs Travers, Sergeant. I'll just pop along there then, thank you.' Stephen turned and rushed out of the police station.

'Must be some dressing gown,' Neville said to himself returning to his crossword.

Emily Travers was startled on hearing such urgent knocking at the front door. She wasn't expecting anyone and most of her friends and neighbours would just walk in. Nobody locked their doors around these parts when they were at home, although lately Emily had insisted that the doors be locked up tight at night, at least until those murders up at the Manor House had been properly solved anyway.

She was very surprised to see Stephen Mountjoy standing on her doorstep as she answered the door. 'Why Mr Mountjoy!' she exclaimed. 'What can I do for you, Sir?'

'Good morning to you, Mrs Travers. Is Inspector Stewart here by any chance?'

'No, I'm afraid he has gone away for a couple of days, he didn't say where to, but if it is a police matter then Sergeant Bailey will be at the station.'

'Oh no, nothing like that. It's just that there's been a bit of a misunderstanding. Lady Mountjoy mistakenly gave away a dressing gown of mine into the jumble and Inspector Stewart bought it yesterday. I now need to buy it back. I'm sure the Inspector would understand.'

'Oh, I see. Well, I don't recall him coming in with anything last night, but I will certainly go upstairs and have a look in his room for you. I'm sure that he would be happy to return it to you free of charge.

'Now won't you step in out of the cold, Mr Mountjoy? Take a seat in the hallway here and I'll be back before you know it.'

Stephen sat down, anxious to have the dressing gown returned to him.

A few minutes later, Emily Travers came back down the stairs, empty handed. 'I'm afraid it is not among his things, Mr Mountjoy. I can only assume that he has taken it with him. But don't worry, he'll be back on New Year's Eve and I'm sure he'll be more than happy to return it to you then.'

'Yes well, thank you, Mrs Travers. Sorry to have disturbed you.'

Stephen hurriedly took his leave and started walking back to the Manor House with a plan formulating inside his head.

Lady Serena had insisted that everyone be present for dinner that evening. She was feeling triumphant that everything was completely ready for the jumble sale, a day early.

Everything was now in the hands of the curate and the ladies who would be manning the stalls on the day which meant that the occupants of the Manor House could all enjoy a free day tomorrow.

'I thought that we might take a drive out somewhere tomorrow afternoon, dear,' she announced to Lord David. 'Most of the snow has cleared. Show Clarissa a bit of the countryside. James, you will accompany us, won't you?'

'Yes, capital idea,' Colonel James agreed. 'You and I can snuggle up under a blanket in the back of the Rolls to keep warm can't we, Clarissa?' He winked at the bashful looking opera singer.

'What if the Inspector calls?' Lord David asked.

'Well, he hasn't been around today, has he?' Serena retorted.

'He is away until New Year's Eve apparently,' Stephen told them. 'But nobody knows where.'

'And how do you know that?' his mother asked him.

'I went to the police station to retrieve my dressing gown, didn't I?' Stephen countered.

'Oh, for heaven's sake, Stephen, will you stop going on about that old dressing gown. It's been sold for a good cause, and I refuse to let you even bring it back into this house. Let that be an end to the matter.

'Now, I think we might have a four for Bridge after dinner. Mummy, did you wish to play?'

Sonia, quite unnoticed by her daughter or anyone else at the table, had hardly eaten anything throughout dinner. 'No,' she declared. 'I have some letters that I would like to finish so shall retire to my room shortly.'

'That's fine. David, James, Clarissa and I shall play. Stephen, can you and Amelia play that silly Chinese game with just two people?'

'Actually, Mummy, I thought Stephen and I could work on some of my ideas for the riding school after dinner.'

'Fine, if that's what you want. Well, let's get started. Coffee, brandy and cigars in the drawing room then, Jameson. Oh, and do bring some of that marvellous Turkish delight.'

The four for Bridge went through to the drawing room whilst Amelia dragged Stephen off to the library.

Sonia dragged herself tentatively to her feet. The last few days had really taken their toll on her, and she was losing the will to fight on much longer. Grimacing, she climbed the stairs to her room and sat down at her desk to compose the most important letter that she would ever write.

CHAPTER EIGHTEEN

As far as its owners were concerned, everything had now reverted completely to normal at the Manor House and so the breakfast gong sounded at the usual time on the morning of December thirtieth. The meal was well underway, but Sonia had not yet appeared.

'Unusual for mummy to be late down for breakfast. Perhaps after the excitement of the last few days, she has decided to breakfast in her room,' Lady Serena contemplated. 'Alice, has Mrs Ferguson rung down for a tray this morning?'

'Not that I know of, Lady Mountjoy. I'll go and check, shall I?'

'Yes, please do, Alice.'

Alice returned a few minutes later. 'Mrs Ferguson hasn't rung for a tray, Milady,' she advised. 'Shall I go upstairs and check on her?'

'Yes, Alice, do.'

Alice scuttled out of the dining room and up the stairs whilst everyone continued with their breakfasts.

A few minutes later, a piercing scream was heard followed by complete silence.

'Good grief, was that Alice?' Lord David asked. 'James, you come with me. The rest of you stay here.'

Lord David ran out of the room and up the stairs faster than he had moved in years, swiftly followed by his brother. They reached Sonia's room to find Alice deathly pale and shaking by the door, unable to move. Colonel James moved her into a chair just outside the room before joining his brother who had already approached the bed where Sonia lay.

The old lady was lying face up with her eyes closed, quite

obviously deceased. Lord David thought he had never seen his mother-in-law look so at peace.

James had wandered over to the desk and was the first to break the silence as he picked up an envelope. 'David look, she has written a letter addressed to Inspector Stewart. What shall we do?'

'Well, to start with, let's return downstairs. Bring that letter with you, James. Alice, are you alright my dear, you've had a bad shock? Here, take my arm and let's get you back downstairs.'

Slowly they descended to the dining room where Lord David handed Alice off to Jameson.

'She's had a bad shock, Jameson. Ask cook to make her a strong cup of tea with lots of sugar.'

'Yes, Milord.' Jameson led a still shaky Alice from the room.

'Whatever is it? Whatever is the matter?' Lady Serena asked.

Lord David sat down. 'I'm afraid it's your mother, my dear. She has died during the night.'

Lady Serena turned pale as a look of shock spread over her face.

'Oh, my dear, how awful,' Clarissa declared.

'Amelia, Clarissa, would you take Lady Serena into the morning room please?' Lord David asked them. 'I think a little brandy might be in order as well.'

He waited until the ladies had left the dining room before continuing. 'Stephen, could you go and fetch Doctor Hollis please? Take the Rolls and bring him back in it. He will do whatever is necessary and with complete discretion.'

'Yes Father,' Stephen acknowledged and immediately left the dining room.

'James, please deliver that letter to the police station. I realise that Inspector Stewart is away but make sure it is placed in the hands of Sergeant Bailey. On your way back here, could you stop at the Gate House and let Lady Eliza and Susan know of this latest tragedy. Ask them if they could please inform the curate of Mrs Ferguson's death and the fact that there will be no Mountjoy presence at the grand jumble sale tomorrow.'

'Of course, David my boy, and may I say how well you are handling all this.'

'James, if this past week had taught us anything, it is that one must simply do the right thing and get on with it. We are Mountjoys and must be prepared to deal with anything and everything that is thrown our way.'

'Yes, Sir. I'll get going straight away.'

As James left, Lord David took a moment with his head in his hands, pondering what fresh hell had just been thrust upon them.

Stephen had run down to the garages and was now on his way to Doctor Hollis's surgery. His mind could not yet register that his beloved grandmother was dead. Of course, he had known that she was ill, but it just seemed such bad timing that she should die now on top of everything else that had happened already at the Manor House this past week. The time for grieving would come later. Right now, he must simply do what was required of him.

Colonel James managed a jog down to the garages where he jumped into his sports car and raced away, therefore arriving at the police station way before Stephen arrived at Doctor Hollis's surgery.

Luckily, it was another quiet morning for Neville, and he was currently seated with a mug of tea and yesterday's crossword puzzle when Colonel James came running into the station, breathless from his exertions. Neville looked up in surprise.

'Good morning, Colonel Mountjoy. Is everything alright?'

'Ah, Sergeant Bailey. Unfortunately, Mrs Ferguson has died in her sleep. Alice, the maid found her in bed this morning after she had failed to appear for breakfast. Anyway, Stephen, my nephew has gone to fetch Doctor Hollis, but I am here to give you this.' James pulled from his coat pocket the envelope that Sonia had addressed to Inspector Stewart and handed it to the bewildered Sergeant.

'This was discovered on the desk in her room, Sergeant. You can see that it is unopened. I trust you will make sure that the Inspector gets it on his return tomorrow?'

'Yes of course, Colonel. I will telephone Doctor Hollis later and please let me know if there is anything I can do. Such sad news. Mrs Ferguson was certainly a character. Please pass on my condolences to the family?'

'Thank you, Sergeant. I must get on now. More calls to make.'

'Of course. Goodbye Colonel.'

James turned and left the station leaving Neville to wonder what on earth Mrs Sonia Ferguson had to tell Inspector Stewart.

Doctor Hollis was just finishing with a patient when Stephen arrived at the surgery. He explained the situation to Darlene, and she fetched the doctor straight away, the latter only pausing to grab his medical bag before joining Stephen for the drive back to the Manor House.

Doctor Hollis was curious. Of course, Mrs Ferguson was ill but the disease that had her in its grasp should not have succeeded yet and her last check-up had revealed a sound heart. Then again, on second thoughts, the events of the last week were enough to cause anyone severe stress. He would miss the spirited old lady, no doubt about that.

The journey to the Manor House was completed in silence, Doctor Hollis deciding that all questions could wait until he had examined the deceased.

Lord David had been watching for their arrival and it was he who opened the front door to them. Grabbing Doctor Hollis's right hand, he shook it vigorously. 'Thank you for coming, Doctor. I'll take you straight up, shall I?'

He led the Doctor up the stairs, leaving Stephen to wander along to the morning room to join the ladies.

Doctor Hollis gazed down at Sonia Ferguson and noted, just as Lord David had earlier, how peaceful the old lady looked. His eye was then drawn to the bedside table and an empty glass, surrounded by a number of empty sachets that had contained the powerful painkiller that he had prescribed for her. He sighed.

'Lord Mountjoy, I'm afraid that I will have to ask Sergeant Bailey to inform the coroner. It very much appears that Mrs Ferguson may have taken an overdose of her prescribed drugs.'

Lord David turned grey in pallor. 'Oh, dear Lord. We are being tested are we not, Doctor Hollis?'

The doctor ignored the question, instead instructing. 'Make sure this door is locked then go and inform the family. I'll take care of everything else and see myself out.'

Doctor Hollis marched out of the room and down the stairs, wondering if it might be time to move once again. This quiet life in the country he had hungered for was proving to be anything but.

Colonel James had gone on to the Gate House as requested by his brother and was greeted there by Susan who answered his ring on the doorbell.

'Why, James, what brings you here? Do come in and have some coffee. Mummy and I were late up this morning and haven't really got going yet.'

'Thank you, my dear. I won't take coffee, but I do need to speak with you both.'

Susan noted the serious expression on James's face. 'Yes. Of course. Mummy is in the front room. Come through right away.'

They both walked in, Susan announcing to her mother, 'It's Colonel James, Mummy. He has something important to tell us.'

'Why, James, has something happened?' Lady Eliza asked him.

'Yes, I'm afraid Lady Serena's mother has died in her sleep.'

'Oh, how dreadful,' Eliza interrupted. 'The poor family, as if they hadn't been through enough already. What can we do to help?'

'Could you let the curate know? Also, for tomorrow. He may need to recruit some more helpers as the Mountjoy family are unlikely to be present.'

'Yes, of course. I shall see right to it,' Eliza agreed.

'Perhaps I should go to the stables and see to the horses,' Susan suggested.

'Yes, I think that is a splendid idea, Susan,' her mother told her.

'Please pass on our condolences to Lady Mountjoy. Susan and I will call tomorrow, after the sale, to pay our respects.'

James nodded in acknowledgement, gave a slight bow and left the Gate House.

'How very odd,' Susan commented. 'I thought the old battle axe seemed as fit as a fiddle. You don't think someone bumped her off as well, do you?'

'Susan really,' Lady Eliza admonished her daughter. 'Show some respect. Besides which the events of this week are enough to send anyone to an early grave. Go and see to those horses and make yourself useful.'

Upset with her daughter, Eliza left the room to prepare herself for a visit to the curate.

Colonel James drove past Doctor Hollis walking back down the driveway as the sports car made its way back to the Manor House. As he entered the house, he met his brother coming down the stairs and on his way into the morning room.

'Ah good, James, you're back. Come with me and we can update everyone.'

James followed his brother into the room where everyone was gathered, including Jameson who was currently serving coffee in the absence of a still shaken Alice.

'Ah, Jameson, you are here too. Good. You can listen to what I have to say as well.

'It would appear that Mrs Ferguson may have taken an overdose of her pain medication. Doctor Hollis is going to inform Sergeant Bailey and the coroner.'

'Oh, the silly woman,' Lady Serena said harshly. 'I do wish you hadn't taken her letter, James. We really need to know what she's written. You shouldn't have sent him David. Now we have to wait for the Inspector and that is really too trying after everything else this week.' Lady Serena sobbed into her lace handkerchief as Clarissa attempted to comfort her.

'There, there, my dear,' David added with little effect. 'Jameson, some brandy for Lady Mountjoy.

'James, I trust you handed over the letter to Sergeant Bailey?'

'Yes, and I've seen Lady Ross and explained everything. Susan has offered to see to the horses. I believe she is at the stables now.'

'I'll go and assist her if I may, please Daddy?'

Half of David thought that Amelia should stay and comfort her mother, but common sense told him that theirs was not that kind of relationship. Besides which, Amelia had been close to her grandmother and would therefore need to deal with this in her own way.

'Yes certainly, Amelia. It's good to keep busy. Clarissa can look after your mother while you are away.'

Amelia rose without a word and left the room.

Lord David addressed his son and his brother. 'Well, Stephen, James, I'm sure there are things we can be getting on with. I have some business in the village. I'll walk down and take Chester with me.'

'Need some company?' James offered.

'No, I would prefer to be alone, thank you, James.'

'Uncle James, I could use your help,' Stephen proffered. 'I thought we could grab Parker and see to that dry stone wall that's been damaged.' Stephen definitely did not want to be alone with his thoughts.

'Yes, capital idea,' James agreed. 'Bit of hard work will take the mind off it all.' James was now counting the days until he could return to London. He sincerely hoped that the Inspector's return the next day would bring nothing but good news. Much as he wanted to be there for his brother, the atmosphere in the Manor House was stifling and to his way of thinking, the family would be best left to heal without him there. So, he would just do his bit before he could make his escape.

Everyone had departed, leaving Lady Serena alone with Clarissa. Even Jameson had gone to inform the servants of the latest occurrence.

'Are you alright, darling?' Clarissa asked tentatively.

'I am with you here,' Serena replied to her friend. 'I know Mummy was ill and I could understand if she took too many powders to end the pain and suffering, to avoid an excruciating death, I can really. But why now, Clarissa? Haven't we all had enough this week? It really is too dreadful of her.

'When this is over, I really think that I must go with you back to London. Get away for a few weeks.'

Clarissa's eyes lit up. 'Yes, you really should, my dear. We'll have a gay old time. Soon have the sparkle back in your eyes and the colour back in your cheeks.'

Lady Serena managed a weak smile and listened to her friend waxing lyrically about all the things they would do together in the Capital.

Amelia was glad to get away to the only place that she found comfort, with the horses. She hadn't yet accepted the fact that her grandmother was dead and was feeling quite numb, apart from the anger she still felt towards her for being admonished in public on Christmas Eve, even though that now made her feel a little guilty. It would be nice to talk to Susan about it all. In the last couple of days, she had found a real friend and rock in the strong, sensible woman.

Susan was already there with shovel in hand when Amelia arrived at the stables.

'Amelia, I really didn't expect to see you what with, you know. I'm so sorry to hear about Sonia, your grandmother.'

'Thank you, Susan. It really hasn't sunk in yet. I just wanted to keep busy.'

'Of course, and if you'd like to be alone, I can leave.'

'No please stay?' Amelia pleaded. 'I would be really grateful for your company.'

'Absolutely. Anything you need.'

Amelia gave her a watery smile and grabbed a shovel.

Lady Eliza had found the curate at home in the vicarage when she called. She brought him up to date on all that had occurred but was surprised at his reaction.

'Oh well, that's it, Lady Ross. The jumble sale cannot possibly go ahead now in light of all the circumstances.'

Lady Eliza was quick to disagree. 'Don't you see that is precisely why it must go ahead. Lord and Lady Mountjoy wish it to be so, and I know that Reverend Smith and Mrs Ferguson would have felt the same way. No Curate. You must open the sale with a prayer for those recently departed. The village needs to come together over this and there is no better place to do it. We could even have a book of condolence, for both of them. You do see that I'm right, don't you?'

And as much as he was disinclined to, the poor curate had to agree.

Lady Eliza left having discussed a few more details, feeling ever so slightly victorious.

Sergeant Bailey's peaceful morning with a pot of tea and a crossword was now completely shattered by the news that Doctor Hollis had delivered. The Sergeant took full control in telephoning the coroner before departing for the Manor House with the doctor, who had insisted on accompanying him.

Jameson opened the door and wordlessly welcomed them inside the house. Lord David had left the key to Sonia's room with him, and this he handed over to Sergeant Bailey who went straight upstairs with Doctor Hollis.

Before this week, the Sergeant had been fortunate enough in the course of his duties, never to have laid eyes on a dead body. Now, in the space of three days, he was looking down on his third, albeit briefly, before his attention turned to the glass and the empty packets of powders on the bedside table.

'I trust this room has not been disturbed at all?' he asked the doctor.

'No. Apart from Colonel Mountjoy removing the letter that he brought to you from her desk, nothing has been touched to my knowledge.'

'Very good. Right well I suggest we leave the room and wait for the coroner.'

And so it was that Sergeant Bailey and Doctor Hollis found themselves seated in the very spot where Sonia had watched everyone arriving at the Manor House on Christmas Eve morning.

Surprised initially at having to return to the Manor House once again, the coroner came and left with Mrs Ferguson but without ceremony.

Doctor Hollis returned to his surgery, so that only Neville remained to gather up any evidence and quietly leave.

So once again, at a time when most families might come together, the inhabitants of the Manor House each spent their evenings in their rooms.

Lord David had insisted that a cold buffet be made available in the dining room, but very little food had been consumed and by whom no one could say.

Only the servants took comfort from each other's company as they helped each other with the kitchen chores. Parker joined Jameson in a seat by the hearth but very little was spoken as each tried to absorb the latest and most upsetting event to happen this Christmastime at the Manor House.

CHAPTER NINETEEN

It had been close to midnight when Tom had finally returned to the village. There were no lights visible at his sister's cottage. Guessing that they would all be asleep, he removed his shoes and tiptoed up the stairs as quietly as he could. Once in the guest room he had been staying in, he quickly undressed and slipped into bed. Despite everything on his mind, he soon fell into a dreamless sleep that complete physical and mental exhaustion brings.

In the morning, upon awakening, Tom felt very refreshed and joined his family in the kitchen for breakfast. Derek Travers had left the cottage a few hours earlier for the bakery, but Tom was greeted happily by his nephew, William, who was busy shovelling porridge into his mouth.

'Uncle Tom, you're back,' the six-year-old greeted him. 'Can you take me sledging later?'

'Don't know about today, son. But maybe tomorrow,' he told his young nephew, who looked crestfallen.

'Now then, William,' his mother Emily stepped in. 'You know how busy Uncle Tom is at the moment. He has a very important job to do.'

William nodded and went back to his porridge.

'And how is my favourite niece this morning?'

Four-year-old Martha Travers ceased from feeding her porridge to the teddy bear she was holding and smiled at Tom, 'Edward Bear won't eat his porridge, Uncle Tom,' she told him.

'Well, perhaps he is full up, Martha and so you should finish it for him.'

Martha nodded and ate a spoonful of porridge.

'How did you get on?' his sister Emily asked as she placed a bowl in front of him.

'Very well thank you, Emily.'

'Well, I hate to tell you this, Tom, but I heard that Sonia Ferguson died in her sleep and was found in bed yesterday morning.'

'Really?' Tom looked at his sister wide eyed with surprise. 'In that case I had best eat this quickly and get to the station.'

Tom gobbled up his porridge and after giving his niece and nephew a kiss on their chubby cheeks, he left the house. He would have liked a cup of tea but was pretty sure that Sergeant Bailey would have a pot on the go.

Sure enough, Neville was already at his desk with a mug in his hand when Tom walked in.

'Good morning, Sergeant. Any tea going?'

'Morning, Sir. Of course, I'll get you a cup.'

'No don't worry, I'll do it. I hear there's been a development whilst I've been away?'

'Yes, Sir. Poor old Mrs Ferguson. Didn't appear for breakfast yesterday morning. The maid, Alice went up to check and found her dead in her bed. Gave her quite a shock, as you can imagine. Stephen Mountjoy fetched Doctor Hollis who noticed empty packets of powder on the bedside table. So, he came to me, and I called the coroner. It would appear that the old lady took an overdose, Sir.

'However, whilst Stephen Mountjoy had gone for the doctor initially, Colonel James came to me with a letter that he and Lord David had found propped up on her desk. It's addressed to you, Sir. I have it here.'

Tom sat down with his tea and took the envelope that Sergeant Bailey held out to him. Inside were three pages covered with Sonia Ferguson's spidery writing. Taking a big gulp of strong tea, he started to read.

Neville sat quietly watching the Inspector's face for any change in expression, but his face remained passive throughout.

He knew better than to ask his superior officer directly, so waited patiently until he had finished reading to receive any orders.

Tom looked up and saw the Sergeant eagerly waiting. 'Right, Sergeant Bailey. I think the time has now arrived to bring the sad events of the last few days to a close. I am going up to the Manor House now. If you could please telephone Doctor Hollis and then Mr Rochester at the bank. Advise them that I have requested their presence at the Manor House immediately. If you then follow along and pick up Parker on the way. Go in via the kitchen entrance and have Jameson, Jane and Alice join also. I want everyone assembled in the morning room. I will go via the Gate House and let Lady Eliza and Susan Ross know. Miss Ross can always collect her mother from the village hall if necessary. I'll walk up, you bring the car, Sergeant and don't take no for an answer from any of them.'

'Yes, Sir.'

Neville lifted the telephone receiver as Tom quickly left the building. The ointment that Doctor Hollis had prescribed for him had worked wonders, enabling him to maintain a fast pace. As he passed the village hall, he slowed down and glanced in, half expecting to find Lady Eliza Ross there. However, still being quite early, only a few of the parish ladies were inside making final preparations, so he continued on.

Susan Ross was sitting on the steps of the Gate House, pulling on her riding boots. 'Good morning, Inspector. So, you have returned I see. Everything all sorted out now?'

'I do believe so, Miss Ross. I would like you and Lady Ross to come up to the Manor House straight away please. Doctor Hollis and Mr Rochester will also be joining us shortly.'

Susan looked at him curiously. 'I must say I'm intrigued, Inspector. I was heading up there anyway to meet Amelia and see to the horses. I'll just go fetch mummy and we'll be up as soon as we can.'

'Thank you, Miss Ross.' Tom gave a slight bow before turning to leave and carried on up the long drive to the Manor House. On ringing the bell, the door was opened by Jameson who was dressed completely in black, indicating that the house was in mourning.

'Good morning, Inspector.'

'Good morning, Mr Jameson. May I have a quiet word with Lord Mountjoy please?'

'Certainly, Sir. If you would care to wait in the library. The family are still at breakfast in the dining room. You have received the news about Mrs Ferguson I take it, Sir?'

'Yes, very sad news, Jameson. Please tell Lord Mountjoy to finish his breakfast and not to rush.'

'Very good, Sir.'

Jameson headed off to the dining room as Tom opened the door to the library and took a seat in one of the comfortable armchairs by the hearth. He did not have long to wait before Lord David appeared.

Lady Serena, eager to know what was contained in her mother's letter, had demanded that he leave his breakfast and enter the library straightaway.

'Inspector Stewart. We are all very relieved that you have returned. I take it that you have been made aware of the sad passing of Lady Serena's mother. Now tell me, have you read the letter she left you?'

'Yes, Sir and that is one of the reasons why I am here now. My condolences to you and Lady Mountjoy. Now, I appreciate how difficult this will be, but I have asked for Doctor Hollis; Mr Rochester; Lady Ross; Miss Ross; Parker; Jameson; Alice and Jane to join with you all in the morning room. I fully intend to bring everything to a close and you can then be left to grieve and make the required arrangements.'

'Yes, well that would bring some peace of mind I dare say, Inspector. Come along to the morning room and I'll inform the others and arrange for coffee to be served.'

'Well, what did he say?' Lady Serena demanded to know as soon as her husband walked into the dining room.

'He wants to talk to everybody again. Bring everything to a close. Doctor Hollis, Mr Rochester, Lady Eliza and Susan are on their way up here apparently and he has also requested the presence of Parker, Jameson, Alice and Jane.'

'Yes, that's all very well and good but what about Mummy's letter?'

'He didn't say anything about it to me, but I believe it will inform part of this meeting.'

'Oh, how dreadful. Well, I suppose we will just have to get it over with. Better go into the morning room, everyone.'

Tom had been staring out of the large window across the beautiful gardens as they all walked in. He turned as he heard the door open, interested to note the facial expressions being displayed.

Lord David and Colonel James looked blank as they came in and sat down. Lady Serena Mountjoy looked quite annoyed whilst her friend Clarissa displayed a mixture of boredom and curiosity. Stephen and Amelia's expressions displayed a mixture of shock and resignation but then they had just lost their grandmother on top of everything else.

Tom spoke first. 'May I pass on my sincere condolences, Lady Mountjoy?'

'Thank you, Inspector. But I must ask is this absolutely necessary given the current circumstances, we are grieving here you know?'

'Yes, and I appreciate that, Lady Mountjoy. But we are talking about murder. So, if you can just bear with me for one last time and I will then leave you in peace to grieve.'

'Very well, Inspector and when will the others arrive?'

'Anytime now, Lady Mountjoy. Sergeant Bailey has been rounding them all up. In fact, I will go outside now and wait for them.' Anything to escape any further wrath from Lady Mountjoy.

Due to the jumble sale taking place in the village right then, Doctor Hollis and Mr Rochester were having very quiet mornings and so both were quite happy to leave their posts immediately. Sergeant Bailey arranged to drive to both the bank and the surgery and transport them up to the Manor House. Neither man had questioned why, knowing that the Sergeant would simply be carrying out Inspector Stewart's orders. The Inspector himself was waiting for them at the top of the steps as they arrived.

'Gentlemen, thank you for coming. I'll take you through to the morning room. Mr Rochester, I assume you've heard the sad news about Mrs Ferguson?'

George nodded.

'I'll go round for the servants then, Sir,' Neville advised.

'Very good, Sergeant.' As Neville departed, Tom spotted Lady Eliza Ross and her daughter Susan Ross walking up the drive. Both had taken the time to change and were now dressed all in black as a mark of respect to Sonia Ferguson.

Tom greeted them. 'Ladies, thank you for your prompt arrival. Let me take you all through to the morning room.' They all followed silently, Tom opening the door of the morning room for them to walk through. Lady Eliza opened her mouth to speak but was silenced by Lady Serena.

'This is not the time for your condolences, please take a seat everyone and let's just get this over and done with.'

Lady Eliza ignored the obvious put down and took a seat on the sofa, next to Colonel James. Susan, Doctor Hollis and George Rochester sat down in the hard backed chairs that had been brought into the room and placed between the various sofas and armchairs.

Sergeant Bailey entered the room with Parker, Jameson, Alice and Jane. The maids were carrying trays of coffee, crockery and a large plate of cook's delicious homemade shortbread.

'Leave those trays on the sideboard,' Lady Serena ordered. 'We shan't want them yet.'

Jane and Alice did as they were requested, before joining Parker and Jameson in the four chairs that had been placed slightly outside of the inner circle.

Tom nodded at Neville, who was standing by the door, indicating that the Sergeant should remain in place there. Then he began to address his audience.

'Ladies and gentlemen. Thank you all for arriving here so promptly today, particularly under such sad circumstances. However, murder is a very serious business. But now, after an extensive investigation, undertaken by Sergeant Bailey and myself, I am in a position to reveal the truth behind the three deaths that have occurred at the Manor House this week. Logically, I should begin with the death of Reverend Smith, what with his being the first. But in this case, it is not the best place to start.

'As some of you are aware, Mrs Ferguson left a letter addressed to me which, due to my absence from the village, I only received this morning. I apologise if this causes you further upset Lady Mountjoy, but I would like to read this letter to you all now.'

'Oh, just get on with it, Inspector,' Lady Serena barked at him.

'As you wish.' Tom gave a respectful bow, cleared his throat and commenced.

'*Dear Inspector Stewart,*

By the time you read this letter I will have left this mortal coil and, to make things quite clear, death will be by my own hand as I will have taken an overdose of my pain medication.

Death for me is very close anyway and, to my mind, not something to be feared and so I choose not to spend one moment longer with a pain that will only increase before nature takes its course.

As a God-fearing woman, I am aware that this is the time when I must confess my sins and therefore there is something, a secret that I have been keeping for a while now, that I really must confess to you.

You see, Inspector, it was I who killed Robert Milroy. The fact that he died on Christmas Day right after Reverend Smith was murdered is pure coincidence. Let me explain.

For some time, I had become increasingly worried about the influence Robert Milroy was having over my granddaughter, Amelia. By early summer, I was quite convinced that he was also supplying

Amelia with some kind of opiate. I knew Lord David would never fire the man on my suspicions, but even if he had seen sense and let him go, wouldn't he just have started up elsewhere, supplying more drugs and in doing so, ruining more lives?

So, I decided to do the world a favour and get rid of him. It was sometime in September I think when I saw him carrying a batch of cook's homemade lemonade down to the stables. I waited until he and Amelia were out riding the horses. David and Stephen had been repairing a drystone wall somewhere on the estate and Serena was off helping some charitable cause somewhere.

I was more mobile then, so simply took a walk down to the stables and placed some of my powders into one of the bottles on the shelf, knowing that within a week or two he would have drunk them all, even if mine was the last one.

However, what I could not have planned for was that the weather could have turned so chilly for September and therefore he did not drink any lemonade at all.

For a while I despaired, especially as I was left without any pain medication. I even tried to convince Doctor Hollis that he had been short in my prescription but of course he wasn't having any of it. So, I just had to wait and keep trying to get Amelia out of Milroy's grasp.

Can you imagine my surprise when the man finally drank the drugged bottle on Christmas Day?

Of course, the family are more than happy to believe that Milroy killed Reverend Smith and then killed himself, but I know that you don't believe that for one minute Inspector and based on what I have witnessed so far, I would not be at all surprised if you suspected me!

Anyway, he was dead, and I watched my granddaughter fall apart. But then a remarkable thing happened. With the help of two horses and Susan Ross, Amelia became a new person. Brighter, more confident and with plans to establish a riding school. I now know that she will be alright and that it is time for me to say goodbye.

I wish you every success in finding your killer, Inspector Stewart and I have absolutely no doubt that you will.

Yours very sincerely
Sonia Ferguson

Tom folded the letter and looked up, awaiting a reaction. Not unexpectedly, it was from Lady Mountjoy.

'Amelia, were you really taking drugs supplied by the chauffeur?' She barked at her daughter.

'Yes, Mummy. Just for a little while to help with my nerves but that's all in the past now and this really isn't the time or place. We can talk about it later.'

Lady Serena huffed and turned her attention back to the Inspector. 'Well, that's really upset the applecart then hasn't it, Inspector Stewart? My own mother is a murderer who then commits suicide. I suppose you are now going to tell us that it was not Milroy who killed Reverend Smith?'

'Let's go back to the beginning, Lady Mountjoy. Reverend Smith arrives here on Christmas Eve just as he has done every Christmas Eve for the last few years. But soon, a noticeable change in his behaviour occurs. We know that heavy snow had been forecast and as a precaution, the Reverend had given a copy of his sermon to Thomas Mason, the curate, just in case he was unable to return for the midnight service. But at this stage, no snow had fallen at all. So, to all intents and purposes, he would be leading that service as usual. Therefore, what was the reason that he took to drinking?

'The answer lies in a conversation I later had with the curate. He told me about a big chunk of land, belonging to the church, that had been loaned to the family and the Manor estate during the war. This land was worked by the WLA, but no documents were ever signed and as far as the church was concerned, the land was theirs again, whenever they required it for the reason it had been originally purchased, and that was for burial purposes.

'Reverend Smith believed that the land had been left idle for too long and, after consulting the church hierarchy, had agreed that the land was to be turned into a community plot for the whole village. Whether it is to become a park, or allotments, or a mixture of both is yet to be established.

'Now the Reverend had been around the family enough to

know that you all considered that land to be part of the Manor estate and he therefore anticipated a very difficult conversation explaining how the church was planning on taking the land back and, as the curate told me, was in need of some 'Dutch courage', hence the imbibing. However, the Reverend was just not used to alcohol at all, so that even after a couple of glasses, his tongue started to run away with him.

'Firstly, he referred to the groundsman Nathaniel Parker as Nathan Parkes. Now, for reasons that no longer matter and also assisted by the church, Mr Parker did use to be Nathan Parkes. Being part of the church, the Reverend could certainly have known or discovered this fact. But he would also have been sworn to secrecy. This then tells us the Reverend's state of mind at this stage but no reason to suspect that Mr Parker would have needed to kill him.

'Then the conversation turns to Lord Mountjoy's new antiques business and, once again, the Reverend pipes up that he has seen some of your antique statues in the antique shop in the village, which you flatly denied Lord Mountjoy, insisting that you did not deal in statues and also did not supply any antiques to the village shop.'

Lord David's face started to turn slightly red as Tom continued.

'As part of my inquiries, I spoke to Mr Arthur Pentelow, the owner of the antique shop, and he informed me that he was holding a couple of statues that you had brought to him with the arrangement that he would take a percentage of the profit when they sold. However, he did not think that they would ever sell as you had priced them as originals, and they are merely replicas.'

'Yes, well now they are in the village jumble sale. May have made a mistake with those, easily done,' Lord David blustered. 'Bit embarrassing to be called out at my own dinner table on Christmas Eve, what? And by the Reverend, no less. Still, might have been a bit embarrassed but not enough to kill the chap.'

'Yes, I quite agree, Lord Mountjoy. But we can now see that with further imbibing, Reverend Smith is growing in confidence and ready to challenge anyone and everyone with what he imagines could be their possible secrets.

'Straight after lunch, he does this again whilst the gentlemen are shooting. Doctor Hollis, Mr Rochester and the Reverend have taken a few shots and are now watching the family shooting. Reverend Smith makes a few polite enquiries of Mr Rochester and his family to discover that his fiancée is spending Christmas and the New Year in Yorkshire. Upon hearing that, he immediately turned to Doctor Hollis to ask if he had ever spent time in Yorkshire, to which the doctor replied that he hadn't. The Reverend then curiously went on to add that he thought he sometimes detected a Yorkshire accent when the doctor spoke. Something that nobody else had noticed, I hasten to add. Doctor Hollis duly explained to Reverend Smith that he had not spent any time in Yorkshire.

'By this point, the Reverend is having a whale of a time and it is quite obvious by the time he descends for dinner, that no one will be leaving the Manor House to attend a church service that evening.

'So, what does he do? He accepts one of Colonel James Mountjoy's very strong cocktails. At this point Stephen, you approached him and pulled him aside hoping to get his signature on a document you had with you. What was that please?'

'Don't you know, Inspector?' Stephen snapped back at him.

'Well, yes, I do. But I'd like you to explain it to everyone, please?'

'Very well. It was a deed of transfer that I'd had drawn up for the piece of land in question. It should have been carried out at the start of the war, but it wasn't, and I just wanted to make it official as that land rightfully belongs to the Manor estate.'

'And would I be correct in thinking that you wish to sell the land off?'

'Well, yes. The estate needs the funds. Look, I would have been more than happy to sell that land back to the church, but the old beggar wasn't having any of it. I fully intend to contact the Bishop in the New Year to resolve this. I don't think Reverend Smith had the authority anyway.'

'Maybe not. But you can't have been too pleased that he turned you down flat like that.'

'Arrogant little nobody,' Stephen retorted. 'I was going to teach him a lesson.'

'Stephen, please?' Lady Serena admonished. 'The poor man is dead.'

'Thank you, Lady Mountjoy,' Tom acknowledged.

'So, Stephen. We understand how you were feeling at this stage but what about the Reverend? He had just attained a small victory and must have been feeling very powerful and confident as he once again indulged in some fine wine. Imagine his delight when Colonel Mountjoy eggs him on to tell some stories from the confessional, so to speak. Now this is where things become really interesting.

'When I interviewed Mrs Ferguson, God rest her soul, she revealed that Reverend Smith had previously performed a very unchristian act in turning an unmarried, expectant housemaid out of the vicarage where he was at the time. Both mother and baby consequently died as a result of this action. It was even rumoured that he might have been the father of the child. That can't be proven, but I have checked about a former housemaid in his employ and unfortunately that was indeed true. Although the Reverend apparently always claimed that she left of her own accord so as not to bring any shame in a house of God. Even if that were true, it is evident that he did little or nothing to find or assist the girl and showed a vindictive side to his personality that now displays itself here.

'He also demonstrated this a little later with you, Miss Llewellyn-Jones. Firstly, complimenting you on your colourful kaftan and how it suited your figure before asking you if all opera singers are fat to make them sing better. Hardly the question a gentleman would ask, is it?'

'Oh, I put him in his place though, Inspector,' Clarissa told him. 'Let him know that I was lovely and slim when I was younger.'

'Indeed,' Tom continued. 'Because he was next overheard to say, 'But I thought', indicating something he thought he knew. He didn't of course, but I did some research anyway. It turns out that there was another English opera star about your age. She married young but kept her maiden name on the stage for a while and then retired to raise a family.'

'Oh, you mean Anna Cartwright, Inspector. I was her understudy in Madame Butterfly for a season. Went on a few times for her when her morning sickness appeared in the evening, on occasion. That's what got me my big break. I took over the role from Anna. You don't mean.......?'

'Yes. I think he had mistaken you for Anna Cartwright and was therefore making assumptions that you'd been the expectant one who had left the stage in disgrace.'

'Well really. What a nasty little man. No wonder someone killed him. Not that it was me, Inspector. Goodness, I didn't even realise.'

Clarissa looked quite flustered and extracting a colourful fan from inside her sleeve began waving it in front of her face.

'No that's quite alright, Miss Llewellyn-Jones. The Reverend was simply trying to get a reaction, revelling in the power and control he felt having taken back the land from the Manor House. He continued to do this in the stories he told over dinner. We may never know if any of them were true, but he certainly adapted them to insinuate that they could apply to someone in this household.'

'Are you going to explain all this, Inspector?' Lady Serena asked somewhat impatiently.

'Indeed, I am, Lady Mountjoy. Let's start with the tale of the housemaid eager to tell Reverend Smith her suspicions that the two senior servants, presumably the butler and the cook, who claim to be married and employed in the house that she herself works in, are not married at all and the butler, in fact, already has a wife but nobody knows where she is. Jameson was in the dining room at this point.'

'Yes, Sir, I was, Sir and so shocked to hear such a scandalous tale that I dropped a knife. Quite a clatter it made.'

'Yes, and I think that Reverend Smith was making an insinuation purely based on the fact that your dear lady wife continues to use the name Trelawney.'

'Avoids confusion, Sir. Happens in most houses with a married couple.'

'Indeed, it does, Mr Jameson. But the Reverend obviously did not know that, hence the insinuation.' Tom gave Jameson a slight nod to indicate that his secret would remain safe before moving on.

'He is then encouraged to tell a tale about a scandal above stairs and the next story, I believe is aimed at Lady Mountjoy.'

'Well really,' she declared. After all the kindness we have shown that man.'

'What exactly are you referring to?' Lord David asked.

'The story of the lady of a rather fine estate who had borne her husband the son he so craved, a few years earlier. Although, having been somewhat indiscreet in her younger years, the lady could no longer be certain that the child was her husband's now that the boy had grown. She was sure that her husband would suspect this also.'

'And he was insinuating that the lady was ME?' Lady Serena bellowed. 'How dare he try to ruin my good name like that. I've never heard anything like it. Why would the stupid little man even think something like that?'

'I believe that he had spotted, as indeed have Mr Rochester and myself, a facial characteristic that Stephen shares with the Colonel.'

Lord David burst out laughing. 'The old, raised eyebrow. Our father had that too. Missed me out, but James inherited and Stephen too. As James was overseas at the time my son was conceived and entered into this world, I can assure you, Inspector, of no impropriety there.'

'Yes, thank you, Lord Mountjoy,' Tom cut him off. 'But you see the Reverend had a captive audience at this point and even though he was shut down at the dinner table, he was encouraged once again when the ladies had left the room and his next tale was aimed at Doctor Hollis.'

The doctor stirred uncomfortably in his chair.

'Oh yes I remember that one,' Lord David suddenly piped up. 'Some ridiculous story about a doctor's wife from up north somewhere, claiming that her husband was trying to poison her for no reason whatsoever and she later died of a gastric complaint. Even claimed that he had gone to the police, and they wouldn't listen to him either. I certainly didn't give any credence to this or the tale he told straight after. Who was that aimed at? Lady Eliza and myself I suppose. Having an affair, forging a will. Too ridiculous for words.'

'Yes, quite so. But even the reactions here today in this room, prove just how upsetting these tales could be. Let's for the moment take all of these stories and surmises out of the equation and what are we left with? Where is the motive for killing Reverend Smith? Who had a reason and who had been angry, indeed very angry, earlier in the day?'

As Tom looked around the room, he saw a lot of puzzled and curious faces.

'A couple of days ago, I called into the village hall where the collected jumble was beginning to accumulate and spoke to Lady Ross. Whilst I was there, it just so happens that I came across this dressing gown.'

Tom extracted said dressing gown from a bag he had brought in with him. 'Rather splendid, isn't it? Not like any dressing gown that I've ever owned before. Lady Ross allowed me to purchase it before the sale, but don't worry, I made a most generous donation.'

Lady Eliza nodded her agreement.

'I believe this was yours, Mr Mountjoy?'

'Yes, it was. But I have a new one now. I hadn't worn that one in quite some time. I think Mummy found it in the bottom of my wardrobe which is why it ended up in the jumble sale in the first place.'

'Yes. I understand that Mr Mountjoy. But what I don't understand is this dark stain on the right cuff here.' Tom held the sleeve up for everyone to see. 'How do you account for that, Mr Mountjoy?'

'I really can't say,' he blustered.

'No, I thought that might be the case. So, I had it tested, and it turns out that it is in fact a blood stain and, furthermore, that it matches the blood of Reverend Smith.'

'Well, I don't know how it got there.' Stephen shouted out. 'Obviously, the killer stole it from my room and wore it to bash the Reverend over the head and then put it back in my room to frame me. I told you; I didn't wear it anymore.'

'If that is the case, Mr Mountjoy, why did you go to the village hall to try to retrieve it? Not only that, but when you discovered that it was I who had purchased it, you called on Sergeant Bailey at the station and at my sister's house in an attempt to buy it back. Can you explain that Mr Mountjoy?'

Stephen turned puce and stood up. 'I don't have to explain anything,' he bellowed at Tom.

'Sit down, Stephen and calm down,' Lord David ordered his son. 'Inspector Stewart, perhaps you could fill us in whilst my son is calming himself?'

'Certainly, Lord Mountjoy. I believe that your son Stephen returned to the drawing room after everyone had retired on Christmas Eve, wearing this dressing gown. I suspect that this was to have one last try at persuading Reverend Smith to sign the paper that would hand over the church land to the Manor estate. However, having drunk so much alcohol throughout the day and evening, the Reverend was pretty much in an alcohol induced coma and you could not wake him up. Mr Mountjoy, I put it to you that this made you so angry that you finally reached the end of your tether. You grabbed the candlestick and bashed him on the back of the head where he had fallen slightly forward. You may have thought that you didn't hit him that hard, yet when you checked there was no pulse, even though there was very little blood. Then you panicked. So, you moved the body and hid it behind the Christmas tree. Now instead of simply wiping the candlestick clean and replacing it on the sideboard, you decided to place it in a rarely used room in the servant's quarters. Whether or not you knew Mr Parker was sleeping up there, I do not know. If not, it must have been quite a surprise. But I suspect you did and were trying to frame either Mr Parker or Mr Milroy. You must have thought it was your lucky day when Mr Milroy himself turned up dead as well, even though it turns out that he never slept in that room. The dressing gown you tossed at the bottom of your wardrobe and carried on as normal until you realised that it was missing and on its way to the jumble sale.'

'Is this true, Stephen?' Lord David demanded before adding, 'And don't even think about lying to me, my boy.'

Stephen hung his head. 'Yes, it's all true,' he whispered. 'Exactly as Inspector Stewart described it. But I didn't mean to kill him. He just made me so angry. Who did he think he was dealing with, trying to take that land back?'

Lord David had turned grey, and his shoulders slumped. Lady Serena however, sat up proud and erect.

'Inspector Stewart, much as I love my son, this family will always do the right thing. You must arrest him if you must.'

'Of course, Lady Mountjoy and whilst your son has certainly committed a number of crimes here, he was not the one who murdered Reverend Smith.'

'What the dickens do you mean, Inspector?' Lady Serena asked puzzledly.

'It's all about the lack of blood really, Lady Mountjoy. You see when your son hit him, he was already dead.'

'Do you know who killed him, Inspector, or is this simply one almighty fishing expedition?'

'Bear with me, Lady Mountjoy, all will be revealed. So, if Mr Mountjoy with his strong motive and murderous intent did not kill him, then we must re-examine the stories that the Reverend had been telling earlier. What if, amongst all those ridiculous tales, one was actually the truth? Then there would be a motive.

Now what had intrigued me the most, was the conversation that took place on the Christmas Eve afternoon shoot. I don't know whether it was pure coincidence or if Reverend Smith had previously been told about Mr Rochester's fiancée being in Yorkshire with family for Christmas, or not.'

'Oh, I can answer that, Inspector,' Lady Serena piped up. 'I told him that about a month ago when he enquired who would be at the Manor for Christmas this year. So, he didn't need to ask the question, he already knew.'

'Right. Well, thank you for that, Lady Mountjoy. That confirms what I already suspected that he was purely looking for a way of bringing the subject of Yorkshire into the conversation. He could then ask you, Doctor Hollis if you had ever been to Yorkshire and also accuse you of having a hint of a Yorkshire accent, even though, as I have stated previously, to the rest of us this is not evident in the slightest. All of which of course you denied, but all of which was the Reverend's way of letting you know that he recognised you from his time in the North of England.'

'That's ridiculous,' Doctor Hollis countered. 'I'd never met that man before in my life before I came here and that was direct from Harley Street, as you well know.'

'Yes. But what about before that time? Anyway, Reverend Smith was convinced that you are the doctor whose wife thought was trying to kill her and so, after dinner when the ladies have left the room and egged on by the Colonel, he told the story. Only, what if this time it is the absolute truth? Unbeknownst to you, your wife did go to see him, and he did go to the police.'

'But I am not married, Inspector Stewart. I have never had a wife.'

'No, Doctor Hollis has never had a wife, that's very true. Furthermore, I had previously been inclined to dismiss everything the Reverend had said until something made me change my mind.'

'And pray tell, what might that have been?' Doctor Hollis

asked haughtily.

'It was when I came to the surgery to consult you about my leg. Very good ointment by the way. It's done the trick very well. As your receptionist went to check with you that you would be able to see me, I glanced through the magazines on the table and found a copy of *Life in Yorkshire*. When your receptionist, Darlene isn't it, returned she took it from me advising that it had been placed in reception by mistake, that it was your private subscription and should have gone straight to your residence. And so, I ask myself, why would you subscribe to a magazine from Yorkshire, unless you had some connection with the county and then why would you be so evasive or even lie about it?

'Certainly, something that should be investigated. So, I made some inquiries and found the case that the Reverend had referred to, only to find that it did not involve a Doctor John Hollis at all, but a Doctor Arnold Bennett. A young doctor in his first practice who charmed and married a rich, older widow, who he had treated after her first husband died. Had, in fact, treated the husband as well. This doctor involved himself in the community, indeed a very popular young fellow, and then his wife became ill and died. Nothing found to be suspicious in that death though and the police quickly dismissed the report from the vicar of another parish. Totally grief stricken, Doctor Bennett left his practice and the area and was never heard from again. Nobody knew where he had gone.

'However, Reverend Smith was not the only person that Mrs Bennett had confided in. She had written a long letter confiding in her sister, who was overseas with her husband at the time. Unfortunately, the letter took time to reach her, after several delays and misdirection's. So that by the time it did, Mrs Bennett was dead.

'Her sister returned to England and showed the police the letter, insisting on an exhumation. Her husband had some weight with the Home Office and consequently, Mrs Bennett's first husband's body was exhumed as well. Traces of arsenic were found in both bodies and the police have been looking for the, now very rich, Doctor Arnold Bennett ever since.

'Shortly after Doctor Bennett left Yorkshire, a Doctor Christopher Cousins opened a practice in Harley Street, with all sorts of modern treatments on offer. Such a success is he that news spreads and people start to come from far and wide. In fact, a Mrs McDonald from Surbiton in Surrey, told me that her old Aunt in Yorkshire had been planning to travel to Harley Street for a consultation. But Doctor Cousins upped and left suddenly. Practically did a moonlight flit. Could they possibly be the same man I asked myself?

'From appearances, no. Doctor Bennett was a slim, sandy haired, youthful looking young man. Doctor Cousins was older looking with black hair and a long beard. Doctor Hollis here wears spectacles, has a slight paunch and the hair is definitely a mousey shade, beginning to turn grey.

'Of course, a few years have gone by since Doctor Bennett was in Yorkshire and we all age and can even change our appearance. But what has never changed about you Doctor Hollis and indeed what we can never alter is the eyes. Doctors Arnold Bennett, Christopher Cousins and John Hollis all have the same trusting eyes. You might have been able to brush off the Reverend's crazy story if only you hadn't told everyone that you had practiced in Harley Street before this. If, after recognising you, Reverend Smith had decided to follow that up, it would have revealed that no John Hollis had ever practiced in Harley Street. No, you simply could not take the risk. So, on the night of Christmas Eve you retire to your room and even though you had no medical bag with you, you had some supplies.

'You then waited at the top of the stairs until you heard the door to the drawing room open and went back down on the pretext of getting some reading material. I assume you must have left your copy of *Life in Yorkshire* at home. Luckily for you, Stephen Mountjoy was just exiting the drawing room, leaving the Reverend Smith alone on the sofa. All it took was a quick jab in the neck with a hypodermic needle, then pick up a magazine and re-join Stephen at the bottom of the stairs. You even made a comment about expecting the Reverend to still be on the sofa the next morning, and that is truly what you expected to see.

'As the doctor in the house, you could have claimed that he had died of a heart attack brought on by all the alcohol he had consumed. I cannot begin to imagine your surprise the next morning when he had vanished.'

Doctor Hollis puffed out his chest. 'There was no surprise, Inspector because this is all just a fantastic tale and just as ridiculous as the ones that the Reverend was telling. Besides which, you haven't presented a shred of evidence.'

'Perhaps, perhaps. But do you know the other characteristic that does not change besides a person's eyes, Doctor Hollis? That would be fingerprints. I have yours from the ointment that you gave me, and it just so happens that they match the prints taken by the Yorkshire police from Doctor Arnold Bennett after the death of his wife, purely for elimination purposes, you understand.

'Sergeant Bailey, please handcuff Doctor Hollis and take him out the front door. There you will find two officers from the Yorkshire police constabulary who have driven through the night to come and collect him and will advise him of his right to remain silent, etc.'

Doctor Hollis glared at Tom but submitted to the handcuffs being placed on him. As Sergeant Bailey led him from the room, Clarissa was the first to speak.

'By Jove how clever of you, Inspector. Imagine, we have been in the presence of a triple murderer.'

'Yes, thank you, Inspector,' Lord David added. 'But may I ask you what you intend to do about Stephen?'

'Well, by rights I should arrest him, Lord Mountjoy. But I really can't see what good it would do. Your family has been through enough this past week. But take this as an official warning, Mr Mountjoy. One more foot out of line with regards to this land business and I'll be down on you like a ton of hot bricks.'

'He won't,' Lady Serena assured Tom. 'We will sort this out professionally and amicably.'

'Yes, thank you, Inspector,' Stephen added. 'I promise you I will never step out of line again.'

'No promises required, Mr Mountjoy. Just make sure that you don't.

'Now I must take my leave. I'll wish you all a Happy New Year. I'll be returning to London after the New Year's celebrations. I'll see myself out now. George, why don't you come with me?'

After everything that had just been revealed, George was eager to get back to the sanctity of his own home and a rather large whisky. He rose from his chair and followed Tom out of the room, leaving behind a roomful of stunned and silent people.

'Well, I think you've given them all quite a shock there, Tom.'

'Yes, murder will do that, George, and this has been as complicated and confusing as any case I have investigated.'

'I can quite understand that' George confided. 'Do you have time for a quick drink before heading home? I must confess that I do still have a few things that I'm not clear on.'

'Be glad to, George, especially as it's the last opportunity we'll have before I return to the city. Besides which, I do owe you after failing to appear the other evening,'

'Well, that's understandable. I suppose you had to go all the way up to Yorkshire?'

'Indeed, I did, George whilst my colleagues at the Yard were working the Harley Street angle.'

'Here we are,' George acknowledged on arrival at the front door of his cottage.

Leading Tom through to the sitting room he asked, 'What will you have, Tom, whisky?'

'Yes, thank you, George. It is New Year's Eve after all, and I do feel rather in need of it.'

'Well, that's quite understandable after what your Christmas break has turned into.' Taking a seat either side of the fireplace, George raised his glass and said, 'Here's to 1931. Let's hope it begins better than this year has ended.'

'I will certainly drink to that.' Tom raised his glass and took a long drink.

'So, two murders and a suicide eh, Tom?'

'Quite so. But do you know, George that if only it hadn't snowed none of this might have happened.'

'Really, now what makes you say that?'

'Well, let's take Robert Milroy for starters. If he hadn't worked up a thirst on those skis, he wouldn't have drunk that bottle of lemonade. Pure bad luck that he drank the one containing the drugs anyway.

'Now I originally thought, as did Sonia Ferguson, that Amelia was addicted to opiates. But now I am convinced that she was only an occasional user, and I would surmise that those occasions were around the times of painful memories, anniversaries, birthdays and the like. So, Christmas must have been a particularly tough time for a grieving widow. I really don't think that addiction would have escaped Lord and Lady Mountjoy unnoticed and of course when I first met her, she had also been sedated the night before so gave all the appearances of an addict.

'However, Susan Ross might have gone riding with her under any circumstances, to pass the time on this visit, so the idea of the riding school could have materialised and suddenly Amelia becomes the proverbial butterfly emerging from the cocoon. Sonia, being a sensible woman, would have then found a way to retrieve those bottles so no harm done. Probably would have laughed to herself in a 'what was I thinking' way. But then it snowed. Milroy died and Sonia did what she thought was the right thing. Confessed to me and ended her own pain and suffering.

'I still think that Reverend Smith would have taken a lunchtime drink to build up the courage to tell the family that the church was reclaiming the land but then sobered up enough to deliver the midnight service. But it snowed.

'I believe he may have thought something about Doctor Hollis was familiar, hence asking the question during the shoot. But I don't think the doctor was too concerned at that point. Emboldened by having got away with two murders and successfully moved away again, this time from Harley Street. Maybe later, perhaps in his room before dinner he realised that if the Reverend decided to follow up on his suspicions, he would discover that there had never been a Doctor Hollis in Harley Street. But at that point, if anything, another moonlight flit would probably have been his solution. Forge some new papers and start again. Maybe even abroad this time. He is certainly wealthy enough. But it snowed, and so the Reverend kept on imbibing and made up those ridiculous stories to hide the one that was actually true. A very dangerous and foolish game to play and I do not believe for one second that a sober Reverend would have done it.'

'Was that the only story that was true though, Tom?'

'Why do you ask, George?'

'Well, it was just the look on Lady Eliza Ross's face and that of her daughter, Susan, when the tale of the adulterous wife and the forged will were revealed.'

'Oh, of course. Yes, I did speak to Lady Ross about that. Apparently, in his very last hours, Lord Ross did ramble about changing his will, but he was a very sick man. Susan Ross knew about this. Easy enough to spot the affection and mild flirtation between Lord David and Lady Eliza, but an affair? No, Lord David is too terrified of Lady Serena's wrath for that.'

George chuckled. 'Hell, hath no fury like a woman scorned, eh? I see what you're saying, Tom. But Stephen did later have an attempt at murdering the Reverend.'

'Indeed, he did. But he had come back down to the drawing room to find the man passed out, not suspecting he was already dead. If he had been conscious, a conversation and a way forward might have been achieved.'

'So, we can blame the snow, can we?' George asked.

Tom smiled. 'Yes, very droll, George. Nobody wished for such a heavy snowfall on Christmas Eve, but unfortunate things happen in life all the time. It's how we react to these things that's important. All actions have consequences. Ultimately, the Reverend's actions cost him his life as did Milroy's, for if he hadn't provided Amelia with opiates, he would still be alive but then how many people's lives in the future might he have ruined? Plus, a dangerous man who had already killed twice will now receive the punishment he deserves because he chose to kill and not to leave.'

'Yes, quite astonishing. I still can't quite believe it. From appearances you would never credit it. What have you learned about the man?'

'Well, I'm sure that more will be discovered in the weeks and months ahead, but I do know that he turned up in Yorkshire as newly qualified MD and joined the practice of an older doctor who was due to retire in a couple of years. Much as he did here. He was certainly a visionary and had great ideas about the future of medicine. Wanted to experiment with herbs and suchlike, but the old doctor wouldn't stand for it. Besides which, he was so poor that he couldn't afford to dabble himself.

'Then, as luck would have it, a wealthy couple move to the area. The old doctor's patient list was full, so young Doctor Arnold Bennett takes them on. The husband is somewhat older than his wife and not in the best of health, so how easy it is to charm the wife and become a rock in her hour of need, whilst adding small amounts of arsenic to the husband's medication.

'Nothing was suspected when he died and so, after a suitable period of mourning, the widow becomes Mrs Doctor Arnold Bennett, and the old doctor also retires. Now the doctor has means but not an entire fortune at his will and he needs funds so desperately for his vision. So, he sets about giving small doses of arsenic to his wife. After all, he has got away with it once.

'He probably always planned to go to Harley Street once the deed was done, which he duly does as Doctor Christopher Cousins. There he gets to work on his remedies with obvious success as he has a thriving practice. So much so, that he is told that someone from Yorkshire will be coming to see him. Although he has changed his appearance, he knows that he is a wanted man and cannot risk any chance of exposure, no matter how small. So, off he goes again, shaving off the beard, dying the hair, adding spectacles and a little weight gain to fill out the cheeks. Then Doctor John Hollis arrives in a small village in the West Country.'

'All for the sake of new remedies?'

'A bit of a God complex, I think. All powerful, healing the world. To him killing was absolutely justifiable if it got him to where he needed to be. Mind you, if all the remedies were as good as the ointment he gave me, he was definitely on to something. I'd better get that analysed, don't want my leg to drop off.' Tom stood. 'Well, George. Thanks for the drink but I'd best go now and join the family. They've seen seldom little of me this past week.'

George rose, took Tom's hand and shook it warmly. 'It's been wonderful to see you again, old friend. Let's not leave it so long next time.'

'Absolutely, and I must meet that fiancée of yours. Happy New Year, George.'

'Happy New Year, Tom.'

Epilogue – 15th January 1931

Tom approached his desk in Scotland Yard. So far it had been a quiet start to the year and a much-needed chance to look at the cases in the unsolved pile. Late yesterday evening, he had discovered a promising lead and was looking forward to following that up this morning. He was surprised to find a small package on his desk, postmarked from the West Country.

Removing his winter coat, gloves and muffler, Tom sat down and unwrapped the parcel. Inside was an envelope addressed to Inspector Stewart which was resting on top of a tin, which when Tom removed the lid, revealed itself to be full of delicious looking shortbread. He smiled, replaced the lid and opened the envelope with the letter opener on his desk.

Manor House
8th January 1931

Dear Inspector Stewart,

I hope you won't mind me writing to you like this. Agnes was disappointed that you didn't get the chance to call and say goodbye before you left, 'specially as she'd baked you some shortbread to say, 'Happy New Year'. I told her I'd send it on to you 'cause I know how much you would like it and it also gave me the chance to send this note.

I wanted to say thank you once again for keeping mine and Agnes's secret. It sure gave me a shock when the Reverend said what he said and I'm sure her Ladyship wouldn't really mind, 'specially with everything that's gone on.

It's all had a huge impact on the family but in a good way it would seem. Miss Susan Ross has decided not to return to London but is investing some money in Miss Amelia's new riding school instead and they intend to run it together. According to Lord David there is an understanding between Susan and Stephen now. That will be good for them both and she will keep him grounded.

The family are returning the disputed land back to the church and making big plans for the existing land with talk of pigs, sheep, hens and a market garden. Quite a buzz about it there is as well. Colonel James, Lord David and Stephen are determined to make a success of things. Lady Ross has lent them the money to get started and will be involved in the day to day running as well. I'm sure she'll keep them all in hand and make sure things run smoothly. That's what Lord David thinks anyway. He is also relieved that it will solve his problems at the bank and that should satisfy Mr Rochester as well, shouldn't it? Lord David also told me that he thinks Colonel James has definitely set his cap at Lady Eliza now.

You might bump into Lady Serena in London, Sir. She has gone there with Miss Llewellyn-Jones. Apparently, she is going to manage her career for a while. Lord David thinks she will be very good at that. Plus, she will get to travel which she has always wanted to do, and her earnings can help repay Lady Ross, so she is doing her bit for the Manor estate too.

Poor old Doctor Forbes has had to come out of retirement for a while until a replacement for Doctor Hollis, or whatever his name was, can be found. Poor old Darlene had to be treated for shock. I think she might have thought she'd found her future husband so to discover he'd murdered three people; well, you can imagine the distress.

There isn't a replacement for Reverend Smith yet, but the curate is doing a fine job holding the fort so to speak. He led the services for both the Reverend's and Mrs Ferguson's funerals. Lovely services they were too.

Well, I think that's all the news Inspector. Agnes says to call in next time you are down this way for a visit.

With very best wishes

Alexander Jameson

Tom smiled. Good old Jameson, family retainer and confidante. He sincerely hoped that the plans for the Manor estate succeeded and perhaps a little visit at Eastertime could be on the cards. After all things should be well underway by then. Besides which his niece and nephew would be on school holidays, and he really hadn't spent enough time with them over the Christmas and New Year period. 'Also,' he thought out loud. 'I bet Agnes makes a mean hot cross bun.'

The end

ACKNOWLEDGMENTS

I have always wanted to write a 'Golden Age' crime novel since reading all the great authors as a young girl. I cannot begin to describe how much fun it was writing the story and I truly hope that it is worthy. A big 'thank you' to Margaret Johnstone and Mike Linane for some invaluable feedback and input.

Detective Inspector Thomas Stewart is named after my maternal grandfather. He wasn't a police detective but did fight and was wounded in the war. He also has a rugby field named after him at Minehead Barbarians Rugby Club.

On 8th September 2022, I was editing this book when I learned of the sad passing of Her Majesty Queen Elizabeth II. At the time this story is set, her grandfather King George V is on the throne and four-year-old Elizabeth is not yet destined to become Queen. To me Her Majesty was truly inspiring, and I very humbly dedicate this book to her with sincere thanks.

Sandra Love 2023

ALSO, BY SANDRA LOVE

The Special Ones

Whatever happened to Jeremy Issot?
Five former friends are asking themselves that question forty years on from when he was last seen, as they all return to their old hometown to attend the funeral of much beloved teacher and mentor, Michael Linane.

When Jeremy's remains are discovered after the funeral, secrets and lies that have been hidden for nearly forty years are uncovered.

Do the five former best friends of Jeremy have something to hide? Detective Inspector Lesley Hughes and Detective Sergeant Danny Collins intend to find out.

COMING NEXT BY SANDRA LOVE

Murder in Springtime

Detective Inspector Thomas Stewart of Scotland Yard returns to the West Country to stay with his sister Emily Travers and her family for the Easter holidays.

Not only is he determined to spend more time with his nephew and niece, William and Martha, but he has also been unexpectedly invited to the Easter wedding of Stephen Mountjoy and Susan Ross from the Manor House.

The whole village had turned out to witness this happy event. But who is the mysterious stranger who slips into the back of the church during the service?

Inspector Stewart alongside Sergeant Bailey will need to uncover the stranger's identity when he is discovered stabbed through the heart in the village church on Easter Sunday morning.

Printed in Great Britain
by Amazon